Cartel Rising

WCP Publishing

<<<>>>

Fort Worth, Texas

Printed in the United States of America

Paxton, Guillermo

Cartel Rising/ Paxton – 3rd Edition

ISBN: 978-0-9771993-0-3

1. Cartel Rising – Crime – Fiction. 2. Organized Crime – New Author –

Paxton Books – Fiction.
1. Title

Cover designed by Daria Skliarova and Thomas Olson

Author photograph by John Browning

WCP Publishing

For More Information, Visit *paxtonbooks.com*

Cartel Rising

Guillermo Paxton

<<<>>>

For my family, both American and Mexican, and Heliodoro Juárez, a true gem among lawyers in Mexico…

Prologue

A HALO OF smoke from the bartender's seemingly endless supply of cigarettes surrounded Eduardo "Lalo" Torres, the sole patron at the only bar in Mapimí, Mexico. The tiny building boasted dusty concrete floors, swinging-wooden front doors, and two brands of beer, which was adequate for the locals. Seven metal card tables, marked with blocked lettering spelling "TECATE" on their faded red tops, perched unsteadily on the cracked floor, their straight-back chairs pushed away from them by the drinkers from the night before. Rusty circles, caused by the condensation of many drinks that had rested upon them over the years, stood out like shadowed eyes, vaguely overlapping one another.

Lalo sat at one of the room's battered tables, his back to the wall. The seat gave him a good view of the front doors and a bit of the street beyond, which meant he didn't have to look over his shoulder every five minutes.

Three months earlier, a gunshot wound in the leg had brought Lalo to Mapimí after he'd driven several hours south from El Paso. Bleeding heavily and weary from his attempt to concentrate on his driving, he allowed sleep to trickle into his consciousness. A screeching horn and glaring headlights saved him from a near crash, convincing him to stop at the next small town he saw before blood loss killed him. When he saw the sign for Mapimí, he pulled off the main road and into the town.

After treatment by the town's doctor, Lalo began the recovery process, made small talk with some of the locals, and learned about the area.

Mapimí, with a population of about 10,000, had not changed much over the last hundred years. Most people still rode horses because they could not afford cars, and telephones were a luxury. Some of the townspeople still carried pistols belted at their sides, ignoring Mexican law prohibiting ownership of firearms. Cobblestone streets constructed in the late forties were the only non-dirt roads in Mapimí and, like most towns in Mexico, Mapimí was built around the church and plaza. Mining had once been the main industry, but after a boom in the fifties, the mining ran out and so did the economy. The main job-producing business of the town now was a Tyson chicken processing plant close by, where very modest wages could be made in exchange for long hours of hard work.

Lalo found the townspeople tended to avoid him, maybe because of the intensity in his stare or perhaps because they thought he was a narco, a drug dealer. Lalo's silk shirts and eighteen-karat gold chain cost more than the average citizen of Mapimí made in a year. That day, he wore a dark green silk shirt, black

Levi's 501s, ostrich skin boots, and a matching black felt Stetson. A gold scorpion hung from a gold chain around his thin neck, adding to his mystique. No one asked, but even if someone had the courage to ask him, Lalo would tell no one what he did for a living. His profession was far more complicated than that of a narco. And far more important.

Leaning back against the straight back of the chair, he filled his shot glass full of Hornitos tequila. After contemplating it for a moment, as if the future could be observed within its golden depths, Lalo tossed it back in one swallow. He'd learned from the bartender that the adobe bar, constructed in 1898, was almost identical to its original structure. Other than the cement floor redone by each generation, the electrical lines and plumbing were the only things new in it. Reddish-brown adobe bricks appeared through many holes in the interior walls, and the only decorations were a few bull-fighting posters hung up by the current owner's father sometime in the 1950s. An Old West-style hitching post stood outside the small cantina for those who came by horse.

Behind the bar, Porfirio, the bartender, lit another cigarette off the burning end of the one in his mouth. Many of the locals joked he wouldn't live much past his current fifty years with his tremendous nicotine addiction. His protruding belly was a monument to many years of chicharrons and beer, and his balding head accented the long scar running from his right cheek down to his neck. Fortunately, since his was the only bar in Mapimí, sales were always good.

Porfirio stepped from behind the bar and dropped some coins into the slot in the outdated jukebox in a corner of the bar. The instruments of mariachis filled the room, and the strong baritone voice of Vicente Fernández sung of women and their betrayals. Lalo let the music wash over him, as he tossed back another shot of well-contemplated tequila. The rest of the evening would have been spent exactly the same way, but the atmosphere changed the moment three men dressed in long leather coats entered the bar.

Lalo knew they were there for him. No one else in Mapimí had enemies like Lalo did. Their long coats in the middle of the August heat were a dead giveaway that they carried more than just beer money in their pockets. Lalo's hand instinctively dropped to his .44, sliding it from beneath the light jacket he wore. His empty glass crashed to the floor, shattering as he upended the table, crouching behind it and shooting the man furthest to the left twice.

The two remaining assassins pulled weapons from the concealment of their long coats and ducked for cover, firing while pushing over another of the tables. Lalo dove behind the wooden bar, still shooting, and scrambled over Porfirio, who hunkered down on the stone floor. Mariachi music could be heard in between the thundering sound of gunfire. Lalo was breathing hard as his adrenalin continued to rise and his heart pounded in his head, crowding out all of the other sounds in the room.

Bullets cracked across the bar, shattering the big mirror and showering Lalo with broken glass. He scurried to the end of the bar, peered around it, and fired off three rounds, wounding a man who collapsed in a spray of blood and tissue. Dropping the empty .44, Lalo pulled out the .380 holstered in his boot, leaning around the bar to find the other gunman. He spotted the man cowering in the scant protection of a chair and got off two quick shots. The man fired his sawed-off shotgun back, rolling behind an overturned table, and Lalo felt a rush of heat and pain as a buckshot tore at his face. His right eye went dark, and he clutched at his ringing right ear for a moment before anger took him. He decided he would take the final bastard with him to Hell.

He sprang from his hiding place, firing repeatedly at the upended table, watching with grim satisfaction as his bullets created pockmarks in the metal. Finally, the man rolled to the floor, the gun falling from his dead fingers.

Lalo stumbled and fell, not feeling the hurt anymore, his pain threshold having long been passed. Clutching his pounding head, he stumbled to his feet. Porfirio waved frantically, his mouth moving in a silent shout, but the ringing in Lalo's ears deafened him. The meaning of the barkeeper's frenzied pantomime became clear when terrible, sharp pains pierced Lalo's back. He turned as he fell, catching a glimpse of the first assassin he'd shot. The thug stood with a triumphant grin and a smoking pistol in his bloodstained hand.

As Lalo willed his hand to raise his own weapon, the man's grin disappeared in a burst of blood and brains. Lalo looked back toward the bar. Porfirio stood there proudly, blowing smoke from the dual barrels of an old shotgun he must have kept behind the bar. Lalo tried to smile back with what was left of his face, but darkness tore at the edge of his consciousness, sucking him under in a wave of pain.

He vaguely noticed Fernando Garcia, the town's excuse for a sheriff, peering inside. Although he was not a bad man, the sheriff wasn't a particularly brave person, an important trait for law enforcement to have. Porfirio hurried over and motioned to Lalo, gesturing excitedly in Spanish. The two men carried Lalo outside in a blanket Fernando brought in from his pickup, carefully placed him in the pickup's bed, and rushed him to the only doctor in town – Jose Baeza, the same man who'd treated him for his leg injury when he had first arrived in Mapimí.

"I knew the day you got here it wouldn't be the last I saw of you, Lalo," Doctor Baeza said, shaking his head. "I only hope you can survive this one." Lalo barely heard him say. His consciousness seeped from his head like the blood from his wounds.

The old man set about his work, looking up to bark at the bartender. "Porfirio!"

A startled Porfirio jumped at the normally calm doctor's shout, "Huh?"

"Put out that damn cigarette!"

Obeying, Porfirio spit out the half-smoked cigarette and smashed it on the floor with his mule-skin boot. Smoke trailed upwards from the crushed butt, almost as if making its final rebellious statement in the face of its impending extinction. Lalo watched it rise lazily toward the ceiling just before he passed out under the anesthetic.

Chapter 1 (Lalo)

AT TWELVE, LALO spent a lot of time on his beloved bike, the only true freedom he knew. As he headed to the 7-Eleven like he normally did, the streets were clear, and a red traffic light blinked lazily in the darkness. He rode on and off the street, alternating between sidewalk and pavement, dodging parked cars, dogs, people, and some parts of town. Socorro, a small New Mexico town about an hour south of Albuquerque, had big-city drug problems, and he avoided certain areas religiously.

Harold the Marinet[AS2] greeted Lalo, as he walked into the 7-Eleven, and Lalo waved. He didn't know Harold's real last name. The man wore an old but taken care of white Havana shirt and blue jeans. What Lalo knew of Harold came from the badass Marine infantry tattoos the man wore like medals and his Vietnam veteran attitude, along with a hundred or so tales of death to go with each tattoo. Lalo enjoyed the tales Harold spun, gesturing to add flavor to the already colorful stories, the endings were always similar – Harold snapping someone's neck, slicing someone's throat to avoid enemy detection, or escaping sure death. Lalo recognized good bull when he heard it. It was fun, just the same. The 7-Eleven clerk was a different story. He looked like he swallowed every story – hook, line, and sinker.

At about two in the morning, deciding he needed to go home, Lalo pulled himself away from the riveting stories. It was Friday; no school the next day, but his eyes had drifted shut repeatedly during the last few stories. Harold followed him out of the convenience store. When Lalo looked up at the older man to say goodbye, Harold's large, beefy hand fell to Lalo's shoulder. Surprised, Lalo shook away from the man and glared. Harold the vet raised his hands up and made the V sign with them. When he saw Lalo had relaxed, he continued.

"You know, Lalo, you're very special."

"Thanks." Lalo disliked the way Harold seemed to keep moving closer.

"No, really," Harold smiled, his yellow, cigar-smoke-stained teeth glinting in the dim light. "Do you believe in witchcraft?"

The man's broad face, warmed with liquor and memories, glistened in the yellow light from the bug bulb on the outer wall of the building.

"Yeah, sure, I guess." Lalo shifted uncomfortably, wondering how to get away without hurting Harold's feelings.

"Well, it's real. It really works. And I can prove it. I'm a fifth level warlock, a powerful magician." Harold released Lalo's shoulder to brush a hand across his graying flat-top hair. "You have the gift to become a powerful warlock yourself. I can help you."

Lalo stayed quiet, unsure of Harold's intentions, wondering if the watered-down liquor he'd been drinking had finally broken his war-ravaged mind.

"All we have to do is an incantation," Harold went on with hand on Lalo's shoulder again, moving him away from the glass front of the store, further into the shadows. "Are you interested in releasing the powers within you?"

"Maybe." Lalo's feet moved reluctantly, but he couldn't seem to break the spell of Harold's voice.

"We'll drive out to the bosque, build a fire, get naked, and perform a spell. Then you'll see. No real magic works with clothes on."

Lalo's eyes widened, and finally he could move, given incentive as Harold's words sank in. He backed away from the man he'd considered his friend.

Harold chuckled, a grating sound like rocks mating. "Don't worry, boy. I'm no fag. It's just that really important spells have to be performed in the nude." He leaned close, whispering, "And you won't be able to tell anyone what we're doing. It'll have to be in complete secrecy. A blood oath."

Even at twelve, Lalo's common sense dictated that going alone to the woods with any adult was bad, and he sure as hell didn't want to see some forty-year-old dude naked, much less be naked with him. He politely declined the generous offer, grabbed his BMX with yellow mag wheels, and rode off as fast as he could, making a mental note to find a new midnight hangout. He hid his bike under the trailer house his mom rented, a place where the skirting was loose. His mom didn't allow the bike inside. His mom's white Pontiac Sunbird wasn't parked outside, so he used his key and entered the dark, lonely mobile home.

Whenever he had time, Lalo spent it with his favorite people and only friends – the superheroes from his comic books. Working odd jobs around town earned him enough money for a few comics a week. Batman, Daredevil, and Spiderman were his favorites, with GI Joe a strong runner-up. In a world where bad guys and good guys had clear roles in life, Lalo clearly preferred a black-and-white existence painted in comic book color to his reality. Lalo longed to be an adult, to be a superhero. Wouldn't it be great to be bitten by a radioactive spider? He grinned at the thought.

Lalo stayed busy doing yard work for his comics' money or riding his bike all over town. It was during the week when his mom was home that there were problems. She would normally arrive home high, raising hell, waking up Lalo, and throwing a fit. This Sunday night was no exception, and Lalo decided this Sunday would be the last time she would see her son.

Earlier that day, he'd found his mother's stash of small, white pills marked with little crosses and flushed them down the toilet. Methamphetamines. He watched them swirl down the drain with the dirty water, and then he sat down to wait. When his mom Alicia showed up and couldn't find her pick-me-ups, she went into a rage, ranting as she tore the living room apart looking for her drugs. Her breath reeked of smoke and onions.

"Where's my stash, you little pendejo? Tell me or I'll beat it out of you, little asshole!"

Alicia turned and walked purposefully to the kitchen. Lalo followed, his eyes widening with fear when he saw her pull out a meat cleaver. It wasn't so she could tenderize meat; it was meant to tenderize him.

He ran then, slamming and locking his bedroom door, listening as she mindlessly beat on the wood for several hours with the meat cleaver, her enraged state fueling her mania. The combination of drugs and alcohol in her system prevented her from thinking of a way to actually open the door.

He curled himself into a small corner and cried softly, wishing his father was still around to save him, imagining he had telepathic powers and that somehow his dad would hear him from wherever he was, coming to save Lalo from the monster that was his mother. Sometime after four a.m., the house grew quiet, and he drifted through nightmares until warm sunlight pried at his eyelids. Alicia was a hard worker, no matter how bad an addict she was, so Lalo knew she'd gone to her job. He packed his things and left, turning to glance one more time at the trailer that had kind of been his home. Shrugging, he hopped on his bike and pedaled to the train tracks that ran through the center of town.

A train going to El Paso passed through Socorro, so he hopped on one of the southbound trains while it was stopped, pulling his bike up with him into the boxcar. He'd taken all of the money he had found in the house, maybe thirty dollars in mostly quarters for the laundry, and packed some apples to eat. Tears rolled down his cheeks, as he cried silently, partly because he was only a child and knew the decision he was making was beyond his maturity, and partly for the relief he felt to finally be leaving behind the torture that was living with his mother. Many hours later, he arrived in El Paso, where the old downtown section was linked to the border of Mexico by a bridge. Long shadows were cast by the caboose in the late afternoon sun. He gently tossed his bike down and climbed out, hearing a lot of movement in the rail yard and men speaking Spanish. Thinking he might get some help from his Uncle Luis, Lalo set off to find his mother's brother, a man he barely remembered meeting years ago.

After getting confusing directions from various passersby, he finally arrived at the address he had for his uncle. Tío Luis lived in what local El Pasoans called El Segundo Barrio, the second neighborhood, an area full of graffiti, gangs, drugs, and violence. Lalo knocked strongly on the old, wooden door. An older man, probably in his late forties, answered.

"What can I help you with, hijo?"

"Tío Luis? I'm Lalo, Alicia's son." Lalo looked up pleadingly at the man.

"God damn Alicia. Come on in, son."

After Lalo briefly narrated what had happened, Tío Luis made Lalo a sandwich, with white bread, mayonnaise, and a single slice of bologna. Lalo gulped the sandwich down, as if it had been a year since he last ate. Luis had lived there for about fifteen years, and he explained to Lalo that it was the only area he could afford. It was a small, two-story home, two bedrooms below and one above. The living room was decorated in the seventies, a lime-green sofa and a black-and-white television hadn't changed since. The bathroom was a disaster and probably hadn't been cleaned since Luis' wife had died. With his three sons, it was already a full house, but Luis said he'd make room for him. *Donde caben dos caben tres,* he'd said, where two fit, three would as well. When Luis called Lalo's cousins down and told them about Lalo, the expression on their faces manifested their disapproval of sharing their limited space, and the fists and fingers they threw at him when Luis wasn't looking made Lalo understand they would make his stay as uncomfortable as possible.

Alienated by his cousins and lonely in his new home, Lalo kept to himself most of the time, spending it usually in the backyard. One day, his oldest cousin, Enrique, showed up at the house with three of his gang-banging friends. Gangsters – cholos – wore well-ironed Dickies, Stacy Adams shoes, and nice shirts buttoned only at the top. They spent hours ironing their clothes, starching their creases, and making certain everything was perfectly aligned, including the bandanas folded neatly and stuck in the back pocket, half hanging out to show their pride for their colors.

"Hey, primito, ¿qué onda, loco?" Enrique said.

Lalo cringed, knowing ridicule and torture were soon to follow. And he hated being called "little cousin."

"Nothing, Enrique, nothing's going on."

"Oh, well, that's where you're wrong, primito. Something is going on. Do you know what?" Enrique asked, winking at his three friends.

Lalo knew his answer would trigger whatever they planned against him. Not wanting to reply, but knowing he would be punished if he didn't, he said, "N-no. What?"

"Titty twisters!"

The teens tackled the younger boy, knocking him on his backside. They grabbed Lalo's chest and twisted. Powerless against their attack, he was humiliated and angry at the feeling of helplessness that overwhelmed him.

The boys finally tired of the game and got off him. Lalo, swallowing his fear and refusing to let them see him cry, struggled to his feet. He faced his cousin, drawing himself up proudly. "I want to be initiated," he said.

The boys laughed.

"I have the right," Lalo insisted. "I live in this barrio. I'm your cousin, Enrique. Kids are always giving me shit at school because you're a part of Los Fatherless, so they think I am too. But I'm not, so no one has my back. I get my ass beat by them, and no one helps. I'm at home, and you and your friends beat my ass too. I've had enough of this shit. I want in." He took a deep breath after the long speech.

Enrique stared at his cousin. Lalo knew the truth in his words could not be ignored. Enrique nodded, slightly, but enough to affirm Lalo's decision.

"Ok, primito, esta bien. Just remember, you asked for it. And no telling my dad."

The five boys walked about a block and a half down the street from their house, Enrique whistling purposefully. One by one, boys emerged from nowhere and followed.

As they walked along the cracked sidewalk in the hot, dry El Paso sun, Lalo took in his surroundings, seeing them intensely as if for the first time. Three-story apartment buildings, Southwest-style duplexes, and houses were scattered along the street like an abstract painting. Mexican music blared from open windows, and mothers screamed at children in Spanish to clean up this or that, to get in the house, or to take care of their younger siblings. The aroma of boiling beans and freshly cooked flour tortillas filled the air, mingling with the more subtle smell of tobacco and marijuana.

A church just off of Delta Street had been burned down in a huge riot about a year before Lalo moved to El Segundo Barrio. The impromptu parade gathered in back of the charred ruins, and one of the boys spray-painted a sign that once had said in Spanish, "All are welcome here." They waited intently for Enrique to speak.

"My primito wants to be Los Fatherless. He thinks he's man enough now. Each of us had to pass through initiation, and so does he. Just because he is my cousin doesn't give him any special rights, so I want you to make it as hard for him as it was for each of you."

Lalo felt his adrenalin rising, fear clouding his vision and hearing. Was he doing the right thing? Maybe if he just told them he was sorry...

"Okay, primito, I hope you know what you're getting into."

No, Lalo thought. *I really didn't. Oh crap, what was I thinking? I can't back out now.* "Simon" was all that came out of Lalo's mouth, Spanish slang for yes. George, another of Lalo's cousins appeared in front of him, showing a wide, horrendous grin. The youngest of Lalo's cousins, Felipe, also emerged. No one, not even his dad, called him Felipe. Payaso was all he ever heard anyone call him, his constant jokes and pranks earning him that nickname of clown.

The almost friendly faces morphed into frowns, signaling the dark violence upon them. The beating began.

Fists and feet were all Lalo knew for what seemed like an eternity, even though the beating took less than two minutes. He fell down, feeling the kicks to his stomach and ribs, some harder than others. He had to get up, or he would not be allowed in. Summoning all his strength, he struggled back to his feet. He was knocked down twice more, and both times he forced himself back to a standing position.

Then, as suddenly as the raining fury began, it was over. Kicks became hugs and welcomes; fists became handshakes. Legs still shaking, Lalo gratefully accepted the joint passed to him and took his first hit of marijuana, the smoke causing him to cough and gag simultaneously. The other boys laughed.

A few weeks after his initiation into Los Fatherless, Lalo stopped at the local boys' club he passed nearly every day walking back from the bus stop. The club had a free boxing program run by the Police Athletic League. Lalo knew if he wanted to survive in El Segundo, he would have to be tough. After speaking with the coach, he joined the club and made boxing his number one priority. In the first six months of training, he never missed a single practice.

Eddie, Lalo's boxing coach and a retired police officer, frowned after Lalo's brief punching flurry.

"Turn that fist over when you jab. Keep your shoulder in front of your chin as you hit."

The smell of sweat, mixed with the sounds of the timer bell going off every three minutes, boxers jumping rope and fists pounding the heavy bags and the speed bags formed a collage of familiar stimulants Lalo now knew as the boxing gym experience. His powers of observation were far superior to other people, especially kids of his own age; Lalo already knew every boxer's strong and weak points. As the years passed, Lalo became a local favorite. His height and lankiness made him difficult to fight by the shorter fighters of the same weight class. That, combined with his speed and intelligence, made him a winner at the state golden gloves tournament. At age fifteen, he headed to Los Angeles with coach Eddie to represent Texas in his weight division at the nationals.

"In the yellow trunks and black shirt, Guillermo Smith, 6 and 0, 4 by the way of knockout."

A few people clapped and cheered.

"In the blue trunks and white shirt, Eduardo 'Lalo' Torres, 32-5-2, 6 by knockout."

A slow rumble turned into a collage of cheers and clapping throughout the entire stadium. The winner of this fight would go on to fight for the championship in the Junior Olympics. Lalo had just defeated the last two of his opponents by out-pointing them, and by the way the people cheered him on, the spectators obviously thought he would do the same to Smith, a boxer out of New Mexico.

Lalo studied his opponent. About two inches shorter than Lalo, the young man had a very light complexion and was more muscular than him. To have made it all the way to the Junior Olympics with so few fights in his record, Lalo knew this kid was either very dangerous or very lucky. Whatever the case may have been, Lalo was not going to take any chances. Lalo stared hard at Smith as they touched gloves, and Smith returned the stare with a goofy smile, confusing Lalo.

The bell rang. Lalo opened the round with a series of left jabs and right crosses to the head. Lalo's strengths had always been his speed and intelligence, and he planned to capitalize on both. Smith took what Lalo dished out to him and returned with a surprisingly powerful jab that went right through Lalo's defenses. Tears clouded Lalo's vision, an automatic reaction to the blow to his nose. Smith followed with a straight right, blocked by Lalo's guard, and a left hook to his liver. Lalo doubled in pain and began throwing jabs to ensure Smith couldn't finish him off. Smith's lack of experience became evident to Lalo when he backed up, obviously unaware as to how bad Lalo had actually been hurt. He barely made it through the first round.

The second round belonged to Lalo. Experience and speed outclassed Smith, and he ended the round way ahead on points.

Eddie wiped the sweat off of Lalo's face with a dry towel. "Just keep doing what you're doing, Lalo, and you can win by points. Don't let that kid in, whatever you do. You can out-point him; he's too inexperienced."

Lalo had no intention of letting Smith hit him like he did in the first round. The bell rang, and he moved to the center of the ring confident he would win the third round like he had the second. He threw a flurry of combinations and then stepped out and around Smith. The kid couldn't catch up to him. After Lalo heard the thirty-second mark, he moved in on Smith. As Lalo followed his left jab with a right cross, Smith countered with a devastating double left hook: first to his liver, then to Lalo's head, hitting directly on the temple. He literally saw stars and barely felt the right cross that finished him. When he finally realized what had happened, Lalo was on the ring's floor, his eyes being checked by the tournament's doctor, an older man in a gray suit, matching his gray hair. Lalo felt flush, as he realized he had been knocked out.

"He'll be alright, coach," the doctor told Eddie.

Lalo returned home from Los Angeles the hero of the barrio, despite his loss.

"C'mon Lalo. Let's box!" Enrique prodded Lalo in the backyard of their home. He threw a few sloppy jabs in the air, close to Lalo's face.

Lalo shook his head. "I don't think that's a good idea, primo."

"What, even after all that boxing, you're still scared?"

Lalo answered his cousin with a flurry of punches. The larger Enrique tried vainly to defend himself, but he was down on the ground, nose bleeding in a few seconds. The other cousins and a few friends who had gathered around were disappointed to see their leader knocked down by a younger and smaller kid.

"Shit, Lalo. My respects, man. You can fucking box!"

Everything changed for Lalo with his cousins; they treated him like a brother. Every dance, fight, or other extracurricular activity they always invited him, nothing at all like when he had first arrived, and they had made him feel like a burden. Lalo felt good he finally had a real family. He rarely thought about his mother anymore, and he definitely didn't miss her. His memories from Socorro seemed like they were from another person's life. Being the local boxing hero had its downfalls, though. Someone was always trying to make a name for themselves by way of Lalo.

"Hey motherfucker, pinche joto, you think you're bad because you can box? I'd like to see you fight me, you pussy, you won't last a minute!"

Lalo couldn't believe Ricky Martinez was threatening him in front of the school, right in front of everyone. Was he crazy? Lalo knew he had to be; after all, it had been just three weeks earlier since he beat the hell out of one of Ricky's cousins, a kid known to be a vicious fighter on the street.

"Are you high, Ricky? You know I'll kick your ass." Lalo started toward him.

"Not here. At six, in back of the 7-Eleven."

"Simon. Dumbass."

Lalo was walking toward the 7-Eleven through the alley that linked the street to the back of the store. Graffiti and trash decorated the walls and ground. Waiting around the corner were Ricky and four other guys. A flash of metal in Ricky's hand caught Lalo's eye, and he knew he was being ambushed. He began to run back from the way he had come, and two other cholos were blocking the way, one wielding a bat. Resigned to his fate, Lalo grabbed a large rock from the ground and prepared himself for whatever was to come. Ricky grinned, a hideous, dangerous smile, that of a killer. A gunshot surprised them all, and Lalo turned around while checking himself to see if he had been shot.

Enrique had the two other cholos who had blocked Lalo's escape by gunpoint. Payaso and George took their weapons. Lalo felt relief flow throughout his body, and he walked as coolly as he could toward his cousins. Enrique smiled.

"Hermano, you can't trust anybody, especially not to fight a straight fight, and extra-especially when it is one of the Thunderbirds," Enrique said, referring to the rival gang that the other boys were a part of.

Lalo slapped Enrique's hand, then George's and Payaso's as well. "Thanks for the *paro*, brothers. Vamanos, before la chota gets here!" Everyone ran.

Lalo felt happy, complete. He finally had a family.

Chapter 2

The 15-year-old girl's coming-of-age dance pulsed with lively music and laughter, and the sound infected Lalo, causing him to want to dance. His cousins were seated near the door of the ballroom, drinking Presidente Brandy in small glasses, refilling them often. They faced the dance floor, shouting encouragement from their chairs.

"What a great quinceañera! Look at Lalo, ese vato. What a heina he's got!"

Lalo smiled at the jealousy in Enrique's voice, enjoying the rhythm of the music moving his body. He looked around the ballroom. As common in quinceañeras, whole families attended, even their little kids. The youngest children slept despite the noise, sprawled out on chairs placed together like a cot. The girl Lalo danced with had light skin, reddish-brown hair, and green eyes. At fifteen, she already had the body of a woman. All Lalo could do was admire her beauty and hope for some extracurricular activities after the dance. Lalo smiled as he mentally asked himself if he could be in love.

"What's your name?" Lalo smiled genuinely at the girl and twirled her around to the beat of the song.

"Manuela. I'm the quinceañera girl's cousin."

Lalo smiled again. "You're beautiful, you know that?"

Manuela blushed, turning her head slightly, Lalo's penetrating stare was too strong for her. A little girl, probably around six or seven, ran up to the couple, tugging on Manuela's dress.

"What's up, Galilea?"

The young girl motioned with her index finger for the other girl to bend down so she could tell Manuela something in her ear. Manuela laughed after young Galilea had finished whispering to her, and Lalo noted that she had a slight gap between her two front teeth, like Manuela. Galilea ran back to the table she had just come from. Lalo contemplated the gap in Manuela's teeth, and, after a minute, decided it just made her more attractive. Lalo finally broke the silence. "So, what did the little girl say?"

"The little girl is my niece. She said you are cute."

Lalo smiled. "And what do you think?"

"I-" Manuela was abruptly interrupted by shattering glass followed by the ominous sounds of gunfire. Lalo instinctively pushed Manuela down for cover, involuntarily inhaling a puff of dust, as they hit the ground. He coughed, rolling away from the girl beneath him, and lay coughing for a moment to clear his throat.

Screams broke the powerful silence. Lalo scrambled to his feet and ran to his cousins. Enrique, George, and Payaso lay covered in blood, eyes staring straight up in that cold way only corpses can. Lalo tried frantically to revive them, but his efforts were in vain. Tears poured down his cheeks, and he lost himself in his grief until Manuela and her mother dragged him away, weeping.

Time for Lalo moved much like the passing of great, bilious thunderclouds in a windless sky. The horrible event was ever present in his mind, like the remnants of a terrible nightmare when one just wakes. Two days later, he sat in the St. Ignatius Catholic Church, his face tight from the many tears that had dried on his face. As he looked around the church, a strange sense of peace came about him. The priest spoke of great losses to the living and the greater rewards of everlasting life, and Lalo wondered if any of his cousins would have the latter. He stared at the many statues throughout the church, but in particular at the one of the archangels he knew to be called Michael. As a matter of fact, he couldn't take his eyes off of him. Lalo blinked hard when an incredibly bright light shone all around the statue, and for just a moment, the angel seemed to look right at him. A hand on his shoulder pulled him away from his "vision."

"C'mon Lalo, time to go." Tío Luis talked to Lalo without looking him in the eyes. Lalo hoped his uncle knew in his heart at least that he had no fault in what had happened, but his uncle's attitude was a little aloof. Lalo was certainly not going to ask, though, because that would make the already difficult situation even worse. On the way out of the service, Luis stopped and shook hands with a man that was apparently the brother of an El Paso cop.

"Don't worry, primo, Rocha will stop by your house in a few days. He would have come but he is deep in an investigation."

"I understand. Tell him it would be appreciated. The cops in Juarez consider this just another gang shooting. You know they don't care if cholos kill cholos. Unless it's their kids, of course." The anguish and frustration that Lalo heard in his uncle's voice made him angry. He was angry at the killers, the cops and even himself.

A few days later, Lalo and Tio Luis were sitting at their tiny kitchen table having coffee when someone knocked on the door.

"Lalo, get the door, it's a friend." Lalo obeyed his uncle and answered the door.

Rocha impressed Lalo. Although he was short, only about 5'7", Rocha's presence seemed larger than life, like he was somehow invincible. He was built like a tank- barrel-chested, with arms like Howitzers. He gave Lalo a warm, inviting smile, and Lalo let him in. Rocha and Tío Luis hugged, and they went to the kitchen. Lalo listened at the door.

"Luis," Rocha said, "you know your friendship means a lot to me."

"As yours does to me."

"Look, I did get some information on who is responsible. But it isn't anything substantial, rumors at best. Some of this you might not like hearing."

"I understand. I promise I won't hold anything you tell me against you. You are my friend, and I won't hold a grudge against a friend for honesty." Luis placed a reassuring hand on Rocha's strong shoulder. Lalo thought Luis seemed so small in front of the other man, skinny, almost frail.

"Your boys were apparently members of Los Fatherless. A lot of gangs here in El Paso have sister gangs in Juárez, and gang members jump around from border to border, causing problems on both sides. They hang out on one side while the other side cools down. You get what I mean?"

Luis nodded.

"Seems a rival gang leader knew Enrique and your boys were going to be at this quinceañera and planned an ambush. Rumor has it they were deliberately seated by the door for that purpose. For the ambush."

Rocha paused when Luis began to sob. Luis got control of himself and looked up at Rocha. "No, don't stop. Please go on."

"His name is Chito Sandoval, but I don't have much else. They say he's about twenty years old. I did some digging on this side of the border. He's got a long juvenile record. You know, there really isn't any way I can prove any of this. With a little money, I know a few officers in Juárez who will…"

"No, no, not without proof," interrupted Luis, knowing that Rocha was inferring that Luis might want to set up a hit on this Sandoval character. "At least I have a little to go on now."

"What are you going to do?"

"For now, just leave it in the hands of God. There's already been enough bloodshed."

"I think that is probably the best thing to do, at least for now, Luis. I'll keep putting pressure on the Juárez police. Brother, I'll never forget what you did for me. If you need anything, *anything*, just say the word. Even if that means taking care of this ourselves."

Luis shook his head. "Thanks, my friend, but I wouldn't ever ask you to do anything like that. What happened in 'nam could have happened the other way around, and I know you would have done the same for me. You don't owe me anything. Just let me know if there's any progress." Luis showed Rocha out.

Lalo clenched his fists tightly, not believing his uncle wasn't going to do anything. He had heard about Sandoval before, and if Luis didn't plan to do anything, Lalo would. Later that night, Lalo snuck into Enrique's room and began looking for the gun he knew Enrique had kept hidden there. The bedroom light suddenly came on and Lalo jumped, startled.

"Looking for this?" Tío Luis asked, holding a small .22 handgun in his hand.

"Shit, Uncle, I can't let Sandoval get away with this!"

"Damn it Lalo! Listen, I'm their father, and if anyone is hurt by this, it's me. First, I lost my wife, your Tía Anjelica, now them!" Luis calmed down. "Obviously, you overheard my conversation with Jeremiah, so you know he said that all he had was rumors."

"Yeah, I heard, but I know that vato. Of course he did it!"

"So now you're going to go out there and shoot him? What if he kills you first? You think he's not expecting retaliation? What if you succeed?" Luis stared down his nephew. "Do you know what it's like in a Mexican jail? Have you killed anyone before?" Luis paused and looked at Lalo, already knowing the answer. "Well, I have." Luis stopped for a moment, apparently swallowing back some particularly ugly memories. "Vietnam. You have no idea what it's like. Taking someone's life changes you forever, in ways you can't imagine." Luis placed his hand onto Lalo's trembling shoulder. "I've lost nearly all my family. I don't want you to ruin your life, or worse, lose it. And I don't want to lose you."

The tears in Tío Luis' eyes were contagious, and Lalo cried with him. The two men embraced in their mutual mourning.

Chapter 3 (Memo)

"Mijo, just promise me, ok? That's all I ask. I don't care what you choose to do, just don't become a pro boxer."

Seventeen-year-old Guillermo Smith gritted his teeth, swallowed back tears and frustration, and promised his dying mom he wouldn't. He'd lost his father a year earlier in a car accident. Before his death, Randy Smith had always supported his son's boxing. By sixteen, just after a year and a half of boxing, no one in the boy's weight class would fight him, and his record was already 23-0, 18 by knockout. Now he sat in a metal chair that he had moved closer to the hospital bed where his dying mother lay, holding her thin, fragile hand in his. Memo, as his friends called him, winced at the smell of disinfectants and sick people overwhelming his nostrils, and he suddenly felt nauseous.

At sixteen, Memo was a light-heavyweight and often had to fight guys in their twenties, even heavyweights, just to get an amateur fight, and he was already being recruited by the pros. When the local boxing community found out Memo's mom was dying of cervical cancer, promoters literally waited like vultures for the chance to grab hold of what would likely be a newly emancipated minor. He now was only a few months away from turning eighteen.

"Ok, Mijo. I'm glad. I know you'll keep your promise to mama."

Three days later, Memo's mom died, and he kept his promise. After sending away all the promoters, managers, and other gentlemen of questionable morals, Memo began looking for work. After graduating from high school, he went to work for the sheriff of Doña Ana County in Las Cruces, New Mexico, primarily painting and other types of handiwork. Sheriff Lester Sanchez had been a close friend of Memo's father. Memo assumed the sheriff treated him like family because he didn't have a son of his own. Memo was doing the final touch-up on one of the interior walls when the sheriff called to him. Les was dressed in a white polo that barely covered his very corpulent body and a pair of brown slacks. He had reddish-brown hair and freckles, a trait surely inherited from some Spanish ancestors. He was taller than Memo, about 6'3", and weighed easily a good 300 pounds.

"Memo, son, when you get done with that wall, come here. I need to talk to you."

"Okay." He dabbed the paint over a crack to cover it, then took his brush to the faucet to rinse the latex out.

"Done," he said, coming over to the sheriff. "What's up?"

"You're eighteen in two days, right?" Sheriff Sanchez squinted through his glasses at him.

"Yeah."

"Well, I was thinking. The locals look up to you, especially the kids. You've always been a kind of local hero, you know, boxing and stuff."

"Okay," Memo said. "So?"

"So, I was thinking you'd be a good example for them to follow. You don't do drugs, never really been in any serious trouble, and you stick to your principles. I think you'd make a good deputy."

Memo thought about it for a moment. He really had never considered being a cop, but his current work as a handyman wasn't at all satisfying. The opportunity the sheriff was offering him was an actual profession, something that would have made his mother and father proud. He nodded.

Sheriff Sanchez smiled. "Monday morning, I want to see you at the office so we can get your paperwork going."

After paperwork and a physical, Les signed him up for the police academy in Santa Fe. Les had obviously timed his offer because the academy started a week after his initial physical exam. Memo figured that the wily sheriff probably thought it better for him to not have much time to recant his decision, but he wouldn't have. The more he thought about being a cop the more he liked the idea, not just wearing a uniform and a badge, but an actual opportunity to help and protect the community.

Memo was in great shape, and he had no problem beating all the other cadets in running, pushups, pullups, sit-ups, and self-defense. Even the book part of the training – laws and ethics – was a breeze for him, and he completed top of the class. When Memo got back from the police academy, everyone congratulated him, and the sheriff was thrilled. His first day of work, a nervous Memo showed up and reported for duty.

"Hey, Memo, come here." The burly sheriff ordered Memo.

A new girl had started working for the sheriff's department.

"Yes sir."

"Meet my new secretary. Her name is Rosa."

As the months passed and his OJT training was over, Memo didn't care to be in the office, preferring to be in his patrol car where the action was. But the new girl, with her oriental-looking eyes and her slim waist, made report-writing an almost pleasurable experience. Memo took every opportunity to flirt with Rosa and the two hit it off from the get-go. She was always quiet and seemingly shy. Memo was just the opposite, always joking and the life of the party. After Memo's nineteenth birthday he asked Rosa out, they dated for two weeks and were married at the courthouse, the sheriff and one of Rosa's friends as witnesses.

They exemplified the old adage of opposites attract, yet they had one thing in common – neither had their parents. Rosa had been orphaned at just seven years of age and had grown up with her grandmother in El Paso. When she had turned sixteen, she joined the Job Corps, and through that organization had landed the job at the Sheriff's Department. As time progressed and their differences became more pronounced, Memo found himself wondering if they had gotten married just so they could have a family of their own and to stifle the loneliness each one had felt.

After a few months of marriage, Memo and Rosa were at a friend's birthday party. Memo had a few drinks; he was certainly not drunk, but jovial as was his nature. Grabbing one of the balloons filled with helium, Memo sucked out the gas and began singing some very serious, romantic Mexican songs, which was met with the crowds' approving laughter and applause. Rosa glared at Memo. She got closer to him, pulling hard on his arm. She was much shorter than he, so he bent to hear whatever she planned to whisper.

"You're making an ass of yourself. Let's go, right now."

"Why should we go, honey? Don't be like that."

"If we don't go right now, I'll leave by myself."

"I've got the car keys," Memo answered Rosa, jokingly dangling them in front of her.

"I'll walk." Rosa turned around and walked out of the party.

Memo sensed the marital bliss the couple had barely experienced was already at an end.

The next morning, he sat at the table in the sheriff's dining room, and Les' mom sat across from him. She was short, light-skinned, and her hair was almost completely white. The wrinkles in her face were accentuated by the large moles on her chin, giving her the classical "witch" look. She wore a very simple, black widow dress, although Les' father had passed away some twenty years ago. Memo had been discussing his marital problems with her while he was waiting for the sheriff to finish changing.

"I know this old man, Memo, and I think he could help," Merlinda told him. "He sees the future."

"A witch, huh?" Memo laughed. "How much does he charge?"

"No, he's not like that." Merlinda frowned, looking over her shoulder uneasily, making sure her disapproving son wasn't looking. "He takes whatever you can give, food, stuff like that. And he's not a witch."

"Why do I need to see him?" he asked her, wondering why she looked so concerned about Les.

"He has strong magic, Memo," she whispered. "He can help you find your way through the troubles you face in your life. His name is Candelario. Go to him. I'll go with you if you want. Come see me when you get a chance. Just don't tell Les; he might get mad at me."

"Okay."

After Memo's shift was over, he picked up Merlinda, not really knowing why he was doing it. He thought perhaps it was curiosity or the sheer desperation of his situation, but whatever the reason, he felt it was something he *had* to do. A few miles outside of Las Cruces, a seemingly abandoned mobile home stood alone on a hill at the end of a dirt road. As his truck bumped along the gravel road, he and Merlinda felt the jolting motion in their bones. As they pulled up beside the trailer,

Memo noticed a collection of crows watching from a nearby fence. Their chatter set his nerves on edge as he stepped up on the porch, knocking on the door quietly. As he entered, Memo noticed that there were no electric or telephone lines going to the trailer.

"Enter." The voice embodied wisdom, age, and something strangely calming.

Once he and Merlinda were inside the trailer, Memo felt peace and tranquility all around him, contrary to the shambles that were the reality of the living room. The white-haired man sitting on a ratty old green-colored easy chair seemed so old, his wrinkles deep, and Memo bet that if asked the man probably wouldn't even remember when he was born. He smiled when Memo entered, a surprisingly youthful smile like the sunrise on a cold winter's morning, rays of warmth emanating from it. His eyes held almost no color, the milky pale of the completely blind, reminding Memo of David Carradine's monk-teacher from the TV show *Kung Fu*. He wore a dirty, graying once-white T-shirt, stained with food and dirt, and a pair of old brown slacks, like the kind one would find at the local goodwill. He did not wear shoes, and his toenails curled under his toes. After an informal introduction, Candelario began praying while walking around Memo in a circular fashion, his blindness apparently not much of a handicap to him. Memo felt chills crawl up and down his spine.

"You are tormented by a terrible marriage; your wife is a miserable person, who loves no one, and she will make you miserable." He paused, thoughtfully, then continued, "you will leave her, and one day and will meet a much younger woman. She will be your life mate, and you will be very happy together."

Candelario's words penetrated deeply into Memo's skepticism, although he would refuse to admit it for a long time after. How could the old man know his entire problem without Memo saying anything? He hadn't even told the old man of his marriage, much less the troubles he was having.

"What do I owe you, sir?"

"Whatever you are able to give without hardship. Just not money."

Since Memo hadn't brought anything, he told Candelario he'd return with food later. After dropping off the sheriff's mom, he stopped at the local grocery store and picked up some food. When he showed back up at the trailer, the old man smiled and nodded. Memo didn't like owing anybody anything, so until he returned with some fruits and sweet Mexican bread, he just didn't feel right. He couldn't explain how the man knew so much about Memo's problem; he obviously hadn't spoken with Merlinda, with no telephone and without transportation, how could he have?

"I'm glad you are back, young man. There were a few things I didn't want to tell you in front of Merlinda. Things that she doesn't need to know."

"Like what?" Memo felt the chills he had experienced during his first "reading" once again.

"Everyone has a destiny to complete. What people don't understand is there are many ways to complete the same destiny. You are destined to be rich and powerful."

Memo laughed under his breath, finding that hard to believe. Not anymore, not now that he quit boxing and became a cop.

"I hear the lack of faith, and I understand. Youth is both a precious gift and a terrible curse. As young people, we have the capacity and energy to do great things, but we lack the maturity and concentration and many never reach their potential. Once we have maturity, we lack energy and time to do those things, and we waste much time trying to regain our youth. Hijo, you are not like this. Your future is full of many opportunities and one day you will have great power. Remember to always treat people justly, with respect and give back to the community. It will be your saving grace…"

Chapter 4

Patrolling in the outskirts of Doña Ana County was by far Memo's favorite area to work. Gangster parties, drug deals by the local mafia, and all kinds of sexual activities were always taking place on the off-roads. Most of the other deputies stuck close to Las Cruces, the main city in the county, home of some 70,000 inhabitants. The local police department took care of the 911 calls and patrolling of the town, and was actually pretty busy, so Memo didn't see any need for hanging around there too. Others were more focused on officer safety and having backup close by was important to them. For Memo, the exhilaration of being alone on a potentially dangerous traffic stop outweighed the risks.

Highway 70 was frequently traveled, but not as much as Interstate 25. Since I-25 was usually covered by the State Highway Patrol, Memo made it a rule to use Hwy. 70 on his way from town to town. Over the last few years, he had picked up many arrests on that road, from DUIs to drug charges and felony warrants.

Memo enjoyed the cool, desert November night. He rolled down his cruiser's window and poked his head out to stare at the cloudless sky. The stars were as bright as he'd ever seen them, with less than a quarter moon to illuminate the road before him. As he sat on the side of the highway, like a hawk waiting for his prey to pass by, Memo saw a blue Ford Bronco with a headlight out. Calling the plate in on the radio, Memo hit his overheads to alert the driver to stop. Getting out of his patrol car, Memo was careful to watch for any sudden movements or suspicious activities of any sort. The driver was Mexican, and Memo spoke to him in Spanish.

"Good evening. May I see your license and registration?" His breath turned to vapor, as he spoke.

"Well sir, you see, I seem to have misplaced my paperwork," the thin driver, about twenty years old, said. He was obviously nervous, his voice breaking as he spoke.

Memo used his flashlight to see the rest of the interior. Dirty sneakers were barely noticeable behind the backseat, and Memo saw one twitch, ever so slightly. The Bronco was an old 1984 model, two-door with a lot of space in the back.

"Okay, I see you all back there. I need you each to show me your hands. No sudden movements."

As sets of hands appeared, pair by pair, Memo realized there were probably a dozen people held up in the back of the Ford. Memo had everyone get out, and he searched the vehicle. No one seemed to be transporting any drugs with them, so Memo didn't really care to bust them. Other deputies would call the Border Patrol and have them pick up all of the illegals that they happen upon, but that was not something Memo could bring himself to do.

"Who is in charge here?"

No one answered. Memo gave them a stern look.

"No one is in charge, officer. We all put our savings together and bought this truck, and I was driving, but we have been taking turns."

"You can tell someone else that story, 'cause I'm not buying it. One of you guys is the Coyote, and I know it. I'm not going to bust you, though. You've got a headlight out. You might get stopped again along the way, and they probably won't be as nice as I am. Good luck." Memo walked toward his patrol car.

The young man walked toward him. "You-you are just letting us go?"

"That was my plan, but I can still call La Migra if you want."

"N-no sir! Thank you!"

"By the way, you might want to find a place to park until daylight. Unless you have a spare headlight, which I doubt you do."

Memo left them to their luck. It was one thing to not turn them in, but he wasn't going to help them any more than what he did. About thirty minutes later, Memo pulled over a gray Caprice that was driving 30 miles below the speed limit. An overweight Mexican man was driving and asked Memo in Spanish what he had done wrong, his breath reeking of liquor.

"Sir, step outside of the vehicle."

The man stumbled out, tripping and falling once he had exited the car. Another unit rolled up behind Memo's car, and a chubby deputy in his fifties walked up, laughing.

"Looks like you got another DUI, Memo. Good job."

"Thanks Gilberto. You think we should have him do some tests?"

"Sure. It will be fun."

After Memo explained to the man how to walk a straight line, counting out loud his ten steps and making a 180-degree turn, the man asked him to explain again.

Still not understanding, the man began walking, not toe to heel as explained, and kept walking, long after his ten steps were up.

"Thirteen! Fourteen! Fifteen!" the man shouted after each step, each number louder than the last. The drunk appeared to be comically marching, almost goose-stepping..

"That's good, you can stop now," Memo ordered the obviously distraught man.

"Okay, the last test is for you to put your hands straight back, separated, thumbs straight up, leaning forward slightly."

Sneering, the man obeyed. Memo deftly placed the handcuffs on him before the drunk had a chance to react. The other deputy laughed.

"I never get tired of that trick."

After Memo placed him in the back of the patrol car, he did a vehicle inventory on the drunken man's car and called for a tow truck.

At the sheriff's office, the intoxicated arrestee consented to a breath test, blowing a .21, well above the .1 limit set by state statute. Memo smiled, knowing it was a good arrest that would never go to court. Any court-appointed defense attorney would tell this man to plead.

Jack Newsome, a newly appointed undersheriff, stopped Memo as he left the office.

"Memo, I want to talk to you about something." Memo felt a shiver down his spine, wondering what he was in trouble for.

"Yes sir?" Memo was surprised to see the undersheriff there so late.

"I understand that a few years ago you were quite the boxer."

"I had my moments."

"I heard you had a lot more than that."

"Well, not anymore. I'm a cop now. That's all I've got time for."

"Les and I were talking, and we'd like you to consider going to the International Police Olympics held in Canada next year. It would be nice to put Las Cruces on the map, you know, and besides-"

"There's always the next sheriff's election coming up, too," Memo interrupted.

"Exactly. What do you say?"

"I'll have to think about it. Tell you tomorrow."

Memo thought about it all the way home. He did miss the excitement of the competition, training, and everything else involved with boxing. And this was still an *amateur* competition, so he wouldn't be breaking his promise. When he arrived home, he found, and not to his surprise, Rosa furious with him.

"Where were you? I called the jail, and they said you had left hours ago? Who were you with? Are you cheating on me?"

"Whoa, relax, would you? I was at the jail about an hour ago, so I seriously doubt the jailers told you 'hours ago.' After I processed a drunk, Jack wanted…"

"Jack?" Rosa interrupted. "What would Jack be doing there so late? Why are you lying?"

"Damn, Rosa, I'm trying to explain!" Every day, Memo was interrogated by his wife, and he was at his wit's end. "Look, I'm going to bed. Leave me alone. I've got court in the morning."

Unknowingly, Rosa had helped make up Memo's mind about boxing. Any extra time he could spend away from the house, the better.

A few weeks later, while patrolling Interstate 25, the highway linking El Paso to Albuquerque, Memo spotted a blue 1987 Buick with Colorado license plates. After he passed by Memo's patrol car, the driver, a Caucasian male, did a double take and took the next exit from the highway into an farm-laden area where few outsiders traveled. Memo followed, looking for a traffic violation. Inexplicably, the man stopped on the side of the road, emergency flashers on.

Memo pulled behind the parked car. Turning on his bar lights, he called in to indicate his location and the reason for leaving his unit. Approaching the Buick, he noted the man was fidgeting nervously at the steering wheel.

Pushing his sunglasses up his nose, Memo leaned down to speak to the driver. "What seems to be the problem sir?"

"N-n-nothing, sir, I just got tired, that's all."

The heavyset man was sweating, his long hair and curly beard damp with moisture. In farmer-type overalls and sandals, he looked like a hippie crossed with Farmer John.

"Where are you coming from?" Memo began the interviewing techniques learned from last week's class, noting the herbal scent of marijuana wafting through the window of the car.

"Just coming back from visiting my daughter in Phoenix, officer," the driver replied.

Memo smiled. "I hope you had a good visit. How long were you there for?"

The man furrowed his brow, then answered. "Just a day."

"Quick visit. And where are you headed now?"

"Colorado Springs. I just pulled over to rest for a minute, maybe get out and walk around." The man placed his hand on the door, as if to open it.

Memo stopped his movement. "Please stay in the car for now, sir."

Something about the man's story bothered Memo, so he made a bit more conversation and finally asked the man to step out of the car.

"Did I do something wrong, officer?"

"No," Memo reassured him. "I just want to make sure you're awake and ready to drive again. So you drove all the way from Colorado Springs to Phoenix just for a day visit?"

The man's face reflected worry. He nodded his head.

"How old is your daughter?"

"She's twenty. She just turned twenty. I went for her birthday." Farmer Hippie John now looked like he was satisfied with his answer and the worry disappeared.

"Sir, that's a what, a twelve hour drive? Why so quick?"

"Well, uh, I needed to get back to work."

"That's reasonable. What do you do?"

The man looked worried again. "I work in, uh, a grocery store."

"Hey, what's your daughter's birthday?"

The man looked like a kid that was just caught arm-deep in a cookie jar. He turned a bright red and Memo could almost see him trying to calculate what his fictitious daughter's birthday should have been. Memo had already done the math, before he had even asked the question, and when the man came up with his answer, it was off. "Sir, mind if I look in your car?"

"What?" The man's face drained of color. "Search my car?"

"Well, that wasn't really my intention, but now that you mention it, a cursory search would be good," Memo said with a smile. "You don't mind, now, do you?"

"Yeah, sure."

Memo pulled out his ticket pad and held one of the consent-to-search forms he now kept handy out for the driver to sign. If possible, the man paled even more, but he signed without protesting.

"Thank you, sir." He handed the carbon copy back. "Would you please open your trunk and then step to the side of the car and wait for me?"

After the driver opened the trunk and moved to the front of his car, Memo lifted the trunk. Surprisingly, the marijuana lay in clear view in a large plastic bag, as if it were groceries just bought from the store. In a canvas suitcase, Memo found another smaller package, probably the driver's personal stash. When it was weighed later, the total load of marijuana came 42 pounds – 38 for selling and another four for the driver. It was a decent amount for his first drug bust on the highway.

After a few weeks of fighting with Rosa, some intense training at the boxing gym, and some uneventful days patrolling, Memo got on a plane for Canada. The International Police Olympics in Quebec were a blur for Memo. The nights he spent partying, and the days he spent fighting, two things he enjoyed immensely. Les and Memo were the only two from the department that could go, so they shared the hotel.

"Damn, Memo, how the hell do you do it? I mean, I see it, but I can't believe my own eyes. You drink until four or five in the morning at the strip clubs, and God only knows what else, then you go and beat the crap out of whatever opponent they put you against."

"I've always been lucky with boxing, Les."

"More than that. You're a natural."

"It doesn't matter. This is the last time I box for a long time."

Memo had told Les years ago about his promise to his mother, and he was glad Les didn't choose to bring it up now. Memo finished lacing up his boxing shoes and sweats. Memo had one more opponent to face, and he would take home the gold.

"In this corner, from El Paso, Texas, Eduardo Torres, narcotics officer for the El Paso Police Department. And in the other corner, although at this point, I doubt there is any reason to introduce him, Guillermo Smith from the Doña Ana, New Mexico, Sheriff's Department."

The crowd cheered frantically, anticipating another bloody beating and subsequent knockout.

When the bell rang, Memo's opponent threw a few jabs and moved laterally out of Memo's reach. About two inches taller than Memo, and with a slightly longer reach, the cop from El Paso was obviously in great shape. He moved quickly in and out, hitting Memo with a fast flurry. Feeling every bit of the alcohol he had drank the night before and his lack of conditioning, Memo was slowing down. His opponent obviously saw that Memo was tiring and moved in more often, bobbing and weaving, causing Memo to miss with his powerful hook.

After what seemed like an eternity, the round ended. Les acted as Memo's corner man, shaking his head as Memo practically fell down on the stool in the ring.

"You don't look so good, Memo."

"Yeah, I realize that. He's got me beat by points, and if he keeps this speed up, he'll keep that lead."

"What are you going to do?"

"He knows I can hit, so he's careful. I'm going to make him confident he can beat me. It might take this entire next round, but I guarantee he'll think he's got me by the end."

"Okay, if you say so. Hopefully he doesn't beat you for real…"

Breathing heavily, Memo felt every punch his counterpart threw at him. It wasn't just that the guy hit hard; Memo was so out of shape, and the punishment was wearing on him. The bell rang, and Memo knew now if he didn't knock this guy out, he'd lose.

"Les, get the towel and hold it in your hands. I don't care how much blood you see, or how bad it seems, just hold it, and act like you are about to throw it in."

Les smiled, understanding. "You got it."

When Memo stepped out of his corner for the third round, he purposely held his guard lower, below his chin, and moved very slowly. A slight grin appeared on the face of his opponent, and Memo knew he had fallen for it. As soon as the bell rang, the cop from El Paso came out with everything he had, forcing Memo against the ropes. Memo took several shots to the head, and blood went everywhere. The crowd roared, but Memo could barely hear it. As the ref moved in to stop the fight, Memo let loose with every hook and uppercut he had. And he didn't stop until he saw his opponent on the floor of the ring, his body limp.

The crowd stood up. The gymnasium was filled with clapping, cheering, and cries of passion. It had been the best fight that many of them had ever seen and probably ever would see. Two Aztec warriors had battled for their lives.

Les and Memo returned to home, Memo's gold medal helping Les win his election. Why people voted for any other reason than for putting the right person in office seemed a mystery to Memo, but nevertheless he was happy with the results. Rosa didn't seem to care one way or the other, neither about the gold medal nor the election.

"Happy now?" Rosa asked Memo, as he was drifting off to sleep.

"Huh?"

"Happy you won your stupid tournament? Happy you got away from me? Did you screw a lot of Canadian women?"

"Ay, Rosa, let me get some sleep, will you? I've got to work in the morning."

In reality, he had been with a few Canadian girls, and while he did feel bad about cheating, her attitude almost seemed to justify what he had done.

"Sure." She went to the living room of their mobile home, and Memo finally went to sleep, albeit a troubled and difficult one.

Memo stood in front of a room, something like an empty warehouse, with many people observing. A sweating man, literally shaking with fear, stood in front of him. The drops of his sweat hitting the cement floor was the only sound in the room, an exaggerated sound, like the way huge raindrops would sound from inside a car as they hit the roof. The gun that Memo carried seemed to have a mind of its own, and Memo, powerless to the weapon's will, lifted it and pointed it at the man's head. With a terrible fear that came from the very deepest part of his soul, as the man pleaded for his life, Memo squeezed the trigger, the gun unfeeling in respect to the man's cries for mercy.

Memo awoke with a start, a bad feeling in his gut. It was probably just the nightmare, he thought. Yet the feeling lingered all through breakfast and his drive to work.

As Memo drove into the parking area of the Sheriff's Department, an unmarked border patrol unit pulled away. When he entered the office, the new secretary looked down at her feet, avoiding his eyes. She had been hired after Rosa quit, something Memo had to insist on because of her jealous fits she often had, even at work.

"What's wrong, Janet? You look like your best friend just died."

"No Memo, nothing's wrong. Les needs to see you."

"Okay." Memo wondered why she said "needs" instead of wants. He knocked on the sheriff's door and waited. "Pasa." Memo entered the office and stood at a chair in front of Les' desk.

"Hey Les. You wanted to see me?"

"Memo, sit down. We need to talk."

Memo felt a heat rushing throughout his body.

"What's up, Les? What's wrong?"

"The border patrol was here. They have been investigating you for about a year now."

"Me? What did I do?" Memo felt the heat rise up through his body to his face, turning his ears a reddish color.

"It is more like what you didn't do. I told them there was no way you were running wetbacks."

"You know I wouldn't do that."

"I know, son, but you can't stop a vehicle with a bunch of illegals and not do anything about it. We're law *enforcement*, for crying out loud."

"Les, I'm a cop, not a border patrol agent. I'd never want that job. How can you blame people who want to work for a better life for themselves and their families? My mom crossed over illegally herself. What the hell do you expect me to do?"

"Damn, son. This is going to be a lot of shit. The border patrol pulls a lot of weight around here."

"No, this won't be a problem, Les. I'll resign. You are a good friend to me, and you don't need this shit on account of me."

"Look, Memo, you're my best officer and my friend, as well. Why don't you think about it for a few days? I don't know how, but somehow, we'll deal with this. I might just have to suspend you for a while. I have another meeting with them on Tuesday as to their suggestions for disciplinary actions, those demanding bastards."

"All right, I'll wait to see what they want done."

All afternoon on patrol, Memo replayed the day's earlier events through his mind's eye. Between Rosa's constant paranoia and now this, it seemed there would be no place for him to feel relaxed anymore. At least when he didn't have problems at work, he was able to temporarily forget about the ones he had at home. Afternoon turned to nighttime, and Memo was asked over the car radio to cover some of the night shift. One of the other deputies' wives was in labor. Memo responded with a "10-4."

Memo answered a distress call from an undercover agent in Anthony, N.M., the town that bordered Texas but still part of Doña Ana County. When he saw the gaunt young man standing outside of the mobile home, he recognized him immediately from their fight in Canada. The El Paso narc was dressed in a black cotton shirt, black wranglers, and black boots. Memo didn't say anything to him about the fight, though, it not being the right place or time. The guy was definitely a badass, Memo decided. He had taken out two drug dealers by himself.

"¿Todo en orden? ¿Necesitas ayuda?" Memo asked the other man, wanting to make sure everything was secure and in order. Memo had asked him in Spanish because he liked for people who didn't know him to know he was Mexican; his light complexion and last name didn't exactly help with that, but his flawless Spanish did.

"Yeah. The state police are on their way to handle the investigation. You can take off."

Obviously, the El Paso cop wasn't thrilled about seeing Memo again.

"When they show up, I'll leave."

The two men stood in silence waiting for the state police, the lack of conversation like a steel wall between them. Both seemed relieved when the state police unit finally arrived. Memo left without saying a word.

The following days before the sheriff's upcoming meeting with the head of the border patrol for the region seemed more like weeks, every minute a tension-filled eternity. Having the entire weekend to mull over the situation, Memo made a hard decision.

Early Monday morning Memo was in Les' office, a worried expression on the sheriff's face.

"No, Les, you know how the BP is. They won't settle for a simple suspension. They will ruin any chances you have to get re-elected if you protect me. I'll resign; it is the best thing I can do. Honestly, I could use a change of scenery. Rosa's driving me crazy too."

Les nodded understandingly.

"Are you sure you want to do this?"

"Yeah. I'll deal with it. I know when it's time to move on. Could you do me just one favor though? Can you pay me for a month? Just to get me by while I look for work."

Les' eyes were watery. "Of course, I can do that. We're going to miss you."

Chapter 5

"After my cousins were murdered, I lost all interest in school, boxing, even in Manuela."

Lalo paused and looked at the police psychiatrist, Donna Thorne. She was in her mid-thirties, and he had never understood how a woman could be "handsome" until he had met her. She dressed conservatively; she wore a gray suit-like outfit that accentuated her curves just enough to show she had them but not so much so that it would be provocative. Her brownish-blonde hair was short, and she used her makeup sparingly. Noticing Lalo was staring at her, she blushed slightly and looked down at her notes.

"Were the killers ever arrested?" Donna asked.

"No, I can't say they were. That pissed me off too." Lalo remembered the night his uncle had stopped him from trying to kill a guy named Chito. He also remembered night after night suffering a recurring dream, reliving the assassinations of his cousins. Justice didn't seem to exist in Lalo's life. He never knew his father, his mother was a drug addict who'd lost all love for anything that wouldn't get her high, and the only real family he'd ever known had been destroyed. Heartbroken and disillusioned with the whole "cholo" lifestyle, he had wanted to get as far away from El Paso, and his life, as possible.

"I joined the Marines. I boxed in the nationals again, this time for the military. Hell, I won my way all the way to the Olympic tryouts."

"Wow. Did you make the team?"

"No. I gave that dream up. I cross-trained to Marine Recon. It was the hardcore of the hardest of the Corps. And I needed the challenge. Didn't have time to think, to remember. I always slept like a baby."

"In other words, you escaped your pain by immersing yourself in the training. I take it you had nightmares too?"

"Yeah, like I said, until Recon. There was no room for them. By the end of the day, I was too exhausted to dream."

"Actually, Lalo, we always dream. It is kind of like when you use programs to archive or get rid of what you don't need or use in your computer's hard drive."

Lalo sneered.

"Yeah...whatever. I'm not much of a computer person." He remembered getting out of the military. He had no idea what he was going to do for a living. He had applied for various jobs, including the El Paso police. As a Desert Storm veteran, he was a shoo-in, and it was only after he'd been accepted that he realized he'd never really wanted to be a police officer before. As a child, the only profession he'd ever dreamed of was to become Batman or Spiderman. But he didn't have millions of dollars to buy special crime-fighting equipment, and he hadn't been bitten by a radioactive spider, so police work seemed a logical alternative.

He had worked the streets of El Paso for a year and a half, quickly becoming one of the officers with the highest numbers of arrests per month. His record drew attention, and Sergeant Jackson of the narcotics division, one of EPPD's few black officers, approached Lalo about going to work as an undercover officer. Lalo fit the profile, physically thin and wiry, a typical trait of many of the heroin and coke users.

Lalo made buys easily and with few confrontations. A buy was an illegal substance bought by the undercover officer with funds provided to him specifically for that purpose. All "buys" had to be documented. Time, place, suspect's clothing, and even weather conditions had to be reported. Lalo identified suspects' real names by memorizing license plates, addresses, or just being nosy in their homes when he had the chance. Sometimes he had backup for the larger buys, secretly recording his contacts by use of fake beepers or wires. Most of the time he was on his own.

He spent a lot of time meeting people and making potential drug-buy connections in local bars, mingling, playing pool, and drinking. He enjoyed the irony of having a job that gave him all the drinking money he'd ever need and paid him to go spend it. It was one of those first-time buys that ended up with Lalo on a seat talking to a shrink, which is mandatory after any officer-involved shooting. As he narrated to the psychiatrist what had happened, his mind was transported to the past, his memory sharp and clear like a movie playing before his mind's eye.

As he played pool at a local bar named Kumbala's, he got into a friendly game with a couple of likely suspects – Raul and David – he'd met twice previously, but without any real interaction. Raul stood about 5'8", with short dark hair. David had at least four inches on Raul, with long black hair and a biker quality about him.

Raul and David watched Lalo play before making their move. "You like to party, man?"

"Simón," Lalo answered, moving around the table to line up another shot.

"You like soda?" David smirked, glancing over his shoulder as he whispered the slang word for cocaine.

"Do Mexicans like tortillas and beans?" Lalo said, glancing up. He would have said yes to whatever they said. It was almost midnight, and he wanted to make a buy. He'd already determined Raul and David were just users, but he would use them to get to their source, from their source to the next, and follow the sources to the main man. They both smiled at his joke, understanding him perfectly.

"Give us ten minutes, bro, and we'll be back with the onza." Raul smiled, displaying broken, yellowed teeth. The story went that one of the other men at the bar bet Raul he couldn't chew a beer bottle. Apparently, he'd won a lot of money proving he could.

"Orale. If you don't come back, I'll be looking for you," Lalo said, clapping the other man's shoulder with forced good humor.

"Que pues? Don't worry."

As the men left, Lalo peered out of the window of the bar to memorize the license plate of their truck. He didn't trust them. Trusting any junkie was just stupid.

He waited, rolling the license number around in his mind so he wouldn't forget it. He glanced out the window several times but continued his game of pool so as not to look suspicious.

After he'd waited twenty minutes, the bartender shouted last call, indicating the bar was about to shut down. Lalo realized the pair had "burnt" him and had no intentions of coming back. Lalo had given them half the money up front – something he never did on the first buy – but overconfidence caused him to make a rash decision. Now, the only recourse was to hunt the pair down and get the money back. If he didn't, everyone in the small town he was working would hear about it, and people would think he was either a cop or an idiot; either of those options was unacceptable and dangerous. He had to play it through as if he was just a regular guy who had gotten gypped.

Since the two idiots had obligingly described the area where they lived, Lalo knew he could find them.

In the center of the desert, about fifteen minutes north of El Paso, sat the small town of Anthony. It was split into two parts, one on the Texas side of the border and the other on the New Mexico side. Since they had said something about New Mexico laws being more lax than Texas laws, Lalo assumed they were living in the New Mexico side of town. After about an hour of searching, he found their truck parked in front of a mobile home just off a dirt road called Montana Vista. Lalo had jurisdiction in New Mexico as a sworn deputy sheriff because border officers were often sworn on both sides of the line.

Pausing near the front door, Lalo stood and listened for a moment, straining to hear. The two loud distinct voices inside sounded like the two men from the bar, and they appeared to be having a good time. Placing his .380 Smith and Wesson in his waistband conspicuously, he knocked and waited.

A long moment of silence, and then Raul yelled, "Who the fuck is it?"

"Lalo."

"Shit." Lalo heard whispers and chairs scraping, and he laid a hand on the butt of his weapon, waiting for someone to let him in.

Raul opened the door, and Lalo barged in, trying to keep them off guard with his actions.

"Where's Twiddle Dumb, cabrón?" Lalo said.

Startled, Raul said, "What the…" stopping in mid-sentence when he saw the handgun. Immediately, his tone changed.

"He's getting the soda, bro. Calmate." Raul held his empty hands out away from his body, his gaze wary. "We were going to get you after he got back."

"You fucks tried to burn me," Lalo growled, still angry they'd tried to pull something on him. "The bar is closed, and the pinché truck is right outside. You're fucking telling me he's not here?"

Lalo grabbed Raul by the collar of his T-shirt and yanked him toward the single bedroom of the trailer, motioning with the weapon for him to open the closed door. As he did, Lalo placed his free hand in the small of Raul's back and shoved him through. If David was waiting to ambush him, Raul would get hit first. Nothing happened, however, and Raul turned on the light.

"Ya see, vato, no one here." He indicated the empty room, and the open bathroom door to prove it was empty.

Lalo took a quick glance around and into the bathroom, moving cautiously past Raul to check the shower stall. Nothing. Keeping his gun ready, he swept the room again, bending slightly to check under the bed. As he did, he realized the bed held an unusually high mound of covers.

Lalo pointed the pistol at the bed and shouted, "Get up, cabrón, I know you're in the bed!"

The mound came to life, sprouting a 12-gauge shotgun. As David leveled the barrel toward Lalo's chest, Lalo emptied four rounds into him, center mass. Screaming, Raul grabbed an empty beer bottle and rushed Lalo, spitting curses. Lalo used the butt of his .380 to knock the shorter man into a crumpled heap on the floor. He reached over and took the shotgun from David's hands, ignoring the low gurgling sounds coming from the man's shattered chest as he died.

He pulled out his cell phone and called his supervisor.

After Lalo's brief explanation, Sgt. Jackson simply stated, "Oh, shit."

"What do you want me to do?" Lalo asked after several seconds of silence. He glanced down at Raul. Still out cold.

Jackson's voice crackled across the line. "Do you have your badge handy?"

"Yes, sir," Lalo answered, patting his jeans pocket for his leather wallet.

"Well, get it ready and stay put. I'll call an ambulance and the county." Almost as an afterthought, Jackson added, "Are you okay?"

"Yes," Lalo said curtly. He hung up, moving out of the bedroom into the living room, propping open the front door to wait for reinforcements. He kept an eye on Raul, who stirred only briefly when the first siren sounded ten minutes later.

The first uniform showed up, a young deputy sheriff from Doña Ana County. The man's light complexion and last name of Smith didn't ring any bells, and he immediately spoke to Lalo in Spanish. Lalo's Spanish was all right, but this guy had no accent at all. As they spoke, Lalo realized he'd boxed against him a few times and lost. As he recalled, the deputy had a punch like a mule's kick. His pride was still hurt from the tournament, so he decided he didn't need to talk to the deputy and waved him off.

Standing in the driveway outside, as he watched officers and vehicles come and go, Lalo pondered the outcome of the shooting. He felt numb, as if all emotion had been sucked from him by some psychological vampire. One of two things would happen. He'd either be busted down to patrolman or promoted. Oh, and he'd have to see the shrink. Again.

Chapter 6 (Memo)

"Rosa, I want a divorce."

Memo waited for her to react, expecting her to lash out at him in her usually frantic and aggressive manner. Braced for an attack, Memo was surprised when none came.

Rosa blinked twice. "Ok, but I keep the house and the minivan."

It was all they had, but Memo didn't care. He just wanted out. "Consider them yours."

Under the ever-watchful eyes of Rosa, Memo packed all he could into two suitcases. She was shutting the door while he was still crossing the threshold. Memo turned to tell her he'd be back for the rest of his things later, but the slamming door in his face was his only answer. Still, he thought, it had gone a lot better than he'd imagined. Walking to the bus station, Memo felt a sense of freedom he hadn't experienced in years. No job, no home, and no vehicle, and uncertainty lining the horizon of his future, Memo whistled, as he journeyed toward downtown Las Cruces. His new lack of responsibilities liberated him. He knew he couldn't afford the rent in El Paso, not long without a job anyway, and decided his next destination would be the Mexican border city of Juárez, Mexico. The rent would be much cheaper there, as well as the cost of living in general.

The city sprawled in all directions, seemingly without organization, and even lifelong residents didn't know the entire city. Bars, massage parlors, and dining places filled the streets of Juárez. People moved like swarms of ants from one area to another. Memo recalled an article in the El Paso Times stating that with more than a million and a half people from all over Mexico and the world, the border city of Juárez claimed almost three times the population of her sister city, El Paso. Memo asked around near downtown Juarez and found a one-bedroom about ten minutes from the border in a neighborhood called La Chavena. His apartment complex was on a hill and had a great view of the city. He still didn't have a stove, refrigerator, or even a bed. Memo unpacked a sleeping bag he had picked up at an army surplus store. Stomach growling, he exited the apartment in search of food. On the corner of his street, a man sold *tacos al vapor* from a small, mobile stand. Memo bought two and devoured them, then bought a large Carta Blanca beer from a store also on the corner. Night had fallen, and Memo saw that the city truly looked different, a mixture of yellow, white, and orange lights in every direction. A huge star made of lights on a mountain in El Paso seemed to loom over the city of Juárez.

Memo climbed to the roof of his apartment with his beer. He sat, drinking his beer as he observed the twin cities' lights, feeling free but also lonely. A large dog perched on the neighbor's roof barked fiercely at him. Startled, Memo decided to get down before the dog decided to jump over to his roof. Memo laughed; he'd never seen dogs on roofs until he had moved to Juárez.

After Memo crossed the border to El Paso, he picked up a copy of the Times to search for a job in the classified section. Because he was bilingual, with the legal right to work in the States, he found there was plenty of work on the American side of the border. Memo got a job at a telemarketing company selling long distance for AT&T. It was grueling; he was cussed at and hung-up on for forty hours a week, but it earned him a paycheck. It was much better to sit in the air-conditioned cubicles set up for telemarketers than to work in the hot El Paso sun. For Memo, the choice was easy. Every day, he would ride the bus from his humble, one-bedroom apartment in downtown Juárez to the border, a long bridge that went over the Rio Grande, linking Mexico to the United States. After walking the quarter mile over the bridge to the Customs checkpoint, Memo would declare his citizenship, showing his New Mexico driver's license. From there, he would walk another mile and a half to a bus stop where he would then complete his two-hour trip to work. Weekends were a lot better due to the lighter foot traffic over the border, as long as he left early. He usually arrived on Saturdays about fifteen minutes early. He overheard some hecklers as he walked into the office along with another guy.

"Hey pinche Chente, what's up with the boots? Where's your horse?"

Saturday was the one day of the week all employees were allowed to work in regular clothes. During the week, they had to dress business casual. A young man who everyone called "El Chente" was dressed in boots, jeans, a red Resistol shirt, and his Resistol cowboy hat. A couple of cholos were antagonizing him in the breakroom because the majority of the people who worked at the company were not the cowboy types. They called him Chente because he looked a lot like a younger version of a famous Mexican singer of the same name. He had very long sideburns, a thick mustache, and was dark-skinned, much like the singer was when he was younger.

"Hey, I like to wear clothes like this; I am Mexican after all," he responded to the cholos with a very thick accent. Memo walked up to the three men.

"Hey, you two, leave the guy alone. It's a free country; he can wear whatever he wants," Memo told the cholos; he also wore jeans and boots.

"What, you defending your boyfriend?"

Memo smiled. "No, he's not my type. But I can't stand to see a couple of shitheads bullying other people. Why don't you two just fuck off?"

One of the cholos, bald head and tats, started toward Memo. Memo tensed up, ready to counterattack. The other cholo grabbed his friend's arm, holding him back. "Not here," he whispered, "I need this job."

The bald one nodded. "Hey putos, we'll see you after work in the parking lot!"

"Simón, pendejos, we'll be there!" Memo responded. The cholos turned and left the room.

"Why did you do that? It was just words, but now they want to fight me."

"No, they want to fight *me*," Memo corrected him.

"Us. You wanted to help me, so I'm not going to let you fight alone."

Memo smiled. "Es todo, compa," he said, happy the man was ready to back him up, "but don't worry; they don't stand a chance. By the way, my name is Memo." Memo stretched out his hand.

"Rodrigo," said the other man, shaking Memo's hand. "And I hope you're right."

After their shift was over, Memo and Rodrigo walked out to the parking lot together. Waiting by Rodrigo's car were four cholos: the two from the incident earlier and two others. Rodrigo looked over nervously at Memo, but Memo's face didn't change, a half-smile lingered, as if they were about to play a game of basketball or something. The black asphalt of the parking lot smelled strongly of tar, and the streetlamps illuminated the entire area.

The cholos started yelling obscenities at Rodrigo and Memo, and when Rodrigo started to yell back, Memo shut him up with a wave of his hand, his commanding presence automatically taking charge. When the four cholos started toward them and were within striking distance, Memo reacted with some vicious hooks, knocking one by one down, moving with incredible speed. All four of the cholos were down, noses bleeding, and holding the sides of their bodies in pain. Rodrigo looked at Memo, his eyes wide with surprise. Memo turned and smiled, a warm smile, not what Rodrigo would have expected from someone capable of doing that kind of damage.

"See? I told you they wouldn't have a chance."

Rodrigo began picking up and dropping off Memo at the border every day, eliminating two hours of bus time for Memo. Rodrigo was from Cuauhtémoc, Chihuahua, and was definitely more Mexican than American, even after ten years of living in the United States. That drew Memo toward him; their cultures and language were a common ground that bonded them instantly. The two always spoke in Spanish, often to the dismay of several of the non-Spanish speaking managers at work. And both men dressed in boots, jeans, and cowboy hats on Saturdays at work.

"Cuauhtémoc is beautiful. It's in the foothills of the Chihuahua Mountains, and is mostly a farming community. Corn, wheat, and apples are the main products. Well, cheese and other dairy products are too. The Mennonites' farms mostly produce that stuff, and the corn."

"You have Mennonites in Chihuahua?" Memo asked Rodrigo, surprised.

"Yeah, they came from Holland I think, some eighty or ninety years ago. They have farms all around, and most of the work in agriculture around here is because of them. Their Spanish is somewhat hard to understand; they still speak their native language."

"Cool. But you didn't mention the most important thing that should be there."

"What's that?"

"Duh, the women! I hear there are a lot of fine girls in Chihuahua."

"I was saving the best part for last. Everywhere you look in Cuauhtémoc there are beautiful girls."

"Then what the hell are we waiting for? When do we go?" They laughed for a while and planned for a long weekend vacation in Cuauhtémoc.

Rodrigo's car was in poor mechanical condition and would never make the six-hour trip to Cuauhtémoc, so the trip would have to be made by bus. The bus station in Juárez was huge; thousands of people converged upon the city, some to stay, some to go to other destinations, on a daily basis. The tickets were the equivalent of $25 each. The young lady selling the tickets flirted with Memo the entire time they were purchasing the tickets.

"Damn green eyes of yours," Rodrigo blurted out on the bus.

"Excuse me?"

"That's why all these chicks like you. Your green eyes. I see them staring at them all the time. No one cares about my brown eyes here. Just the Gringas in the U.S."

Memo smiled at the comment. It was true; many a woman had complimented his eyes. He had good genes too. Whatever fat that accumulated in his body mostly ended up in his rear end, so he almost always had a thin waist. His six-foot height, green eyes, and well-formed muscles had always made him popular with the women.

The six-hour ride to Cuauhtémoc was without incident. The first two hours were primarily through the desert, and a movie played on the large television screen situated in the front of the bus. Because they had left on a Wednesday, the vehicle was only about half full, to the relief of Memo. Whenever there was a large group of people in a small area, body odors seemed to abound, something Memo couldn't tolerate. Rodrigo snored in the next seat, and Memo envied him. Desert turned into wide, dry valleys, and within its vastness appeared a city, Chihuahua, the capital of the state with the same name. At the bus station in the dry and very dusty city, Memo and Rodrigo changed buses.

"How long do we have to go, Rodrigo?"

"About an hour and a half. You'll like the rest of the trip, though, it's all green and we'll be heading toward the mountains."

"I guess that's why you slept all the way over here. By the way, you've got saliva all over the front of your shirt."

Rodrigo looked down.

"Made you look!"

Rodrigo made a fist like he was going to hit Memo. Assuming the boxing stance, Memo threw a quick jab, barely missing Rodrigo's nose, intentionally. Rodrigo put his hands up, surrendering, and the two men laughed.

Cuauhtémoc had a similar look to a small, Midwestern farming town one might have found in the fifties. The bus stopped downtown where Rodrigo and Memo caught a cab to Rodrigo's grandparents' house, following a paved road converting to a dirt one as they got closer. Memo smiled, enjoying the scenery of humble adobe homes, many painted in bright colors one normally wouldn't see in the States. The home was adobe covered by bright yellow-painted stucco, the door metal with a small window in the middle of the upper portion. As the cab paused in front of the house, an older woman's face appeared in the window, deciding whether or not a welcome person or a bill collector was in front. Smiling when she recognized her grandson, the old lady opened the door and hugged Rodrigo.

"Abuelita, this is my friend, Memo. Can he stay with us for a few days? I invited him to see our town."

"Of course," she said, then whispered to Rodrigo, "he looks like a gringo. Does he speak Spanish?"

Memo answered quickly back, in Spanish. "Of course I do, I'm Mexican. I'm very pleased to meet you. Rodrigo has told me so much about you, especially about how great of a cook you are."

Rodrigo looked at Memo, surprised. Even though he had never said much about his family, Memo knew enough about people in general to say what they would like to hear him say. When she had opened the door, the aroma of red chile sauce had also greeted them. Memo had a talented nose, so he assumed she was a great cook by the way the food smelled.

Smiling, the old lady invited them in. She was wearing a long, dark brown skirt and a black top with a brown shall around her shoulders. She was slightly hunched, making her already short stature even more diminished. Her hair was long, some grey but mostly white.

"You boys want something to eat?"

Both men nodded hungrily.

Memo whispered to Rodrigo. "What are we going to eat?"

"Chilaquiles."

Memo was unfamiliar with the dish, but he didn't want to show his ignorance, so he merely answered with the universal "mmmm." It turned out to be cut up pieces of homemade corn tortillas, lightly fried, with onion and cheese. The red sauce was poured over it, a taste similar to those of enchiladas. The refried beans on the side went well with the chilaquiles, and Memo felt he would soon explode after he finished the final bites of his second plate.

"Your friend *is* Mexican. Look how well he eats."

Beat from the trip, the two rested for a while in the living room, each man laid out on his own couch. Memo slept for a while, and when he awoke, all he could remember of his dreams was the outline of a beautiful girl with long, black hair.

"Hey, Rodrigo, where's the rest of your family?"

Rodrigo's normally happy face turned solemn. "My parents died in a car accident in El Paso when I was seven. My two brothers and I came to live with my grandparents. My brothers are older than me, and they both live in California. My grandpa died three years ago."

Memo frowned, regretting having asked. "I'm sorry to hear that."

"That's life, I guess."

Memo knew all too well that the simple phrase Rodrigo had just uttered was very true, and Memo shared with him his story of his parents' death. Their bond became stronger.

Rodrigo spent most of the day Thursday showing Memo the "sights," the local building's styles, smells, and people. Most of the men in the city dressed in cowboy clothes and drove big trucks with fancy rims cruised the streets. Most of the vegetables and goods were sold market style and small stands lined the local mercado.

"There's going to be a big dance tomorrow, Memo. Do you want to go?"

"Are politicians corrupt? Damn right, I want to go!"

Chapter 7

A musical group known as Los Rieleros Del Norte played at a dance at the Sertoma, one of the larger dance halls in the city. Memo thought the outside of the Sertoma looked just like a huge warehouse, but the inside was filled with cowboys, pretty girls in dresses, and a shiny wood floor to dance on in the center. Around the dance floor, plastic tables with "Carta Blanca" in red, block letters were scattered about. He saw the most beautiful girl there, so tall and thin but also curvaceous; she looked like a supermodel. With long, straight black hair and light brown skin, her large almond-shaped eyes held his and, although Memo did not believe in love at first sight, he felt Cupid's arrow dig into his heart.

"Beautiful, is she not?" Rodrigo handed him a Tecate-brand beer, and Memo took a long sip.

"More than that," he agreed. "Do you know her?"

His friend shook his head. "I've seen her before, but I don't know her name or where she lives. Or even her partner there." He pointed to the dance floor.

She danced gracefully with a short, chubby man several years older than she, and Memo never got a chance to dance with her. He danced with other women there, not really paying attention to any of them, his gaze fixed on the gorgeous woman who'd bewitched him. At the end of the evening, Memo stood at the door, waiting for when the beautiful dark-haired beauty would leave. When the girl and her dancing partner passed by, he told them good night. The girl turned to acknowledge his words, her long hair billowing out, and her radiant smile bemused him the entire journey home.

Rodrigo and Memo returned to their jobs in El Paso. Memo couldn't get the girl he'd seen in Cuauhtémoc out of his head. Deciding he couldn't rest until he could find her again, Memo made plans with Rodrigo to go back there.

"You like that girl that much?"

"No, it's just...I really like your town." Memo lied.

"Yeah right."

"Fine. I can't get her out of my head. Everything in me says to find her and make her mine."

"That's what I thought." Rodrigo said, smiling.

Four months later, at another dance in Cuauhtémoc, Memo saw the couple again. After finding out from one of Rodrigo's cousins that the short, chubby man was only the girl's brother, Memo decided to ask her to dance. She sat at a table with another pretty girl Rodrigo had mentioned he liked.

"Okay, here's the plan, Rodrigo. Let's go together and ask both of the girls to dance. I'll ask the dark-skinned one, and you the one with big breasts."

Rodrigo smiled at the idea probably because Memo had mentioned big breasts and Rodrigo's name in the same sentence.

"Sounds good to me, Memo."

As Memo approached the table, a young man beat him to the supermodel girl, and she accepted his invitation to dance. Memo looked back at Rodrigo who was still sitting back at the table, looking a little drunk; Memo decided to ask the dark-skinned girl's friend to dance.

"Shall we dance?"

The girl was attractive, light-skinned, blue-eyed, and even taller than the other one, but she lacked whatever it was in the other girl that made Memo's heart skip a beat. The only reason he had decided on asking her to dance was so he could get a little closer to the other girl.

"I'd love to."

She talked and talked about God only knew what, her constant banter a drone in Memo's ear as they danced. He stared at the dark-haired girl the whole time he danced with her friend, all the while plotting how to meet her. The two danced until the group rested.

"Would you like to sit down with me? There's room at my table."

"I'd love to, but I'm with a friend. I really don't want to leave him alone like that."

"Well, invite him too." The girl was obviously smitten with him. She had told him her name, but he couldn't remember it for the life of him.

"I'll be right back."

When Memo got over to where Rodrigo still sat, he met the accusation in his friend's eyes.

"Hey, Memo, I thought you liked the other girl," Rodrigo reproached, his words a bit slurred. He lifted his beer again, but Memo stopped him.

"I do," he said. "Go with me to the table. When the group starts playing again, ask the girl you like to dance, and I'll ask the other one."

When the group started to play again, the two put their plan to action. Memo and the black-haired girl danced the rest of the evening. She told him her name was Lucia, and her brother Beto usually escorted her to dances to keep an eye on her for their parents.

"Beto, this is Memo. Memo, this is Beto."

Beto eyed Memo, trying to decide whether he was a predator or not.

Memo extended his hand and shook Beto's firmly.

"Nice to meet you."

Beto, Memo, Lucia, Rodrigo, and the other girl all sat down. Memo still couldn't remember her name.

"Beto, what are you drinking?"

"Tecate."

"Me too. I'll be right back."

Memo went to the bar and ordered six beers. If he knew people, especially a drinking man, free alcohol was a sure way to his heart. When he arrived at the table, six-pack in hand, the somber Beto suddenly smiled. Memo had placed him in his pocket.

Beto invited Memo and Rodrigo to the house after the dance, and they continued to drink until about five the next morning. After waking up on the sofa at Lucia's brother's house the next day, Memo spent the rest of his time in Cuauhtémoc with Lucia, enjoying every moment spent in her presence.

On his last night before returning to El Paso, Memo asked Lucia to walk with him. They wandered through the town in the warm twilight until they came to a small gazebo in the town square. He pulled Lucia up the steps and looked down into her laughing face.

"I know this may seem a bit fast, Lucia," he murmured, reaching out to smooth a strand of dark hair away from her face. "But I love you. Will you marry me?"

Her brown eyes widened, and she stood completely still. "Memo, I don't know what to say."

"Say yes," he urged, drawing her to him. She put a hand on his chest to keep her distance.

"I don't want to hurt you, Memo, but I can't answer you right now."

Her words made his heart ache, but he pressed on. "Why can't you answer?"

"My parents are on the other side," she said softly, the other side meaning the United States. "My father is very traditional and would expect a good future son-in-law to ask his permission to request my hand."

Memo took a deep breath, relief welling up inside him. She didn't say she didn't want to be with him, so hope still held sway.

"When will they return?"

"Beto and I expect them back in two weeks." She smiled up at him, her eyes twinkling. "You may ask my father then, if you like."

Memo swung her up into his arms, kissing her deeply.

Chapter 8

Detective Lalo Torres sat at his new desk in the Homicide Division of the El Paso City Police Department, contemplating which "crap" case he'd start on next. Because he was the junior detective on the squad, the other officers loaded him down with suicides and accidental deaths. Ever since he'd started with the department, homicide had been his goal, so he didn't mind getting the boring cases. Even the John and Jane Does were welcome compared to this stuff, but one day another detective in the division would retire, and he'd move up another notch. He remembered how not that long ago he was almost disqualified from police work entirely because of his former, however brief, gang ties. However, the captain in charge of recruiting also came from El Segundo. He realized that in the barrio one lived, one was automatically associated with that gang, and therefore many kids joined simply for protection from other gang members in other barrios. The Captain decided Lalo's knowledge of gang activity would be an asset to the department rather than a hindrance, and it had served him well in his years on the street.

The intercom on the corner of his scarred wooden desk suddenly came to life, and the chirpy voice of the division's secretary chimed over the speaker.

"Detective Lalo—err, Torres, line four."

Lalo smiled at the secretary's hesitation. He could tell she liked him; her flirtatious demeanor with him was the only slip in her normal professional manner. A bored desk sergeant on the other end of the line gave Lalo details on a new suicide case just reported, and his heart skipped a beat when he recognized the name of the deceased.

Carlos Medina Tenorio, a notorious cocaine dealer in the El Paso-Juárez area, lived in Northern Heights, a wealthy area of the city. Surprised none of the other detectives picked up on this info, Lalo scrambled out to his unmarked unit and sped across town to the opulent home. During Lalo's years as a narcotics undercover agent, he'd never been able to snare Medina. Even the confidential informants could never make a buy from him, even after they swore up and down they had in the past. Two search warrants yielding no evidence ended up in a lawsuit against the department, and Lalo's superiors ordered him to "cease and desist" all investigations of Medina.

The driveway bulged with emergency vehicles, fire, ambulance, and the coroner's black station wagon. Lalo pulled up next to the wagon, parked, and pulled a new notepad out of his glove box. After noting the time, date, and weather conditions, Lalo stepped out of his car. He'd found that details were often what won or lost a court case, so he was quite meticulous about recording them and even used a new pad for every case. Once entered as evidence in a case, anything in the pad was subject to scrutiny, so he carefully kept each case separate to prevent confusion.

Lalo began to sketch the outside layout and worked his way inside the home, greeting the paramedics as they wandered out, their kit closed and stretcher empty. He noted if lights were on or off, door positions, and basic conditions of the home, hoping the other personnel knew better than to touch anything but the victim to avoid contaminating the scene.

Medina had lived like a king. For a moment, Lalo envied the large rooms, expensive furniture, the big screen TV, and every electronic gadget a person could want. When he finally made it to the master bedroom, the grisly scene within made him wonder if all that drug money had really been worth it to Medina. At that moment, he was very glad to not be in Medina's shoes.

Medina slouched in a chair near the bed, his right hand in a death grip on a black Glock 9mm hanging stiffly between his legs, brain matter splattered across the textured silk wall behind him, and a pool of blood had formed on the floor in front of him. One designer shoe hung from his right foot, while the other lay upside down on the floor near the body. Lalo's uncle had once said, "Todos pagan en esta vida," and this drug dealer paid in this life, with his own.

Lalo felt the familiar gag he always felt when viewing scenes like this one. He swallowed hard, took a deep breath, and let it drain from him. Time to get to work. Lalo treated it like he would a murder scene, not wanting to make the mistake that many cops did of assuming something was simply what it appeared to be. Anyway, he felt something was wrong with the scene. It seemed almost too clean, too perfect. He directed the crime scene technicians to their work, much like a choreographer would direct a troop of finely tuned dancers.

A commotion near the door heralded the entrance of Detective Spurgeon, a large man with graying hair and a permanent frown. The fact that Spurgeon walked into an unprocessed crime scene without regard for processing bothered Lalo, but not nearly as much as the fact that a senior detective was coming to check on him.

Spurgeon walked over to stare down at the corpse. "Why are you processing this like a potential homicide? It's obviously a suicide."

Lalo spared him a glance but nodded to the photographer to finish.

"In the Marines, we had a saying, 'assume makes an ass out of you and me.'"

"Don't give me that shit, Lalo. You just want to see if you can find a drug bust out of this. You need to remember you're in homicide now."

"Hey Spurgeon, I don't need you to remind me what department I'm in. I've got no intention of going back to narcotics. I had a lot of fun in narcotics, but homicide has always been my dream."

Spurgeon answered with a sarcastic grunt.

Lalo knew better than to argue the point with this bull-headed man. Spurgeon was a one-opinion type of guy and arguing with him reminded Lalo of arguing with a battleship.

Lalo shrugged and walked away.

Spurgeon followed. "Why do you really care about this piece of human garbage anyway?"

When Lalo said nothing, continuing to make notes in his pad, the other man added, "Even if it wasn't a suicide, someone just did us a favor. Why waste everyone's time?"

"I'm just doing my job," Lalo reminded him, keeping his voice calm. He made a note of the watch lying on the floor near the foot of the bed and a man's ring lying on the bedside table.

"Your job is to investigate homicides," Spurgeon spat. "Not keep my crew busy on an open-and-shut case."

Lalo looked at him, wondering why the older detective minded his investigation so much. "We're almost done here."

He signaled the waiting coroner to come and retrieve the body.

With a disgusted snort, Spurgeon left, brushing past the coroner.

The crime scene was processed for trace evidence. What still bothered Lalo was the scene was unusually clean for a suicide. Lalo knelt down on the hardwood floor, following the cracks from one wall to the other with a magnifying glass. There were no trace particles on the floor around Medina, no hairs or fibers. A bottle of Don Julio Tequila sat on the floor, mostly drained, and a single shot glass beside it. A thumbprint, surely belonging to the deceased, was at a very odd angle on the glass. There were no photos of friends or family nearby, nor a suicide note, things usually indicative of a person who is about to commit suicide. The cleanliness of the crime scene continued to gnaw at Lalo's gut long after he left the scene. Back at the station, Lalo knocked on the division head's door, Captain John Barba. The balding man seated in the office waived him to enter. Barba wore a goatee, and his hard features gave him the appearance of being permanently angry. His suit and tie were impeccable and expensive.

"Captain, I'm thinking we need to do an all-out homicide investigation on the supposed Medina suicide."

"Look, Lalo, I know you're gung ho on investigating a homicide. Spurgeon says this is an open and shut. He's not the smartest white boy around, but he's been in homicide for about sixteen years. He knows a suicide when he sees one. Anyway, even if it wasn't a suicide, since when is it a crime when someone *takes out the trash*. Give it a rest."

Lalo couldn't figure it out why Spurgeon and Barba refused to even consider the "suicide" a homicide. It became his obsession in the weeks to follow, and everyone in his division seemed to know it. After he filled his cup with water in the break room, two fellow detectives made a point to stop on either side of the cooler.

"Hey, whatever happened to the really great detectives?" Reed, a tall, lean blonde-headed detective who always wore cowboy boots asked a shorter, dark-haired Mendoza.

"Why, that's elementary, my dear Watson, just ask our Mexican Sherlock Holmes."

Lalo flashed a sarcastic smile at both of the detectives and gave them the one-finger-salute.

After work, Lalo decided to continue his investigation, although Barba had already officially closed it for him.

"Mrs. Medina, what can you tell me about the day your husband died?" Lalo said.

In between short bouts of sobbing, Mrs. Medina answered. She was dressed in an elegant, and as far as Lalo knew, probably designer black dress, a pearl necklace with matching earrings and bracelet, and shoes probably worth more than his entire week's paycheck.

"He was so happy. He had seemed very upset for several days, but he wouldn't tell me what was wrong. On the day he-he-you know..." She paused and Lalo gave her a reassuring nod. "...well, he just seemed very happy. He told me to go shopping, so I did. He had been very insistent about it."

"Where did he get the gun?"

"Carlos has collected guns since we were first married. He went shooting every weekend with his friend in Juárez."

"What is his name, and how would I contact him?" Lalo readied his pen on the notepad as he waited for the widow to answer, tapping the tip of it gently on the paper.

"Angel Godinez. He owns a restaurant called Guasave's Seafood." Her tears had dried up as they had been talking, and when Lalo looked up at her, she began to cry again, blotting dry her newly wetted eyes daintily.

"Well, ma'am, I guess that will be all for now. Umm, just one more thing. Was your husband a righty or a lefty?"

"Ambidextrous."

Lalo knew Godinez as being a smuggler from some drug busts in El Paso, but he'd never arrested him because he was smart enough to only set up deals in Juárez. Apparently, he and Carlos Medina worked for the same guy, El Soldado, the bloody leader of the Juárez cartel. He drove to Juarez to set up a meeting with Godinez at his restaurant. Godinez happened to be there and agreed to meet with Lalo. He acted friendly enough, offering Lalo his finest table, and even joining him to order lunch. Lalo had almost laughed when he first saw him because the fat, round-bellied man wore more gold than Mr. T, with a white silk shirt open at the neck, beige Wranglers busting at the seams, and a pair of brown ostrich-skin boots with a matching belt.

Lalo ordered a plate of Camarones Empanizados and a Carta Blanca beer. Godinez ordered a large combination seafood plate and a Bohemia. The two talked for a while, a mere pleasantry. They both knew Lalo was there to talk about Medina. Finally, after the meal and one more Carta Blanca, Lalo got to the point.

"I need to know about Carlos." He leaned back and watched the expression on the fat man's face.

"A great loss," the other man said, mopping his sweating brow. "What is it you need to know? Something bothering you? Aren't all you law enforcement people just tickled that you no longer have to deal with Medina?"

Lalo thought for a moment. "Some are, sure. I'm interested in if someone would go through all the trouble to make his murder look like a suicide. I have no proof, yet, but something isn't right."

Godinez shook his head, his double chin still moving even after he had stopped moving. "I seriously doubt Carlos would commit suicide, myself. He was moving up, a respected businessman on both sides of the border."

Lalo suppressed the urge to laugh. *Medina was a respected businessman?* But, without changing expression, he asked, "What can you tell me? Is there a particular direction I should go?"

"Now, you know I do not believe in informing the police about company problems," Godinez replied stiffly. "But in this case, I know nothing to tell. Unless, of course, whoever did it had ties to Carlos' jefe."

"You mean, to avoid retribution from El Soldado."

Godinez' eyes widened, pupil's dilating in the process, almost like those of a cartoon character when shocked or surprised. "Shhhh, detective, remember you are not in El Paso. Juárez belongs to HIM, and we need not mention his name."

"You're right, I won't do it again. Now I just have to prove this was a murder to my boss." Lalo paused, as he decided to take a different approach. "You went target practicing with him. Anything unusual there?"

The other man frowned, as if thinking back to his target practices. "No, not that I can think of. He preferred to use a .45, and although used both hands, he couldn't shoot worth a damn with his right hand."

Lalo leaned forward. "Are you certain about that?"

"Of course, I'm sure." Godinez looked offended. "I shot with him often, and I tell you, he couldn't hit anything with his right hand."

Lalo sat back, forcing himself to look disinterested. He took another sip of his beer and made small talk for another fifteen minutes before excusing himself. Godinez insisted on treating him to lunch, so Lalo left with information, a full belly, and money still in his wallet. Outside the restaurant, as the two men waited for the valet to bring their vehicles, Lalo turned to Godinez and asked, "One last thing. What was Medina's favorite liquor?"

Godinez smiled, as if remembering a good drinking night he may have had with Medina. "Buchanan's, definitely Buchanan's."

There were too many discrepancies with the supposed suicide scene. Now he could prove Medina's death was not a suicide, or at least support his belief that it was a homicide. It took over an hour for Lalo to get through the long line of cars at the bridge that acted as the border crossing from Mexico to the United states. After nearly two hours, Lalo needed to pee so badly that he stopped at the first convenience store he passed. He ran in, ignoring a homeless man's pleas for money. Relieved, he bought water, a coke and a burrito. He handed the food and coke to the homeless guy. The man's grimy hands reached up and took the burrito and soda, not even looking up at Lalo, or uttering a thank you. His hair was long and matted; his clothes were greasy and dirty, and he smelled just like he looked. Lalo sat in the patrol car for a few minutes, drinking his water and observing the people entering and exiting the store. No one even glanced at the homeless man. He was invisible.

When he got back to the station, Lalo went immediately to Barba with the information. Instead of commending Lalo's discovery, Barba gave Lalo a verbal beating that left him feeling very small.

"Listen, Lalo, I like you, really I do. We're from the same roots. So now I'm going to tell you plain and simple, if you want to continue to be a homicide detective, you'll have to stop worrying about drug dealers who committed suicide and start worrying about your job."

For the next few days, Lalo kept a low profile and did what he was told. But he didn't stop thinking. He wondered how Carlos Medina had killed himself with the hand he didn't normally shoot with. He also couldn't understand why no one wanted him to investigate the case, even after he volunteered to do it on his own time. Drug dealers had been murdered before, and when the cases were investigated thoroughly, usually other drug dealers could be arrested for the murder. It was like hitting two birds with one stone. Lalo wondered why this case should be different.

Lalo's radio blared and awoke him from his mental trance. "El Paso, D-14."

"D-14. Go ahead, El Paso."

"D-9 and 10 request back-up at 1107 Delta Drive. They have a murder suspect in custody and need a translator to explain the arrest to the family."

"10-4."

The street was in the neighborhood known as El Segundo Barrio where Lalo's old gang, Los Fatherless, once ruled. Lalo pulled up to the block where the row of single-story apartments were, the only thing really differentiating them from one another were the different pastel colors: pink, lavender and salmon. The detectives had the man in cuffs but were surrounded by his family.

"You cops, you're all racist. My boys aren't doing anything, and you just come and want to arrest everyone. Why don't you just go leave our neighborhood alone like you normally do?" The lady yelled at Spurgeon in Spanish, saliva spewing with every word. Spurgeon's 6'3" stature didn't seem to faze her at all.

"Lady, please just calm down. I don't understand Spanish very well."

Lalo noticed as he walked up to Spurgeon's side that the man actually seemed a lot more intimidated than the five-foot lady he was trying to converse with. Two men, apparently also related to the homicide suspect, walked menacingly up to Lalo and Spurgeon. A small crowd suddenly appeared, yelling profanity at the police officers on site. A patrol car with two uniformed police officers showed up as back-up. When Lalo looked away to motion the two uniforms to go over where he and Spurgeon were, one of the men grabbed Spurgeon. The other man, short and stocky, began punching Lalo. The crowd cheered.

Lalo easily evaded the man's punches to his face by bobbing and weaving. He hurt the man's fist when he blocked his punch with his elbow, then answered the man's short flurry with a left-right combo that hammered him into submission. Spurgeon slammed the man he was wrestling with into the ground and cuffed him. The lady who had been yelling at him when Lalo had first arrived had grabbed a broken beer bottle and was about to hit Lalo with it when Reed, the other detective at the scene, pepper-sprayed her. She immediately dropped to her knees, hands rubbing at her tearing eyes frantically, mucus gushing from her nose. The angry mob vocalized their disapproval.

The sudden cracking sound of a gunshot silenced the crowd. Lalo felt warm liquid running down his leg. Reed yelled frantically that someone had stolen his gun. Lalo looked around, suddenly feeling very weak, and saw one of the suspect's brothers taking aim at Spurgeon. Lalo already had his 9mm in hand and shot the man three times, aiming center mass as he had been taught in the Marines, as well as in the police academy. All of his training had been for a time just like this one- having to defend himself or others despite being wounded and disoriented.

Lalo looked down, saw the blood staining his shirt just below his heart and fell to his knees. His thoughts were surprisingly clear; he pondered the fact of how volatile police work was; when he had arrived at the scene, a few people were arguing, and in just a few minutes, total chaos replaced the repose of a moment before, much like when an auto accident occurs, suddenly and without enough admonition to modify the eventual outcome. His mind started wandering, dreamlike, as the last thing he saw was people running in all directions and Spurgeon's big, round face in front of him, mouthing unheard words.

Chapter 9 (Memo)

Lucia wore a traditional white dress and flowing veil, and Memo sported a western-style suit with crocodile boots and a matching belt. He spent all of his retirement money from the police department to make the day special for his bride. In Mexico, the wedding was one of the most important things in a young woman's life. The religious ceremony and expensive reception made for stronger family and religious ties in the community.

Another of Lucia's brothers, Leo, prepared a pig to make asado, pork in red chile sauce, and chicharrones. After killing and cleaning the pigs, he and another man promptly began to cut up the pig, cutting pieces of the legs into small bits for the asado. A large iron disc that had once been a part of a tractor was used to fry the pieces of skin and fat, making them into chicharrones: the smell of freshly fried pork making Memo very anxious to eat. After the chicharrones were made, the smaller pieces of the pigs' rear end and legs were fried, then Leo drained the excess oil. The red chile sauce was poured in, and he added garlic laurel to it. One of her aunts made Spanish-style rice, while yet another made frijoles charros, a mix of beans, beer, bacon, ham, chicharrones, chile, onions, and cilantro. Memo had bought brandy for each table in the dance hall they had rented, and arrangements for the tables had been made by Leo's wife. A huge cake had been procured as well.

Rodrigo was the only person at the wedding who had been there on the groom's behalf. The reception was a blur of great food and meeting Lucia's seemingly endless number of family members and friends.

Memo had hired a live group known as Innovación to play at the reception and dance; the combination of sax, accordion, and electric guitars provided a harmonic mix. Lucia liked to dance, and Memo knew this costly detail would make her very happy.

The music lasted until about four in the morning, beginning with the traditional waltz. About halfway through, people lined up to dance with the bride and/or the groom, having to clip money to their garments for the privilege of doing so. Memo noticed Lucia refused to dance with one of the guys who had lined up. He left, obviously angry. Memo was dancing, too, so he didn't have time to ask her what that had been all about. When the waltz was over, several of the men and all five of Lucia's brothers grabbed Memo and disrobed him in front of all of the guests, leaving him in underwear. Memo didn't put up a fight; he knew this was just a part of the fun. Several of the female guests, and one or two of the male ones, made comments about his body or whistled. Lucia looked on, jealously. After the dance, Memo and Lucia went to a local tourist attraction for their wedding night called Rancho La Estancia, a large ranch and fancy hotel in a beautiful area in the foothills of the mountains, green with trees and grass. As they drove, Memo asked what had happened with the guy she didn't dance with.

"About two years ago, I had been dating this man named Julio Cesar. He taught Taekwondo at the gym his family owns. We were to be married when two of my brothers died in a car accident."

Memo frowned. He didn't even know she had two more brothers.

"The wedding was postponed. Later I found out that Julio, supposedly a good friend of my brothers, was seen at a dance but only a week after the deaths. Someone in mourning doesn't go to dances, especially when his girlfriend is totally broken-down. I broke off the engagement. There were some really crazy things he did afterwards that only solidified my decision. I swear to you I never expected him at the wedding."

"I believe you. Why hadn't you talked to me about your brothers before?"

"We have a lot to learn about each other, still. I'm sorry."

Memo nodded, totally in agreement. When they arrived at the hotel, Memo swung Lucia up into his arms and carried her into the luxurious suite he'd rented. The room was decorated with several dozen roses he'd ordered to show his love, and the subtle aroma filled the room. After gently laying her upon the king-size bed covered with rose petals, Memo kissed Lucia on the lips, parting them gently with his tongue. She responded, and they embraced in a long, passionate kiss.

Memo slid the long zipper of her wedding dress down and then gently removed it from her slender body. He wanted their wedding night to be a night they would remember for the rest of their lives. Lucia shivered, as he uncovered her satiny skin, her eyes full of moisture and lips trembling. Memo took his time, kissing her lips, her neck, and tracing his way down her body as he removed her clothing. Soon, she reached for him eagerly, drawing his lips back to hers.

Kissing her neck, Memo worked his way down toward her small breasts, circling her nipples with his tongue. Lucia moaned slightly, her nipples hardening. He continued down to her navel, marveling at her flat abdomen. Traveling down further, Lucia gently grabbed his head, pulling him back up. She obviously wasn't ready for that, yet. Memo would respect that, for now. He turned her over, kissing the back of her neck and down her shoulders and back. Knowing he would not be able to go to certain areas because of her lack of experience, Memo turned her over again, kissing her toes and gently sucking on them. Lucia moaned and arched her back slightly. Memo was very happy at the effect, and continued up, missing the seemingly forbidden area. He wanted to take her to all different levels, but he would have to settle for a more traditional approach, for now.

Lucia delivered her virginity to Memo with all her heart and soul, and Memo took it, decisively, with passion and love.

Chapter 10

After a few days at the ranch, the lighthearted newlyweds went to Memo's apartment in Juárez in an old farm pickup he bought from a Mennonite that Lucia's dad worked for.. As they slowly made it through the busy Juárez traffic, they got to know each other better. Their engagement had been a whirlwind. As they spoke, Memo realized how little they knew about each other.

"Tell me about your parents, Memo. You've said so little about them."

Memo took a deep breath. He had many good memories of them, but their loss still hurt. "My dad was a kind man. He loved my mother and me very much. He would have given his life for either of us. He spent every free minute of every day with us." Memo paused for a moment, memories filling his mind.

"My mom. Wow. She was overprotective. She spoiled the hell out of me and my dad. We had freshly made tortillas every day, chicken soup, Vicks when we were sick, and a hug when we were sad. They were the best." He stopped at a red light.

Lucia smiled and hugged Memo.

The neighborhood streets were lined with rundown, one-story houses and apartments, all running together. There were no spaces or yards in between to separate them. On the other side of the street was a clinic run by the social security system in Mexico, much like county hospitals in the States. Graffiti covered everything that could be painted on.

Seeing the look of anguish in Lucia's eyes, Memo said, "Look, it's only temporary. We'll save up and find a better neighborhood as soon as we can."

"My love, I don't care where I live as long as I'm with you."

Memo smiled. His apartment didn't look much better than the neighborhood, with his laundry lying around on the floor and unwashed dishes piled in the tiny kitchen sink. Poor lighting and dirty windows didn't hide the dust layered on every surface.

Upon seeing the condition of his apartment, Lucia said, "This is how you lived? No wonder you wanted to get married so fast!"

The two laughed and settled into the routine of marriage. Memo's commute was much faster now, and it allowed him more free time to spend with Lucia. They did typical things that couples do, eating out, dancing, and the movies.

One evening as Memo returned home from work, the driver of an old Lincoln was blocking the road trying to convince a girl who was walking on the street to get in with him.

Memo pulled alongside him, his window already down, and yelled, "Hey, why don't you go to your ranch to talk, idiot!"

Once he drove around the Lincoln, Memo floored it, passing the other man. To his surprise, the man evidently gave up on the girl and pursued Memo. Not wanting the man to know where he lived, Memo turned a few blocks before the street where his house was and stopped. The car pulled up in front of Memo's truck and stopped. The man climbed out.

Still dressed in business-casual attire with a tie, Memo must not have looked very menacing to the other man, who also was evidently still in his work clothes. He looked like he was some kind of a mechanic, his shirt and pants covered with oil stains.

Memo carried a tire iron in one hand.

"What, you want to fight?" Memo asked.

"Why don't you put down the tire iron and fight like a man?"

The mechanic didn't appear to have any weapons on him, so Memo threw down the tire iron. The mechanic ran toward him, grabbing his tie, but Memo unleashed a flurry of right crosses and left hooks, making short work of the man.

The mechanic, laid out on the cement, begged for mercy while Memo stood hunched over him, still pummeling him with lefts and rights until the man covered his bloody face with his hands and pleaded with him to stop.

A small crowd of children had gathered around to watch.

"I'll stop, but you better not get up until I've left."

"Okay, okay."

Memo walked away, keeping an eye on the man, as he got into his truck and drove off. The mechanic didn't even flinch. Still surging with adrenalin, Memo arrived home, practically yelling to Lucia what had just occurred.

"Baby, you have to quit being so violent," she said. "You never know who might have a gun or a knife. Lots of men don't fight like men. They might use weapons."

"I know. But I saw he wasn't carrying anything."

"You could see into his pockets?"

"Well, no," Memo answered, lowering his head a bit.

"Please, try to be less violent, if not for me or you, for the baby." She placed a hand on her stomach.

"You're pregnant?"

"I confirmed it at the doctor's today. One month."

Memo smiled from ear to ear and hugged Lucia firmly. "That's wonderful, my love."

"I called my mom today to let her know. She wants to stay with me and help out during the pregnancy. Is that alright with you?"

Memo thought about all the extra expenses that would incur with Lucia's mom. Just her mom was one thing, but she would bring her three youngest with her. Not wanting to disappoint Lucia, Memo accepted.

So many people at the apartment made life more difficult, but they did the best they could with Memo's meager earnings from his job in the States. Lucia's mom was very helpful around the house, and she treated Memo like another son. The boys didn't do much around the house, but they didn't cause problems, either. There wasn't too much friction in the family, even within the reduced space of the one-bedroom apartment. Privacy for the couple was almost nonexistent: the tiny kitchen and living room being the only other rooms in the apartment. After work,

Memo often played outside with Lucia's brothers, temporarily escaping the apartment's heat and claustrophobia.

Memo played soccer outside of his home with his three brothers-in-law in the hospital's parking lot in front of his modest apartment. Every night after Memo got home from work, he and the smallest would team up against the two older brothers in what would always become a heated game. As customary in Mexico, when one team or the other made a goal, the team inevitably yelled, "G-o-a-l!"

One night, a thin young man passing by yelled out, "C-u-l-e-r-o-s, shut the fuck up." From his unsteady gait and slurred words, Memo thought the boy might be an addict from a nearby drug hot spot.

"Your momma!" responded Gilberto, one of the two older brothers.

The four continued playing, not thinking anymore of the situation. Omar, the youngest brother, kicked the ball out of the playing area. Jorge and Gilberto ran for it.

"Memo! Come here, quick!" Gilberto yelled out.

Omar and Memo ran toward the other two brothers. Memo saw the two were backed into the corner by the same cholo who'd been yelling profanities at them.

"Be careful, Memo, he's got a knife!"

Memo ran toward the cholo and stopped just a few feet short of him. The kid had a syringe in his hand. Knowing that all kinds of blood-borne diseases could be contracted by the prick of a used needle, Memo didn't take any chances. He stepped quickly to the side of the cholo and kicked him in the arm that held the needle, causing him to drop it. As the cholo turned away to run, Memo kicked the boy in the rear.

"You're in deep shit," the boy yelled as he ran, "I'll be back with my gang!"

Even though the four laughed at the cholo's behavior and the comical kick in the ass, they decided it would be better to go home. As Jorge, Memo's most talkative brother-in-law, recounted the story to Lucia and Memo's mother-in-law later in the evening, somebody began banging loudly on the door, nearly breaking the glass windows. Memo looked outside the window and saw six cholos dressed in baggy pants and undershirts. One was in a white truck parked by the curb, still running, while the other five were standing in front of the door.

Memo's mother-in-law trembled, as she looked out the window. She turned to Memo with fear in her eyes. "Let's just call the police."

"You know there's no time for that. They'd never get here in time," Memo answered, truthfully.

Two of the men at the door again beat on it loudly. Memo thought of Lucy and the baby, and worried about what would happen if they got inside of the apartment.

After going to the bedroom, Memo grabbed the bat he kept by his bedside. The fists banging on the door became more aggressive. Returning to the living room, Memo looked around at the panicked faces of his family and said, "Everyone get away from the door. Don't go outside, no matter what happens." He opened the door and barely stepped outside.

Surprised, one of the cholos in front of the door jumped back and yelled, "Hey, mother fucker, drop the bat!"

Five gangsters were in front of Memo, distancing themselves from his bat. One with his head shaven clean leapt forward, and Memo responded with a short swing to his head.

"Ahh, you fucker!" The cholo jumped back, holding his head where he had been hit.

Any fear Memo may have felt fueled an incredible adrenalin rush, so powerful he couldn't hear what they were yelling at him anymore.

"Back off, or you'll get it!" Memo shouted at them. After seeing they weren't deterred by the bat and realizing they had started to throw rocks at him, Memo called for his brother-in-law.

"Get my gun, Gilberto! Throw it to me!"

Gilberto tossed Memo the Smith and Wesson .357 he kept in the house for protection. Memo aimed the gun at the cholos and yelled, "Leave or I'll shoot!"

The cholos got in the truck, yelling angrily, but still didn't leave. His heart beating thunderously in his ears, Memo was still unable to discern what they were saying to him. Memo aimed at the truck and pulled the trigger, his wife's face in his mind as he did so.

Click! The gun didn't fire. Memo cocked the gun and aimed again.

"This time it will fire, fuckers, you'd better get the hell out of here!"

The cholos finally left, still screaming obscenities at Memo.

As soon as he entered the house, Lucia hugged him with all the strength she could muster, as if her hug had protective powers to magically transform him into an indestructible being.

Looking deep into Memo's eyes, she said, "You could have been killed!"

"What did those men want?" His mother-in-law asked, her eyes wide with fear.

"Whatever they wanted," Memo growled, "they're gone now."

Gilberto came up beside Memo, his face pale. "We should not be here tonight, but I don't know where we can go."

"I know." Memo looked at Lucia. "Gather what you need for the night and get your mother ready. We will find some place to go for tonight and deal with this problem tomorrow. I just want you to be safe."

Lucia nodded, her dark hair swirling around her.

Memo's brother-in-law frowned as the women left the room. "What are we going to do?"

"For now, we're just going to leave," Memo muttered. "Then, I'll worry about where we'll go."

As they were about to step out of the home, Memo's cellular rang.

"Hola," he barked into the phone.

"Memo, what's wrong?"

"Rodrigo, you're just the person I needed to talk to."

Memo filled him in on the evening's events, while keeping a close eye on the street outside. The women sat on the couch, Memo's mother-in-law praying with her ever-present rosary.

"What can I do to help?" Rodrigo said quietly.

"We can't afford a hotel, my friend," Memo said. "I thought maybe you could come get my truck and take it to your house for the night. If those gangster bastards come back, they'll think we're gone. But you'd have to pick me up in the morning."

"No problem, amigo," Rodrigo said. "I'll have to find a ride, so give me a bit. Tomorrow, I can pick you up for work, and after you get your check, we'll find you a different apartment."

When Rodrigo arrived, Memo went outside, his gun in his back pocket. He handed over the keys, and they agreed on a time to meet in the morning. Rodrigo clutched his arm in farewell, got in, and started the truck. Memo turned to walk back toward the front door of his house.

A noise to his left brought his head up. A young Mexican male, slightly overweight, ran toward Memo, yelling and firing a pistol. Memo's instincts took over. He crouched to run behind the minivan parked in front of his neighbor's apartment. The cholo yelled at Memo not to hide, an insane request. Memo pulled out his weapon and carefully walked around the van with the gun pointing forward, his police training taking over.

As Memo moved forward, the cholo jumped into Memo's truck, using Rodrigo as a hostage with the gun to his head. Anger gave Memo's feet wings. He ran as fast as he could toward them, not caring about the truck, but with one thought in his mind: to save Rodrigo.

The old Chevy stick shift was in bad shape, so it took a while to gain any real momentum in first gear. Memo caught up with the vehicle, running alongside the truck at the driver's window. The gangster, still screaming angrily, was trying to control the truck with one hand while shooting at Rodrigo, but for some reason, his gun jammed. Rodrigo's eyes bulged with fear, and the driver cursed even more, shaking the gun before leveling it again at Rodrigo's head.

Memo made a split-second decision and shot the cholo point blank in the jaw, aiming down at an angle so the bullet would not go through his head and hit Rodrigo.

The cholo had no time to react. Bleeding profusely from his left jaw, he slumped forward. Memo snatched open the door and pulled the cholo out of the truck, watching him fall to the ground like a sack of potatoes.

"Go, Rodrigo!" he shouted. "Drive." He threw his gun into the middle of the bench seat.

Rodrigo slid into the driver's seat, still pale and sweaty, and rammed the truck into second gear. He glanced back at Memo.

"Tomorrow."

Memo nodded, waving him on. "Go. I'll call you."

The old truck rattled away, gears grinding as Rodrigo shifted again. Still filled with adrenalin, Memo slowed his pace, leaning down with his hands on his knees to catch his breath. Sirens wailed in the distance, and he waited. The police and paramedics arrived, and the cholo was pronounced dead at the scene.

Chapter 11

Memo sat on a metal chair in a small office belonging to the two detectives working on his case. Handcuffs dug into his wrists, but he ignored them. He'd already related the events to them several times. One of the two detectives left the office, then returned with a thick stack of papers.

"You really did the community a favor, getting rid of that trash. Look," he said, pointing to the paperwork. "Robbery, rape, drug sales and use. He was a real piece of work."

"Really?"

"Yeah. Don't sweat this. You'll be out of jail in no time."

Memo breathed a sigh of relief. The detectives helped him out of the chair and escorted him to the holding cell.

On the way over, a short, curly haired man lunged toward Memo, trying to hit him. One of the detectives got in the way.

"Cut that shit out! Get out of here before I arrest you!"

"Who was that guy?"

"He's the older brother of the guy you shot."

The detective led the curly haired brother by the arm away from Memo, the two speaking in hushed voices. Memo was escorted through a long hallway and stopped in front of a small, plastic desk. The short, balding, chubby guard looked up at the detective, but didn't say anything.

"Here's another prisoner. Take care of him," the detective told the holding cell guard.

"Charge?"

"Homicide."

Memo's heart sunk at the mere word.

"Take off your shoelaces," the guard said.

Memo was locked up in a 10' by 10' cell shared by thirteen other prisoners. The body and foot odors were horrendous, and the single toilet without a seat was only flushed every twelve hours. Despite the odors and the lack of space, the adrenalin crash was stronger, and Memo rolled up into a fetal position, laid his head on his shoes, and fell asleep.

Floating like an angel, Memo's wife opened the cell door and carried him out of the hell he now suffered. In the middle of a long, passionate kiss, Memo awoke to the reality of his shared cell. The sweet aroma of his wife's perfume from the dream gave way to the putrid odors of sweat and feet, causing him to gag slightly. A short, skinny man, missing most of his teeth, laughed.

"You'll get used to it. It just takes a few minutes."

Memo nodded, silently thanking him.

"Your first time in jail?"

"Yeah."

"Homicide, huh? That's a hell of a way to start out."

Memo looked over at the toilet, almost overflowing with material best flushed.

The skinny man, noting the look of disgust in Memo's face, answered the unasked question.

"The toilet is flushed every twelve hours. Water conservation. There isn't even a sink to wash up in. Hungry? Food should be here any minute."

Everyone in the holding cell was given two bologna sandwiches consisting solely of bread and bologna. Four one-gallon jugs of water were left in the cell; no cups were distributed, so the prisoners had to share the jugs. Memo looked down at his dirty hands, and the man with the nasty cold sores on his mouth drank directly from the clear plastic jug. Not having many choices in his current situation, Memo wolfed down the sandwiches. Carefully following the jug the cold sore man had drank from, Memo ensured he drank from another, tilting his head back and letting the water fall into his mouth rather than drinking from it directly.

"What's your name?" the toothless man asked.

Memo answered and asked the same question.

"They call me Jaws." The man said, laughing at his own inappropriate nickname. "You're pretty lucky, really. A lot of times there's at least one hard ass who has been in prison a few times and will give a new guy crap, but I've only seen one guy here right now who is heavy, and he doesn't mess with people unless they mess with him. That's him, in the corner," Jaws said, no longer smiling, using his lips to point. Then, he continued in a whisper, "His name is Arturo. He's a hit man for the mafia."

If no one had told Memo that the gaunt, pock-faced man was a killer for hire, Memo would have never given him a second thought. The nondescript Arturo spoke with no one, and none of the thirteen men who were left in the cell went out of their way to talk to him, either. For some men, their reputation could be almost as good as having a weapon in their hand.

Jaws continued. "Don't worry. This place is a lot worse than the prison. After 72 hours, if a prisoner is still here, they ship him off to El Cereso. It isn't nice, but the facilities are a lot better."

"What about court? Isn't there a trial?"

Jaws laughed. "Not in Mexico. Your case will be seen by a judge, probably in the capital city of Chihuahua, and you'll be sentenced without them ever seeing you. If you have some money for a lawyer, you can appeal, but there is no trial."

Two days had passed. No one had come to see Memo, and he had not been allowed to make any calls. Jaws had been transferred to El Cereso. Even though the detectives who had worked his case assured him he would be exonerated, Memo now wondered if he'd ever see the light of day. Another day passed, and none of the men who had been in the holding cell with him on the first day were still with him.

Then, two guards showed up at the cell's door.

"Guillermo Smith!"

Memo's heart jumped. Maybe his wife was there with a lawyer to get him out of jail, he hoped.

"Yes sir."

"You're out of here."

Memo happily put his shoes on and stood at the door.

"Turn around and place your hands at your back."

Maybe it was a precaution that the guards were handcuffing him again.

The guards roughly pulled Memo out of the cell and marched him to a back door where a windowless van was waiting with seven other prisoners already inside. Memo was headed for prison.

Memo wasn't afraid as the prison guards transported him to the prison in Juárez called El Cereso. Instead, he felt deep sadness at the injustice inflicted upon him and his family. How was his wife, a pregnant woman in a third world country with already low wages, going to possibly make it? It had been hard enough paying the bills on his salary from the States.

The ride bumped and plodded along, and he took advantage of the time to ponder his situation and the choices before him. Before he even arrived at the prison, Memo made an important decision. Somehow, he would find a way to support his wife, even from prison, no matter what it took. His new resolve brought him some peace of mind. He could make this work, even if he didn't know how just yet.

The prisoners were rudely shot forward as the transport truck stopped suddenly in front of the processing area of the Cereso, waking many of them from needed sleep. They were searched as they were herded inside. Memo was surprised when he was led to a cell without changing into some type of uniform. In fact, none of the prisoners wore uniforms. He hadn't even been photographed. Three men, all rough looking, were staring at him.

"What are you in for?" asked the biggest of the three men, spit flying off his tongue with every word he pronounced.

"Homicide."

The other two men looked at each other, then at the bigger man, apparently the leader of the cell.

"If you're lying, we'll find out."

"I don't lie," Memo simply said, staring directly into the man's eyes. They locked stares for a moment, and Memo didn't even blink.

Finally, looking away from Memo, the man spoke again.

"I'm Javier, this is Scar, and he's El Tonto." Javier pointed at each man prospectively.

"Javier, I'm Memo. Now, can you guys tell me what I need to know to survive here?"

Javier and the others laughed at Memo's frankness.

"So, you're American? You have a funny accent."

Memo frowned. He hated when people told him that. His Spanish was flawless, but his light skin and features inherited from his father often caused people in Mexico to believe he was a gringo.

"I'm Mexican," Memo said, and stayed silent. Javier finally broke the silence.

"The two over there are in for being stupid and getting caught dealing drugs. I'm in here because of betrayal."

Memo looked at Javier, the look of intrigue upon his face urging Javier on.

"I was working with a Mexican customs agent. I would bring over from the States electronics, guns, ammo, whatever I could that would bring us a profit. He would let me through, and we would split the profits."

Memo waited patiently while Javier, obviously still upset about what had happened, paused.

"He was being watched. He didn't even warn me, and, when I was passing a load of illegal goods through, he busted me. He whispered to me not to worry: he'd take care of everything. As you can see, he didn't."

Javier and Memo got along very well, and Javier spent a lot of time over the next few days showing Memo the ropes of the prison, who to watch out for, who you could get things from, and so on.

After his first week inside, Lucia came to visit him. She had dark circles under her eyes and was very thin around her six-months-pregnant belly. She cried when she saw him. They embraced and then sat down at a small metal table in a general population room. The prison was incredibly overpopulated. The cells obviously made for two prisoners housed four, and in some parts, even six. The wealthy and powerful had even bigger cells all to themselves.

Memo looked into her eyes. "Why didn't you come and see me before?"

"They didn't let me! I tried to see you when you were in the holding cell, and they wouldn't even let me send you a message." She had a look of indignation as she told Memo about the experience. "They treated me like I was sub-human."

Memo felt a surge of fury rise in him.

"I had brought some money for you," she sobbed, "but the lady guard who searched me took it."

"Bastards," he snarled. "Don't worry about bringing me money. You and the baby need it more than I do."

She looked at him with huge, tear-filled eyes. "I heard it was easier for prisoners when they have money."

Memo longed for the impossible, to grab her, hold her against him, and never let go. He reached up and gently dried the tears that streamed from her eyes. "Don't worry about me," he said. I can take care of myself. How are you doing? You're working, aren't you?"

Lucia hesitated, dropping her gaze. "N-no, no. I got the money from my brother."

Memo knew she was lying, but he didn't press the issue. Instead, he said, "It's too much for you to stay here in Juárez. You need to go back to Cuauhtémoc with your family."

"I can't." She shook her head, her long dark hair flying about her thin shoulders. "I can't be away from you so long."

"You have to think about what's best for the baby."

"No, I won't go." Lucia's tears started again, coursing down her gaunt face in thick rivulets. "I won't leave you."

"Okay, okay," Memo shushed her. "At least don't visit me so often. Once a month is fine. Hey, have you seen Rodrigo?"

Lucia shook her head. "I heard he left town – afraid he would be implicated."

"Some friend. Save his life and that's how he pays me."

After a few hours, Lucia left, looking back yearningly at him as she passed through the outer gates.

Chapter 12

Every week, like clockwork, Lucia visited Memo. Memo knew she was probably working, cleaning someone's house and earning a pitiful fifty dollars a week. He knew he had to help her somehow. He could work in the jail, but it paid so little it wouldn't be much help to her. Desperation clouding every waking moment, Memo almost didn't see a familiar face visiting another prisoner. Curly hair, short, and chubby, the face of the brother of the man Memo killed was etched in his mind forever. The man, who tried to attack him while he was in custody after being first arrested, pointed at Memo and grinned.

Knowing assassins were cheap in a Mexican prison, Memo spent the night making a makeshift weapon, ready to kill again if he was forced to. Memo remembered how his former police department secretly taped prisoners making weapons inside the prison system to show officers why it was important to treat every prisoner with extreme caution. It occurred to Memo what an ironic twist of fate that he, once a police officer dealing with criminals, was now the dangerous prisoner constructing a makeshift knife.

He slept lightly and an unusual silence awakened him to an empty cell.

Night blurred the outlines of objects around him, but when three muscular and very menacing men entered the cell, he wasn't surprised. He jumped out of his bunk, the knife concealed in his waistband, wanting the element of surprise if he was attacked. Memo was hoping they would underestimate him, and a knife in his hand would only escalate their assault.

The men positioned themselves at the exit of the cell, blocking him in. Memo was sure their intent was to release him from the agony of life, something he was not prepared to give up easily. Judging from the tattoos lining every exposed inch of their skin from head to toe, the three were long timers in the prison system. Heart racing, Memo reached for his knife. Fear rose from some deep, primal place within Memo's bowels. When it reached his heart, it was converted into adrenalin, his heart pumping it fiercely throughout his veins. Memo no longer felt fear, but instead fury, cold and pure, like a Japanese Samurai sword made from hard steel.

One of the men lunged for Memo, yelling, "Die, fucking gringo."

Sidestepping, Memo shoved his knife deep into the man's jugular, and watched his eyes widen in horror at the realization of his impending death. Blood coated Memo's hand and the blade, as he pulled it free and circled around the bunk bed with frightening speed and agility to meet the other two men. They rushed Memo, but he avoided their attack. In boxing, Memo had learned to aim his punches where major organs were located, so he thrust the shaft forcefully into the larger man's liver, feeling the other man collapse as attempted to pull the knife back out.

The last man stabbed Memo in the back before he could turn, barely missing his kidney. Memo kicked out, catching the man square in the gut, dropping his makeshift weapon. It hit the cell floor with a splash in a pool of blood. He took up his boxing stance, knowing he'd been cut, but the rage in his heart kept the pain at bay. The man smiled, sure of himself, and took up a stance to mirror Memo's.

"Let's dance, you fucking pig," the assassin said.

Memo drew two of his blood-damp fingers down his left cheek, marking himself a warrior as he faced his opponent, and grinned fiercely.

He saw a tremor of uncertainty slip across the other man's face before his jaw tightened again. Memo attacked, pummeling the guy with a storm of fists. Breaking the man's jaw with a left hook to the head, Memo followed to the body with his left and right hooks. After the man collapsed under the onslaught, Memo finished the job with some swift kicks to the head.

Memo slumped against the wall; his breathing was ragged. Then, he straightened and hauled the bodies out of his cell one by one, tossing a homemade knife contemptuously on top of the last body.

He cleaned the blood from his cell and himself with the four gallons of water, then returned to his bunk as if nothing had occurred.

The investigating guards assumed the men were butchered by a group of other inmates, never suspecting one man was capable of killing all three. A shakedown of the prison revealed nothing, and Memo hid his wound to avoid any link to the deaths, dressing and caring for it himself. The prisoners' code of silence protected him, although his fellow prisoners now made way for him as he moved about.

Memo's roommates were more helpful to him than ever, as if eager to make up for any perceived part in the attack on him. His reputation after the incident catapulted him to fame and power in the prison. The three men he'd butchered were known killers, serving long sentences for multiple murders. The new respect afforded him by the other inmates in the prison made Memo believe his life would improve somewhat at the prison.

Every time Lucia came to visit, guilt tore at his heart. Her pregnancy advanced, rounding out only her belly, leaving her arms and legs stick thin. If only he had money to take care of her and the baby to come, to pay for birthing and good food for them both. Respect from inmates would not put food on her table or milk in the baby's mouth, and despair settled over him again.

The most powerful man in the Cereso, a major drug trafficker named Rafael Carrillo Ortega, sent one of his underlings to bring Memo to meet him. Second-in-command of the Chihuahua Cartel for about five years, "Don Rafa" Ortega claimed membership in the Mexican Mafia and expected people to come to him when he summoned them. Ortega was in the prison more because of politics rather than justice. He'd been arrested after the governor and Rafael's boss decided he was getting too powerful.

Memo told the subordinate if the man wanted to meet him, he could come down to see him in his cell, but he would not go anywhere with people he didn't know. In probably fifteen years, no one had denied Don Rafa anything, but the drug trafficker merely laughed.

One day, after a visit from Lucia, Memo got another call from Don Rafa to come to his cell. This time, with Lucia's gaunt face and thin, pregnant body fresh in his mind, Memo went, hopeful for a business opportunity.

Compared to Memo's simple, shared cell, Don Rafa's cell was more like a suite in a hotel. He had it to himself, with a TV and air conditioning to boot. Four cell phones lay on the desk he had near his bed. He glanced up when Memo entered the cell. The gray in his hair and wrinkles around his eyes revealed Don Rafa's age, probably in his early fifties. He had a comfortable "extra" around his waist, and when he stood up to greet him, Memo noticed his six-foot, 200-pound frame literally towered over the man. Still, Don Rafa had a presence about him, and Memo felt it as if he was in front of a president or a king, in spite of the man's stature.

"Memo. I heard a lot about you. Nice work with the, well, you know, the 'incident,' we'll say. Sit down." Don Rafa sat back down, crossing his legs. Memo couldn't help but stare at the beautiful and obviously expensive ostrich-skin boots he was wearing. Gold jewelry, the Armani shirt, and matching belt all confirmed the man had money, and in jail, it was obvious he was mafia.

"Thanks," Memo said, barely audible, as he sat in an easy chair across from Don Rafa's.

"I hear you have some problems with money, and a pregnant wife too. That's terrible."

Memo winced as if he'd just been slapped.

Don Rafa leaned back in his chair with his beady black eyes fixed on Memo's agonized face. "I'll get to the point. I could use someone like you. I need someone to teach me English and, let's face it, you'd make a great person to have as a bodyguard. No one in the prison will even look at you funny."

Memo looked around the luxurious cell that rivaled suites in fancy hotels, knowing he was defeated. After working against drugs for so many years, he'd have to work for a drug dealer if he wanted his wife to survive.

Don Rafa stood and put his hand on Memo's shoulder.

"I like you. Few men around here are real men. You are. I respect you. I want you with me. On the desk is a paper bag with $10,000 dollars in it. That should help your wife get by for a while. I need some help while I'm here, someone I can count on. I feel you won't let me down. What do you say?" The dollar was by far the preferred currency for the mafia, and this was no chump offer.

Memo got up and shook Don Rafa's hand. Then, he walked over and clutched the bag, sealing the deal. Ten thousand dollars. It felt good in his hand, as if it belonged there. He could deal with a lot of crap for that kind of money.

He turned and strolled out of his new boss's cell.

Chapter 13 (Lalo)

"Mijo. Wake up, baby."

Lalo opened his eyes, squinting at the bright light coming through the window. His wife Manuela leaned over him with concern radiating from her green eyes. He tried to reach up to brush reddish-brown hair away from her pale face, but his arm refused to cooperate, and his hand fell back uselessly on the bed. Dressed simply in a pair of jeans and a red T-shirt, even with dark circles under her eyes probably because she hadn't slept a wink, she was still a knockout to Lalo.

He turned his head toward the window, trying to gauge the time of day. "How long have I been out?"

"Just a day." She smiled at him, but he could see she'd been crying. "All night I worried."

Lalo frowned. "I didn't mean to make you worry. How are the others…"

"Fine," Manuela interrupted him. "You were the only one hurt. Always worried about everyone else, huh, mister hero? Typical."

She smiled again, the worry slipping from her face like rain before the bright sun.

Lalo tried to smile back, but his face hurt, along with every other part of his body. If he ever got run over by a semi, he thought, this is how he would feel.

Another thought struck him. "Isela?"

Manuela patted his arm. "Our daughter is fine. She wanted to be here, but I wanted to make sure you were up first. I didn't want her to think you were dead."

"She's only two. She would have thought I was asleep."

Manuela moved away from him, settling back into the chair pulled up next to the bed. A soda can and open magazine lay on the bed tray pulled next to her chair. "Maybe, but I'll bring her later, okay?"

A nurse bustled into the room with a syringe in one hand. "Awake, I see."

"Just now," Manuela said. "But he's grumpy."

"I'm in pain, mujer," he muttered. "Not grumpy."

"I'm here to fix that." The nurse slipped the needle into his IV connection and pushed the plunger. "Now, lie quiet. You'll feel better soon."

She dropped the used syringe into the marked container on the wall and came back over to the bedside to take his vital signs.

Within moments, Lalo could feel the painkiller dulling his senses. He glanced over at his wife, thankful she was there. As she read her magazine, the brilliant sunlight gave her brown hair a reddish glow, reminding him of when he first saw her.

Lalo met Manuela for the second time when he was still working narcotics. She was a few years younger than him, and even though he'd changed a lot from when he was seventeen, she still recognized him. While Lalo was surveilling Carlos Medina's place, he frequented a local Burrito shop where Manuela worked. She remembered him immediately from the night of the quinceañera and gave him a hug, everyone at the burrito shop staring. He frequented the burrito shop for a few months before they finally went on a date, no thanks to Lalo, though.

She was a straight shooter, and she made the first moves on Lalo. She later told him his shyness stood in their way, and, if she'd waited for him, they would still be just friends. She'd popped the question, and they married. She knew how dedicated he was to his job and how serious a person he was. Lalo didn't joke around very much, and he often took whatever anyone said to heart. A man of his word, he was often disappointed by those who weren't.

Lalo had wanted to get married in court only, but she convinced him they needed a church wedding, too.

"Don't you believe in God, Lalo?"

"It isn't that, mija. I just don't have any use for Him."

"What do you mean!?"

"Well, he hasn't had any use for me, so I feel likewise."

"Lalo, God has a plan for everyone. How else can you explain us meeting again after all those years? And we were both still single. That can't be just a coincidence."

Lalo thought about what she had said. After all those years of constant loss and hardship, Lalo couldn't believe it was all part of God's plan; unless of course, God was one sadistic motherfucker. But it was important to Manuela, so he agreed to the church wedding. Two years later, Isela was born, and she became a daddy's girl almost from the moment of her first breath.

Lalo rested at home after his release from the hospital. When he returned to work, however, he went right back on the Medina case. Barba found out, and after a serious "ass-chewing" session, he threatened him with suspension if he didn't "cease and desist." The chief detective didn't seem to realize that the more he kept Lalo away from the case, the more determined he became to find out why this case pissed so many people off. After all, he was a homicide detective, not a politician.

Even though Lalo's free time was limited, he had always dedicated time to his family. He didn't waste time watching sports on television, drinking with friends, or going to the local strip clubs. Every time he looked into his wife's and daughter's eyes, Lalo felt as if all of the madness and sickness out in the world was just a dream, and their unshakable love for him was the only reality. Their love helped him face the horrors he saw every day, anchoring his heart to them while he tried to make a difference in the world. But he became obsessed with the Medina case, and he began to spend more and more of his free time on it.

After interviewing each potential suspect or witness, Lalo was getting nowhere, so he returned to the most basic question. Who had the most motive for the drug lord's death? Medina's wife had a boyfriend or so went the rumor. Who was he? Tailing Mrs. Medina might expose the lover and any motive he might have. On his own time, Lalo watched the Medina house, waiting for something to break.

After a few nights of boredom, Lalo finally saw movement. A taxi arrived at the house, and Mrs. Medina, all dolled up, got in. Lalo waited a minute and followed. With several newer model vehicles in the two-door garage, Lalo couldn't imagine why she'd use a taxi. Maybe the taxi driver was the lover? A cab driver didn't seem like her style. She was an extremely attractive woman in her early forties, and she looked ten years younger. She went to the gym for two hours a day and made regular visits to the beauty salon.

The cab stopped at a traffic light, and when Lalo stopped as well, the cab suddenly peeled out and ran the light. Following, Lalo almost hit a truck rolling through the intersection. The cab seemed to disappear in the brief moment it took for the truck to pass by. Lalo now felt the wife and the lover more than likely had something to do with the murder. After some futile searching for the cab, Lalo finally went home.

As Lalo got out of his car in front of his home, a Ford Econoline van pulled up to the curb. Several men jumped out and one tasered him before he could react, knocking him to the ground in agonizing shock. The men lifted him into the van and drove away.

"Detective Torres, we're taking you for the ride of your life," said one of the brutes, smiling through broken teeth.

"Yeah. A real cruisin' for a bruisin', you might say," another voice chimed in. It came from a thinner version of the first man, but with better dental hygiene.

"It's good to know such an intellectual bunch has taken an interest in me," Lalo muttered through numb lips.

"Oh, you'll pay for that comment," one of the men growled.

Several broken ribs and smashed teeth later, the men threw Lalo from the moving van onto his front lawn.

"Stay away from the Medina case!" one of the kidnappers yelled, as the van drove off.

Lalo crawled to the house and banged on the door. Manuela screamed when she saw him, helping him drag himself inside before grabbing the phone to call 911 for an ambulance. As he lay there listening to her cry and scream, rocking him against her body, Lalo really didn't feel the pain anymore. He even joked with the ambulance driver, who told him he'd passed his pain threshold and that the strange feelings of blissful numbness were normal. As the numbness wore off on the ride to the hospital, Lalo lost consciousness.

Lalo awoke to incredible pain. The nurses who came in and out of the room didn't seem to notice him. As he tried to speak, Lalo realized his mouth had swollen shut. That alarmed him, and he began to moan loudly, finally getting the attention of one of the nurses. She called for the doctor, who finally appeared at his bedside.

"Hello, Detective, I'm Dr. Bane. Are you in much pain?"

Torres' eyes widened, and he answered with an emphatic, "Hmmm-hmmmm," unable to squeeze out any words.

Dr. Bane took it as a "yes" and ordered up a shot of quien-sabe-que (who knows what), and Lalo drifted off into a happier world.

After a few days, Lalo returned home, his face still swollen, but at least able to talk and eat. Manuela smothered him with kisses when he arrived, then sat him down for a talk.

"You have to stop this, hombre." She stood over him, hands on her full hips.

"Stop what?" Lalo looked up at her. Her expression told him how serious things had gotten.

"This job will kill you," Manuela cried softly. Her dark eyes filled with tears. "We need you, Lalo. I can't lose you."

"You won't," he said, trying to smile. "I've always been a cop, mi corazón. That's what I want to do. You knew that when you married me."

"I didn't know you would try to get yourself killed." She turned away, hurrying up the stairs. Lalo followed her up to his daughter's bedroom.

"Papi!" Isela held her arms out to her father, and Lalo lifted her up.

"Would you like to go to the park for a while?" he asked her, nuzzling her soft baby skin. "Mami, would you like to come?"

Manuela shook her head, motioning them out. "I'll get dinner started. You two go on without me." Lalo noted the somber expression she had while she addressed him, totally unlike her normal demeanor.

The park smelled of fresh-cut grass and fertile earth, and Lalo breathed in deeply. It seemed like a million years since he'd held his daughter in his arms and actually played with her. How could he have gotten so wrapped up in the cop shop that he'd missed how big she'd already grown? Manuela was a stunning lady; he'd forgotten that, too. Maybe she had a point. Maybe he needed to reevaluate his life and his job.

After a week off, he returned to the station, and everyone seemed genuinely glad to see him. Barba didn't even chew him out.

"Lalo, how are you feeling, son?" Barba said as he placed one arm around Lalo's shoulders, and Lalo cringed, not trusting his sincerity. "We thought we were going to lose you. We're glad you're back."

The other detectives gathered around, slapping him on the back or shaking his hand. Spurgeon gave him a hug. Lalo smiled, but it was really his mask of feigned ignorance. He knew some or maybe all of the men in the homicide division were responsible for his beating. After completing a few natural death cases, though, Lalo went straight back to tailing Mrs. Medina. He took all necessary precautions. The bruisers wouldn't find him as easy of a target again.

Lalo couldn't stop investigating the Medina death, his obsession worsening by the day. He had to find out why police were involved. Lalo spent every night watching the Medina house, instead of spending time with his wife and daughter. He followed Mrs. Medina to the beauty salon, to the local boutiques, and to her aerobics class. She seemed very business-as-usual, not at all like a woman who had just lost her husband.

After about a week of surveillance, Lalo got the break he had been hoping for. Captain Barba pulled into the driveway of the Medina's. Barba exited his personal vehicle, seemingly looked straight at Lalo, a half-smile on his face, and entered the home without even knocking. It was obviously not an official visit; he didn't leave until the next morning. Lalo felt sick to his stomach.

After a full day of court, Lalo avoided the office, or more specifically Barba, and went straight home. The aroma of flour tortillas cooking on the stove greeted Lalo at the door of his small home. Manuela stood in the kitchen making dinner while Isela played in her highchair near the table. His wife returned to her task as he sat down at the table, but after a few minutes, she began to talk.

"Mijo, I know we've gone over this before, but...I really wish you'd look for a different job. Look at you! You're in and out of the hospital all the time, you don't have any friends, and your fellow police don't even want you to do your job. And you do all of this for what? How many lives have you saved? How many criminals have you reformed? Has the crime in El Paso gone down just because you joined the force? Don't get me wrong, mi amor. You're a great cop, but your family needs you." She paused for a breath.

Isela nodded, as if she understood everything her mother said.

"Firemen help people," Manuela continued, back in full voice, "and it's still a dangerous job, but at least you won't be getting shot all the time. That is, if you still feel you need to help people. Paramedics help people, too, and they aren't hated. You know what I mean." She finally looked at him over her shoulder, tears pouring down her smooth face.

"We need you, and I can't stand seeing you hurt all the time."

Lalo thought about what Manuela was telling him. He knew she was right. He really hadn't helped too many people over the years. He'd put drug dealers in jail on a regular basis, and yet drugs were as abundant as ever. Murders and violent crimes would always be committed, with or without Lalo as a part of the force. He had become completely obsessed with this case and solving it probably wouldn't make the world any better of a place. Besides, his family meant more to him than any job.

"You're right."

"What?" Manuela said, wiping the tears from her face.

"You are absolutely right," he repeated. "I've spent a lot of time doing nothing. I solve crimes, and criminals still go free. Politics and greed run the department, and I'm one of the few who really cares. What's worse, I'm working for a murderer!"

Manuela's eyes widened, not fully understanding, but astonished, nonetheless.

"Last night, Barba showed up at the widow Medina's house and stayed all night. He's been avoiding me, but now he doesn't care that I know. He has a lot of pull on the force, and the other officers love him. Being the lover of a drug dealer's wife could just be the tip of the iceberg; he probably has other officers working with him, and they all may be tied to the mafia. When I used to work narcotics, Medina always seemed to be a step ahead of me. This might all be related."

"Babe, this is dangerous. If Barba doesn't care that you know what is going on, don't you think it could be because he already has something planned to protect himself?"

"I do, mija, and that is why I am going to resign tomorrow. I should have a good chunk of money in my retirement. We can relocate and look for work with that."

Manuela stared at Lalo with unbelieving eyes.

He grinned at her astonishment. "I mean it."

She ran to him, hugging Lalo with all of her might, showing him how she felt without saying a word. They'd talked about him looking for another profession many times over the last few years, but Lalo held firm to being a cop for the rest of his life. After a few bullet holes and awful pain later, Lalo realized Manuela and Isela needed him more than the rest of the world. There were other ways to help people.

After dinner, Lalo tucked in his little girl. She hugged him with her skinny little arms, and he kissed her goodnight, whispering his love against her tiny ear. He walked downstairs to the kitchen to help Manuela with the dishes, but she shooed him off to take a bath. Reluctantly, he left her to the dishes and climbed into the 19th century bathtub filled to the brim with warm water, its solid metal shell comfortably heated. Taking a sip of the cold beer he had brought with him from the kitchen, Lalo contemplated the life-changing decision he had just made. Perhaps she had been right when she had told him God had a plan for everyone, and his was to take care of his family.

Lalo finished his beer and laid back into the water, submerging his head completely. He liked the silence of it, like a baby within the protective womb of its mother. He opened his eyes and studied the blurry version of the ceiling. Flames and debris replaced the ceiling he was looking at, and the bathtub was rocked violently over. Lalo hit his mouth against the iron faucet as he was tossed around, knocking out a few teeth. He was protected by the tub over him, as the waves of fire and falling pieces of lumber and sheetrock crashed all around him. As sudden as the explosion had erupted, it seemed to be over, and Lalo fought to stay conscious. The tub was incredibly heavy, but the thought of his injured daughter and wife needing his help made him that much stronger, and he somehow lifted the tub and got out from underneath. Naked, he fought his way through the flames to his daughter's room. He saw nothing. Roaring flames devoured the floor and ceiling, but there was nothing recognizable left of the bed and his baby. The smell of seared skin penetrated his nostrils and Lalo vomited.

With a roar, he turned to make his way toward the kitchen. He felt his sanity slipping as the heat around him seared his skin and hair. He lost it completely when he saw what was left of Manuela's body burned on the kitchen floor, one arm flung out as if to reach for him. The pain of his burning feet became easy to ignore, his emotional loss far greater than any amount of physical pain he felt.

Lalo gathered every bit of strength and willpower to keep his wits about him. Why would this happen, now, when he was ready to give it all up? Everyone wanted him to get out of police work, and now that he'd made the decision, the two people he loved the most were taken from him. God's plan. *Of course.*

Through his ringing ears, screaming sirens grew louder, and he realized he shouldn't be there when they arrived. Lalo had no idea how many of his fellow officers were in bed with Barba, and obviously they wanted him dead. With nothing left but a gaping hole in his heart, the only possible action for him now was revenge; obviously that was what God wanted him to do. Why else would He have allowed this to happen? Lalo's mind worked quickly under extreme pressure, an asset from his years as a Marine and a cop, and he knew this devastation would be an opportunity. Lalo tore off the dog tags he always wore, removed his wedding ring, and scattered the objects near the remains of his armchair in the living room. Hopefully the police would think Lalo Torres was a dead man.

Outside in the dark, he crept through the shadows into his neighbor's yard, tears from either the smoke or from his grief clouding his vision. Coughing and gagging at the same time, he grabbed a cotton shirt from the clothesline and an old pair of boots from the back porch. He looked back once, mourning the loss of the two loves of his life in the burning house that once belonged to a man named Lalo. Then he walked away, a new man...different, harder. And now he understood God's plan for him – kill each and every evil mother fucker he could.

He knew where he would go, and what he needed to do. The best way to hide from his enemies would be in plain sight. To be invisible.

Chapter 14 (Memo)

Lucia visited Memo in the courtyard. Passing twenty pesos to the guard in charge, Memo rented a table and chairs. Everything in El Cereso happened as a direct result of a money transaction. Those without money were just out of luck.

Memo studied Lucia's face as she talked to him about her brothers, the lawyer she was looking to get him, her mom, and how she felt with the baby now moving inside her. She had seemingly aged two years in the few months Memo had been incarcerated; lines had appeared just recently in her forehead and the dark circles under her eyes accentuated her paleness, uncharacteristic of her naturally tanned skin. It only served to strengthen his resolve to work for Don Rafa. Memo put the bag of money he had been given into Lucia's hands.

"Memo, where did you get all of this money?" Lucia asked, eyes wide in disbelief, pushing the bag back to him.

"Shhh, I don't want the guards to know about this. Look, at this point it doesn't matter how I got the money. I can't give it back. I'm in this now, and there's no turning back." Memo felt his face turning red as he said the words, finally acknowledging even to himself of what he had done. He urged the bag of money back into her hands.

Tears in her eyes, Lucia nodded, understanding. Memo didn't know whether the tears were of joy for no longer having the financial burden she had or sadness in knowing her husband had crossed over to the dark side. Maybe it hurt her even more knowing he was doing it for her benefit.

"This will cover the birth of the baby, and you can maybe even find a little house close to jail."

Lucia shook her head. "Memo, what have you done?"

Memo didn't answer. After a few hours, Lucia didn't feel well anymore, and the couple kissed, long and passionately. While Memo was with her, he felt like he was himself again: the man who had traveled to Cuauhtémoc and married a woman he had barely just met. Now that she was gone, Memo put his game face back on and played the part of the hardened criminal once again. Returning to his cell, Memo felt drained, the emotion of the last few days' events taking their toll, and he fell into a deep sleep.

Memo stood in what appeared to be a barn, his brothers-in-law with him. He was holding a gun to the head of a young man tied with duct-tape to a chair. The man was crying, begging for his life.

Cocking the gun, Memo knew what was next. He didn't want to fire it, but he was compelled by forces stronger than he was. His finger slowly squeezed the trigger. As blood and brain matter splattered, Memo screamed.

"No!"

Jail cell, not a barn. No brain matter or blood. No gun. Memo sighed with relief, actually happy to be back in the reality of his cell rather than the nightmare world where he had just killed someone in cold blood.

Memo went to Don Rafa's cell.

"Memo! How'd everything go with your wife, son?"

Son. Did he really feel that way, Memo wondered, or was it just a part of his charm?

"Good, thank you, Don Rafa."

"Good. Now, are you ready to work?"

"Yes, but I need to talk to you about something. I need you to know the truth about me."

Don Rafa raised his eyebrows.

"I used to be a cop in the States. I worked a lot of drug cases; I'd get loads on the highway."

"I see…"

Memo prepared himself. Don Rafa would probably call for a few men now, maybe five or ten, and have them beat Memo to death. Or perhaps he would just tell someone to spread the rumor that he used to be a cop, and within a few days, he would be found strung up in his cell, just another jailhouse statistic. Memo looked up and was surprised to see Don Rafa smiling.

"Then we really have a lot of work to do. How much do you know about smuggling?

"I know all about what law enforcement is taught to look for."

"Then teach me, so I can use what they don't look for."

Memo started with the basics, the simple signs that something was amiss. "The keys. If a person only has keys to the car and nothing else, that's a sign something could be wrong. People usually have keys to their apartment, house, maybe a supermarket or video store club card, pictures, something. Also, if the car is recently registered or bought. Temporary tags. If it lacks items that belong to the person or make it unique, like bumper stickers, crayons, or toys in the back seat, trash. Those are the obvious things."

Don Rafa nodded, acknowledging that he understood and for Memo to continue.

"If the stories of multiple passengers match. First, we would separate the passengers and the driver and ask them individually the same questions, later comparing their answers for significant differences. If it was just the driver, we would look for clues to support his story. If he said he was visiting a certain place for an extended period of time but didn't have any luggage, things like that."

Memo went on for hours, the indicatives being innumerous. Don Rafa took it all in, laughing to himself when he realized that many of the things Memo was teaching him were the very reasons his drug loads had been caught or stopped in the States. The two spent weeks going over Memo's knowledge. And Rafa never actually got any "English" classes.

When a large man entered Don Rafa's cell uninvited, Memo's entire demeanor changed, his hands clenched into fists and his smile became a scowl. He had been so absorbed in teaching Don Rafa the basics of English that he hadn't even noticed the man approach. Nor did he have any idea how long the man may have been observing them before he had entered. Memo stood up and touched the small blade he carried in his waistband, making sure it was where it should be. The man turned to Memo and said, "Boy, you better get out of here. I'm here for Don Rafa, not you."

Memo tensed, preparing for an attack. He had no intention of leaving Don Rafa alone with him.

"Have it your way."

The man was taller than Memo and probably about fifty pounds heavier, all in muscle weight. He fell upon Memo with a surprising speed, faster than men who were eighty pounds lighter than he. Memo began throwing hooks and connecting, but the man only grinned as his ridiculously large hands got around Memo's neck, and Memo felt the blood flow depleted from his head. Tiny stars that reminded Memo of when a television station had just gone out filled his eyes. As suddenly as the man had grabbed him, he let loose of Memo. The giant man's attention was now upon Don Rafa, who apparently had just hit him with a chair. Memo reached for the blade in his waistband and was disappointed to find it was no longer where it should have been. The man was now choking the life out of Don Rafa.

Memo leaped upon the man, biting his ear, as he reached around his throat to strangle him. The man violently backed into the bars of the cell, cracking some of Memo's ribs. Memo held on. Don Rafa, recovering, picked something off the floor and rushed toward the monster Memo was riding. Blood spurted out of the giant as

Don Rafa repeatedly thrust the blade that had been Memo's into the man's midsection. Crashing back against the metal bars again, Memo felt another rib break, a strange crackling sound that he not only heard but felt.

The giant was weakening, but he wasn't dead. Don Rafa looked at Memo, as if asking *what the hell do I do now.* Memo squeezed his arm even harder around the incredibly thick-necked man, seemingly to no avail. The giant reached up, grabbing Memo's head, and literally threw Memo off of him.

"Rafa! The knife!"

Don Rafa threw the blade to Memo, and the giant was upon him, large hands pounding Memo's already dizzy head. Memo blindly swung the blade, and one of the giant's fists knocked it out of his hand. Don Rafa dove at the man, but he was knocked unconscious and slumped into the corner of his cell. Memo evaded the giant's punches, bobbing, weaving, and backing up like his life depended upon it. Because it did.

Memo punched back. It didn't matter where he hit the man, wounded or not, he could do no damage to his overly muscled body. *Think Memo. Go for the knees. He can't have any muscle covering his knees.*

Memo straight-kicked the man-giant with all his might in the kneecap, the man's leg literally bending backwards from the force of the blow, wincing in pain and temporarily stopped his forward motion. A normal human being would have been down at that point, the excruciating pain crippling their senses. Memo knew he would still be dangerous, even without a leg, so he scanned the floor for the blade. Finding it, Memo leaped upon the man, his blade reaching for the throat. The giant grabbed Memo's hand that held the blade. Memo began to knee the man in his wounded leg, until a single punch knocked Memo to the floor. Miraculously, Memo stayed conscious and still held the blade.

Don Rafa was up again. He must have noticed the man was wounded in the knee because he found a piece of iron from the chair he had broken on the giant's back and swung it, pounding the giant's knee again and again. Clearing the dizziness from his head, Memo took advantage of the opportunity and ran toward the giant again.

The man grabbed Memo's arm. Not being able to protect his head, Don Rafa swung the small bar, hitting the giant in his temple. After about three hits, the man-giant released Memo's arm. Memo jabbed their would-be killer's in the throat repeatedly. He continued long after the giant man had finally slid to the floor, his blood pooling around him. Don Rafa carefully took the knife from Memo and threw it onto the floor.

The guards arrived. Don Rafa and Memo merely laid back on the cell's floor, laughing, exasperating the pain from his broken ribs.

Weeks passed, and Memo and Don Rafa became close friends. One day, Memo decided to ask Don Rafa something that had bothered him for a long time.

"Don Rafa, can I ask you a rather personal question?"

Don Rafa thought about it for a few seconds, then answered.

"Anything."

"Why are you here?"

Don Rafa laughed. "It's a long story."

"I really want to know."

"Fair enough. About twenty years ago, I was a farmer. I raised cows, grew corn, typical farm stuff. My wife became very ill, breast cancer, and the hospital costs took everything I had. My wife died. I looked at my two daughters and decided from that moment on I would never be too poor to be able to afford the best medical attention any of my family members could ever need. Or for whatever other reason.

I knew a man that went by El Soldado. He had been a sergeant in the Mexican Army, infamous for his torture tactics and overall cruelty when dealing with prisoners. He had been out of the military for a few years, and he was the upcoming cocaine dealer in Ciudad Juárez, then he killed all of the competition within a few weeks' time." Don Rafa paused, as if regressing to some distant point in his past.

Memo didn't interrupt.

"He needed someone to provide him with marijuana. The coke business was good, but he wanted to expand. I agreed, and he set me up with a huge piece of land in the mountains. He could have gotten it from anyone, but instead he decided to use someone who was connected with his family."

Memo wondered what their family connection was, but remained silent.

"We've worked together for twenty years. I was his right-hand man, but my popularity with the people, his own people, made him jealous. And worried."

"He thought you might want all of the business for yourself?" Memo asked.

"Exactly. So, when the Mexican government began pressuring the local and state authorities more and more for the arrest of a major drug dealer, El Soldado gave them-me."

"That's why he didn't have you killed? Two birds with one stone, so to speak?"

"That, and because I was married to one of his sisters."

"So, what do you think of your baby boy?" Lucia asked, tears in her eyes.

Memo's eyes gleamed with tears of joy. He hugged Lucia and the baby. His face was round, eyes were big and expressive, and he laughed at the funny faces Memo was making. The baby's hands and feet were enormous.

"What did you name him?"

"Silly. What do you think? Guillermo."

Memo smiled.

Lucia proceeded to show Memo pictures of their new house. It was small, and not luxurious, but nice. She had pictures of her brothers and mother, and a small baby shower they had held for Lucy. Memo was Memo again, not the Mafioso.

"Lucia, Don Rafa is getting out of jail soon."

"Really? Wasn't he given ten years?"

"You pay the right people off, paperwork can get misplaced, changed, whatever. You know how it is. Money makes the world go around."

"Right. How will that affect us?"

"It means, according to him, when he's out he will have better access to the court system. He says he can get me out."

Lucia made a joyful sound in her throat and hugged Memo tightly, the baby between them.

"Careful, you'll squish little Guillermo."

"Sorry. I'm just, you know, so thrilled. I miss you so much, Memo."

They said their goodbyes, and Memo returned to Don Rafa's cell. He had been transferred ever since the giant assassin incident.

"Everything okay?" Don Rafa asked.

"Oh yeah, just great. I'm a father!"

"Now we have two reasons to celebrate. Memo, how long has it been?"

"Been? For what?"

"A conjugal visit. How long?"

"Let's see. Lucia was four months pregnant, six months, about four months or so."

"How can you take it?"

"It's hard. The transsexuals don't do a thing for me."

"I'm glad they don't," Rafa said, a smirk on his face. "Well, we're going to party tonight. In style." Don Rafa called the guard in charge and began to make arrangements.

Memo was very surprised when two girls, very attractive to say the least, entered the jail cell, bottles of tequila in hand. He felt guilty, but only for a minute. How could he protest such a gift from his boss?

"Memo, meet Stefani and Galilea. ? They are guests at the women's side of this fine motel." Everyone laughed.

The night became a blur of drinking, dancing, and sex. When Memo awoke the next day, Galilea was beside him, naked. Again guilt appeared, filling his heart, but as he stared at the naked girl the emotion was quickly replaced with lust. Her body would rival any swimsuit models'. Her large, yet perky breasts, trim waist, thick legs, and hips were irresistible. Memo was hard, and his dry mouth suddenly became moist, like a man in a desert seeing an oasis. He kissed her on the neck, moving slowly down to her breasts. Galilea awoke, but she didn't protest. He continued down to her vagina, circling her clitoris with his tongue. Galilea moaned, and she pushed his head forcefully into her. He answered her apparent demand, and licked even more fervently, his lusty needs being satisfied more than they had ever been with Lucia. Galilea quickly came, and Memo then slipped his aching member inside her, moving rhythmically in and out. Both of them climaxed together, Galilea moaning so loudly that Memo was afraid the guards would show up. Apparently, Don Rafa had paid them well, so no uninvited guests arrived.

The following day, Don Rafa left the prison, a free man at last.

It was bittersweet for Memo, Don Rafa getting out of jail; he was happy for his friend, but he would miss him. Three months passed before Memo finally knew that Don Rafa hadn't forgotten him.

"Guillermo Smith!" a guard yelled. Memo sat up in his cot.

"Present."

"Grab your stuff. You're out of here!"

Memo couldn't believe his ears and consequently pinched himself to ensure he wasn't dreaming. He quickly collected his things and threw them in a laundry bag. Don Rafa had made good on his promise.

Chapter 15

Galilea called Memo on the cell. "I need to see you. When will you be in Juárez again?"

"I'm here now. What, are you psychic or something?"

"Oh, thank God. Can you–?"

"I'm on my way."

Memo and Galilea had continued their relationship even after Memo had gotten out of jail. His relationship with Lucia was loving and traditional but lacked the spice he got with Galilea. He knew it was wrong; Lucia loved him purely, probably more than any other woman could, and she didn't deserve his infidelity. But the chemistry between Galilea and him was too powerful for him to stop seeing her.

Memo entered the women's side of the prison.

The female guard smiled when she saw him.

"Ok, handsome, assume the position."

She patted him down, paying special attention to the gluteus.

Memo winked at her, as he entered the door to the common room.

"Mi amor!" Galilea screamed, as she ran and hugged him. Then she whispered, "Just want to be sure the rest of these jealous bitches know you are mine."

Memo laughed as they walked to a special room set up for conjugal visits. Another female guard stood at the entrance of the hallway, blocking the way. Memo handed her a twenty-dollar bill and she moved.

"You've got 'til 1700."

"Ok."

After the couple sat down, Memo asked, "Tell me what's wrong."

"You've got to get me out of here."

"We've been over this before. The lawyer said–" Memo started.

"I know what he said. It's different–I'm pregnant."

Turbulent emotions surged through Memo – joy at having a child with a woman he cared for very much, fear of Lucia one day finding out, and despair that he would never have the time to dedicate to his illegitimate child like he would his others. But he did know one thing – no child of his would be born in prison. Memo was glad that money could move mountains in Mexico.

Memo held Galilea in his arms, kissing her forehead, then her eyes, and moved to her lips.

"I'll get you out. Don't worry."

Memo returned home to Cuauhtémoc, his thoughts racing like an out-of-control train.

Picking up his cell phone, he angrily punched in the number of the lawyer he'd hired for Galilea. "This is Guillermo Smith. You're fired."

When Memo arrived at his new, five-bedroom home, Lucia met him at the door and embraced him. The house was a far cry from the tiny apartment he once had shared with his wife, mother-in-law, and Lucia's brothers. After some renovations, the house was now a two story, with a two-car detached garage. The entire property was encircled by a seven-foot wall made of rocks from the local area.

"Mijo, I missed you so much! Thank God you're home safe. I've got some news for you."

He held her away from him. "What? Everything okay with our boy?" he said, reaching down to pat Guillermo on the head.

"Everything's fine," Lucia said, beaming up at him joyfully. "He's going to have a brother."

Memo smiled broadly and grabbed Lucia up into his arms, laughing heartily as he did so. As an only child, Memo had always dreamed of what it would have been like having a brother of his own; Guillermo would have a brother and wouldn't have to experience the loneliness that Memo had. He thought about his other child he would be having with Galilea; they wouldn't even know about each other.

A troubled look fell upon Lucia's face. His face became flush and he wondered if she somehow knew that he had another woman. And worse, that she was pregnant too.

"What's wrong, Lucia?"

"I saw Julio Cesar today."

Memo felt a different heat rush to his head.

"He's a cop now. A detective."

"I see…And did you talk to him?"

"I did." Lucia lowered her head. "But only for a minute. He asked about how I was, and I told him I was happy and that we have a child and are expecting another."

Memo wanted to yell, but he calmed himself before speaking. "So, this bastard knew about my new baby before I did?"

Lucia trembled. "It just came out."

Memo put on his boots and hat, grabbed his gun, and left the house, leaving Lucia in tears, her eyes simultaneously apologizing and pleading with him to stop, although she was powerless to speak. The look on his face scared her to her very core and, though she didn't know it at that moment, Memo didn't care how Lucia felt.

Chapter 16

Lalo read a newspaper with the report about the explosion in his home. It mentioned him as having been a decorated policeman and that his wife and child had died in the explosion. The article also said he was possibly missing, but they had found some teeth and personal items, so it was possible he was dead. The paper was correct in that assumption because, although blood still pumped through his veins, his heart still beat, and oxygen filled his lungs, he really was dead without love and his family.

Revenge became his sole reason for existing. He fell off the grid to live as a homeless person, not taking money from his bank accounts or calling any relatives. He made no movements that could be recorded anywhere. He knew his enemies, who had enormous funds and many friends, could find him through such activities, and without the physical evidence to prove him dead, they'd stop at nothing to track him down. He'd have to be very careful.

Lalo grew a short dark beard, and he wreaked, not something he normally tolerated, much less his new odor of trash, sweat, and grease. He moved like an old man in an old denim jacket he'd traded for, and he only came out at night to scavenge for food and information. The summer sun in El Paso was ruthless. Seeking shade of any sort, Lalo found a box that used to hold a big screen TV. Pulling it to his "spot" in the alley behind an Italian restaurant, Lalo remembered he had always wanted a big screen to watch soccer but had never been able to afford it with his meager cop salary.

Dining was at 10 p.m., when the restaurant threw out the food people left on their plates. Eating was no longer a pleasure for him as it had been when Manuela had lived, and Lalo quickly became accustomed to the cold pasta, sauce, and sometimes pieces of meat mixed with something else – cigarette ashes, soda pop, or God only knew what else.

A putrid mix of feet, sweat, and feces scented the alley. Lalo couldn't become completely accustomed to the constant smell, but he could tolerate it better than when he had first moved into this particular spot. Small packs of dogs sometimes ran by, stealing any food not sufficiently protected.

The police cruisers that drove by completely ignored his existence; he was just another homeless bum. Nights and days ran together into one long day, and Lalo completely lost track of time. When it rained, the cardboard box leaked, wetting Lalo's thin blanket. The humidity made the smells worse. Once in a while, he would sneak into a fast-food restaurant and use the facilities, washing himself wherever he could if he got the bathroom to himself. Sometimes he would just wander the streets, remembering his past life, his loneliness nearly overwhelming all of his other senses. Passersby went out of their way to avoid his fetid path. But his true suffering was not this meager existence; it was the way his mind tortured him with memories of his wife and child, and visions of what he imagined their fear and pain must have been like the night they died. Lalo curled up in his box-house and slept.

Manuela hummed the song she had last heard on the radio, as she washed the dishes. Isela laid in her bed in the fetal position, thumb in her mouth, in the twilight between sleep and awareness. Fire and debris hit them as the house suddenly exploded, the shrapnel from the walls and windows cutting them, the intense flames burning their skin beyond recognition. They screamed, the fear and pain overwhelming. Dying, his wife and daughter's last breaths were for Lalo.

Now awake, Lalo couldn't remember the last time he had soundly slept. He was startled by a little girl, dressed in rags, hair dirty and disheveled, crouched in the far corner of the alley where Lalo stayed. She noisily ate something; when Lalo moved a little closer to see what it was, she snarled at him, a strange glowing in her eyes. She smiled and he saw she was eating a human hand. Appalled, Lalo turned, genuinely frightened by the sight. When he looked back, the girl was gone. There were more visions appearing as the weeks turned to months. The visions would happen day or night, and half the time Lalo wasn't sure that he was really awake.

One night, alone in his box, Lalo stirred, awakened by a blinding light in the alley. Manuela stood there, their dead daughter cradled in her arms, and she pointed a blaming finger at him. Everything became painfully clear to him at that moment. He had more to do, and a consuming need for revenge possessed his spirit. The light around Manuela and Isela grew painfully bright, and he had to squint. As suddenly as they had appeared, his family was gone. With a cry of rage, Lalo leapt up and ran, not quite knowing where to go. The city moved around him until he finally stopped, weak and out of breath, at a park in central El Paso. He dropped onto a park bench, and a newspaper there fluttered against his hand. The date glared up at him.

A year had passed since he'd lost his life, and he'd done nothing but wallow in self-pity. God had punished him greatly because he no longer had wanted to continue to do His work. Remembering his vision of the Archangel Michael when he was a teenager, Lalo realized Manuela had been so very right. Everything that had ever happened to him and the ones he loved were all part of the plan.

All he'd kept from his former life, a .380 Smith and Wesson not destroyed in the fire, what once had seemed to mock him now was clearly yet another sign from God. The gun would be enough to start his mission for God, the message Manuela had been sent to give him. Shedding his last tear, with Manuela's pointing finger of accusation still fresh in his mind, Lalo began to plan and become God's newest Angel of Death.

Chapter 17

Lalo needed money. The only place he could get "invisible" money, without checks, money orders, or banks, were drug dealers. They would now be his primary targets for funds. Lalo remembered Ricky Munoz, a clean-cut Chicano with strong ties to the Mexican Mafia, both from his childhood and later from his days in narcotics. Munoz spent a four-year stint in prison when he was twenty for aggravated battery, and "La M" taught him to deal drugs. Ricky quickly became one of the top middle-level dealers of El Paso when he got out of prison. His garage had been converted into a body shop, serving both as a front for Ricky and his cash, and also a way for him to receive and deliver money and drugs clandestinely.

Lalo knew El Paso was a "source" city, a drop-off point for drug loads from Mexico to the United States – a virtual warehouse for marijuana, cocaine, and heroin. Ricky's shop was just one of many drop-off points Lalo could go after, but, more important than the drugs themselves, at least for now, were the large quantities of untraceable cash Ricky had to transport illegally back to Mexico.

Lalo knew who brought Ricky the cash, so he would simply stake out the house until the right person showed up.

Three nights later, a black Ford Aerostar pulled into Ricky's driveway, windows darkly tinted, a picture of "Calvin" the cartoon pissing on the Chevrolet logo, and a "Support Your Local Police" bumper sticker. Lalo knew this man carried the cash he needed, so he mentally prepared himself for battle. As the man exited the vehicle, Lalo took a position ahead of him behind a tree.

The short fat man jumped from the van and scurried toward the front door with a black duffle bag clutched in his right hand. Lalo noticed a strange black ring, some type of aura around the man's head. He had never seen anything like it before. As the courier entered the house, Lalo deftly snuck up behind him and placed a bullet cleanly into the back of his head. Then, he fired three rounds into the surprised Ricky Munoz' chest, watching the astonishment on his face fade away into despair, then to death. The dark circle around his head faded as well. The bright image of his wife suddenly appeared, the light temporarily blinding Lalo. He felt a strange surge of energy throughout his body, and he went into convulsions.

After Manuela and Isela's image had gone and his convulsions had passed, Lalo made a quick sweep of the house, only to find it empty. How arrogant for a man receiving large quantities of cash and drugs to believe he was untouchable. Too easy, but that was the way of destiny. Lalo had become a part of that destiny, an avenging angel born of revenge more than a year before. He imagined God looking down at the scene below, unhappy lives had to be taken but approving of his dark angel's violent act.

Lalo left on foot, duffel bag in hand. As he got closer to his alley, he dragged the bag in the sand, completing his homeless-man look. When he arrived at his "house," Lalo opened the bag carefully, surprised to find more than $70,000 dollars in cash. *God helps those who help themselves*, Lalo thought. He contemplated how to avenge the death of God's helpless angels, the two beautiful women he'd been blessed with the duty to protect. He'd failed them miserably, and he realized that the money staring up at him could not bring them back, nor could the deaths of a hundred more drug dealers.

Mind whirling with broken thoughts and memories, Lalo realized there was only one way to fight and win this battle: clarity of thought and focus. All thoughts of the Angel women, as he now thought of his wife and child, had to take second place to logical thoughts and plans of war. In his mind, he constructed a giant wall, separating him from his love for the Angels and human need, filling his bunker with purpose and deliberation. His heart broke when he closed the wall around his love.

He fell asleep for an hour, awakened by tortured dreams of the Angels screaming for help, their bodies crumbling apart in a rain of fire, their eyes burning in the flames. Lalo could tolerate no more of the dreams, so he got up and began alternating push-ups and sit-ups. He'd let himself go soft in this half-existence and now would have to be in shape to carry out his mission from God. He realized if he didn't eat soon, he'd probably pass out. Perhaps living as an indigent was no longer convenient. His best bet would be to go to a cheap motel, rent a room, and clean up a bit, if he could find a motel that would accept him in his current state. Barba once told Lalo, "If you have a problem, just squirt some money on it and it will go away." The second motel he stopped at, the Montana Motel, was open to negotiation. Lalo paid a hundred dollars for a room that should have cost him twenty.

Lalo was seeing everyone with either a white, black, or gray aura. He had seen a grayish aura around the motel clerk's head. He now understood it was God's way of allowing Lalo to distinguish among the good, the marginally evil, and the truly evil. After buying some new clothes and taking a hot shower, Lalo felt decidedly better than he had in a long time. While shaving was not an option, being clean was. With his newly found cash, he could start buying equipment to fund his war against God's enemies. Lalo thought about the last few weeks and decided he'd probably gone insane. Shrugging, he quickly returned to his planning and made a list of equipment he would need to kill Satan's spawns.

As the list grew, so did his need for sleep. Soon he was drifting away, a small wooden boat on a huge river. The river flowed calmly, and his wife and daughter were on the other end of the boat, smiling and laughing contentedly. As the river shifted its flow, so did its velocity. Soon it was like a raging bull, angered by a red cape and thousands of people jeering. Water tore the fragile wooden boat in two, separating him from his loved ones. They screamed for Lalo's help, but the torrential waters prevented him from reaching them. As he watched his wife and daughter drown, Lalo tried desperately to escape the awful nightmare. But much like being under anesthesia, he could not escape the nightmare's grasp until it reached its awful conclusion – Manuela and his daughter's lifeless bodies floating to the river's edge as the waters of the river calmed to a normal flow, the sound of its liquid movement mocking Lalo's anguish.

For the next six months, Lalo trained his body and planned his revenge. He rested little, ate only the bare necessity, and slept a total of two to three hours per day. Surveillance was instrumental to planning, providing him with the intelligence he needed to confirm suspicions of guilt or innocence, daily activities of those who were guilty, and when they would be at their weakest points. His first instinct was to mindlessly kill all of the involved parties, but he realized he would need to follow the money trail to find out who was at the top of the drug chain. He needed to know who gave the order to have Lalo killed or whoever stood to profit most by him being out of the picture, or simply the person in charge of this drug operation that paid cops to turn a blind eye. He didn't care who it was; that person and any of their associates had to die.

Lalo knew he'd soon need an apartment for more privacy. He found the perfect one-bedroom apartment with the only access through the alley and moved his operation there. It provided an ideal place to train his body, and hide the weapons and equipment he'd been buying. His landlord was an older man who always wore old Vietnam-style military khakis. His haggard face was apparent below his gray beard, his long, white hair tied back in a loose ponytail. His aura was white.

"It's three hundred a month, including water."

"That's fine. All I ask for is my privacy."

The landlord nodded. "You a vet?"

"Yeah. How'd you know?"

"It's in your eyes, man. Everyone I ever knew who had seen combat in the 'Nam has that same look you have. It's the look of a man who's lost more than he can ever get back."

Lalo nodded, satisfied that he had found the right place to stay a while.

The next several months were one long blur for Lalo. Surveillance, target practice, and stealing from drug dealers were almost daily activities. Every time he was shot at and wasn't hit was just another attestation to his new role as God's archangel. Although he was more than ready to join his wife and daughter in eternal slumber, it seemed that God had made him bullet proof.

A year later, planning and training complete, the enemies' activities well documented, Lalo began God's master plan of revenge. Lalo now knew Barba's every move, as well as that of each and every one of his associates, and he planned every detail of their executions with great pleasure. Beginning with the lowest ranking of Barba's associates, Lalo began murdering them one by one, their auras always black as night.

Some of them were fellow policemen he'd worked with on cases both in the narcotics division and the homicide division. He didn't care. He started with an undercover cop named Juan Castro. Lalo had worked with him on a case or two, and now that he knew Juan had been working in Barba's ring, it made sense why both cases had not resulted in arrests or seizures of any kind. Juan must have alerted their targets beforehand.

Juan lived alone in an apartment complex, which made him an easy target. Waiting in the living room of Juan's two-bedroom apartment after breaking in, Lalo decided to use a switchblade he'd bought at an army surplus store. He wore gloves and tucked his hair under a baseball cap, careful not to leave any evidence behind.

As Juan entered the apartment, Lalo positioned himself behind the door and hit the man over the head with a loose brick that he'd found outside. After he'd tied Juan up, Lalo brought him back to consciousness with smelling salts.

"Hey, Juan, remember me?"

A blank stare was his answer, and Lalo realized he didn't look at all like who he used to be.

"It's me, Lalo Torres." He said it slowly, enjoying the widening of the other man's eyes. "Back from the dead to make sure you and your friends pay for your crimes."

"B-b-ut, how?"

"*How* doesn't matter, Juan. What does matter is *why*. Now, you have an opportunity to repent for your sins."

"But...you died..."

Lalo slammed his fist into Juan's face.

"God brought me back from the dead and I'm here to make sure you repent and pay for your sins. Now, let's get past that, okay?"

Juan nodded, trembling as he did.

"Remember going to church, Juan?"

"Every Sunday, *con mi mama.*" Spittle flew out of his mouth as he spoke.

"Well, I'm the Padre, and it's time to tell me all of your sins. Start from the very beginning and tell me all you know."

"I-I don't know what you're talking about."

Lalo pulled a switchblade out of his pocket, simultaneously flicking out the blade. Juan squirmed like a worm, his hands and feet bound very tightly. Lalo knelt down by his face.

"You know, Juan, I've seen a lot of movies. When people don't cooperate in the movies, they tend to lose things – fingers, toes, things like that. I'd hate to have to do something like that to you. Unlike the movies, I'm pretty sure the pain would be really bad. Really, really bad, Juan." He paused, Juan's eyes tearing up, his face contorted in anguish. Lalo continued, "I've been missing for a long while. Nobody thinks I'm even alive anymore. I have no family, no friends. I lost my wife and child. Nothing to lose, and I'm a fucking ghost. Do you honestly think I'm going to put up with any bullshit from you?"

Lalo placed the knife just above Juan's Adam's apple and Juan sobbed. Lalo was satisfied that Juan finally understood the true nature of his precarious position.t.

"Okay, okay. Look, my uncle Frank is a U.S. Customs Agent. He and Barba had been friends since before high school. Barba was a sergeant in the narcotics unit back then. Tío Frank noticed that all of a sudden Barba had a new ride and kept picking up the check all the time when they went out, so he decided to confront him. Barba didn't admit to being involved in anything at first, but after my uncle explained his pending divorce and the other financial problems he was in, Barba invited him to meet with Carlos Medina, who I know you knew, to help him out financially. With a customs agent at the border providing Medina with intelligence and protection for his drug loads, along with a group of police and border patrol agents, Medina became the most powerful drug trafficker in El Paso."

The light pressure of Lalo's knife produced a small cut, allowing a minute amount of blood to seep out, urging Juan to continue.

Juan kept talking in a desperate attempt to save his life. "Every week, INS issued a warning about a particular vehicle or certain locations of the vehicles to look for, and Frank would always tip Medina to avoid those that week. Occasionally, they set up a burro to take a fall, and Frank would bust a decent load of drugs, never over a hundred pounds, and it was almost always only marijuana. Coke was too valuable to run as a decoy load. Unless Medina had info on a run for one of his enemies. Those were open season."

Juan struggled to move away from the knife blade pressed to his neck because talking made the cut deeper with every word. Lalo let up on the pressure, only a bit.

"Right behind Frank's 'bust,' Medina would run a load of coke, usually a van or a truck, with every conceivable hiding place filled with it. The load would be escorted by Barba or one of his men to safety."

As the flow of blood grew thicker, Juan screamed, "That's all I know, honest. Now let me go, okay? I'll get out of this shit. I promise. Just give me a chance to change. I hate what I've become."

Lalo felt his face crease in an unpleasant smile. "Like my wife and baby were given a chance?"

"Oh, c'mon, man, I got a wife and kids, too. I had nothing to do with that!"

Lalo growled. "Who did?"

Juan grimaced. "I don't know, man, I'd tell you!"

"Prepare to meet the Devil, you son of a bitch." Lalo said, pulling up Juan by his hair. Juan began to scream, but Lalo slit the man's throat from ear to ear before he could, Mafia style. Blood spilled onto Juan's clothes and seeped into the faded carpet of the living room floor. It sprayed over Lalo's face and shirt and he grinned madly. Manuela and Isela's light blinded Lalo, and he fell to his knees, tears running down his face, another murder committed in the name of God's vengeance. A strange surge of energy filled his body. God was pleased with this day's deed; Lalo could feel it. Lalo prayed on his knees, his arms straight up over his head, trembling as he said his words to God.

Lalo rested for a moment after his prayer. As he cleaned up any physical evidence that could have been possibly linked to him, Lalo wondered if he really was insane or if what he was feeling was real. In the end, he thought, it really didn't matter. Insane or not, he was getting rid of the scum of the earth.

Chapter 18

As Rafa drove Memo along the highway connecting Cuauhtémoc with the Mennonite colonies, they passed farms where blond-haired children worked in the fields, the girls wearing large *Little House on the Prairie* bonnets and wide skirts, the boys wearing striped bib-overalls and straw hats.

"Don Rafa, I thought you said we were going to see a man who makes secret compartments. Aren't we in the Mennonite camps?"

Rafa smiled. "We are. I want you to meet a Mennonite named 'the Wire.' He's an ingenious welder; for about the last seven years, he's worked for me, suspending my product in the gas tanks, so when someone hits the tank, it sounds like it's empty, and making compartments that fit around the tire rims. The Wire's *clavos* are second to none."

"I thought the Mennonites were highly religious."

"A lot of them still are. Some of the Mennonites have strayed from their religious background. Their leaders blame it on the Mexican influence."

Rafa paused and chuckled.

"I know many who are alcoholics or even have drug habits. I'm sure that's nothing like the original Mennonites who settled here some eighty years ago. I'm glad we could help the boring bastards."

Like many Mennonites' homes, the Wire's home was a gray, one-story house, built like a typical farmhouse. As soon as he saw him, Memo understood why he was called the Wire. About 6'3", the Wire was all bones, just barely filling out about half of his gray Levi's jeans. He had a nice button-down shirt, gray boots, and a Stetson to match. He spoke with a heavy accent.

"Good to see you, Rafa. Who's here with you?"

"This is Memo. He's my second in command and will be running the operation while I'm gone."

"You're going somewhere?"

"The other side," Rafa answered.

"I haven't been to the United States in a while. I envy you. Well, Memo, welcome to my home."

The two men shook hands. Memo saw a very German-looking plump lady peer out from another room.

"That's my wife. She just got here a month ago from Canada. She still doesn't know a lick of Spanish."

"Sprechen sie Deutsch?" Memo asked the Wire, his four years of German in high school finally being put to use.

"Nein. We don't speak high German. We speak low German. High German is only used in church; our Bible is in high German. Where did you learn to speak it?"

"My grandfather was German. Plus, I took it in school."

"You're good. Said it without an accent."

Rafa smiled, pleased the Wire was impressed. "You see, I told you Memo was an asset to the organization."

The Wire smiled, then wrinkled his forehead as if something worried him.

Rafa asked, "What is it?"

"I just wonder how El Soldado will feel about all this."

"Not to worry. That's on us."

"Okay, Rafa, you know I trust you," the Wire said, then he turned to Memo, "You like beer?"

Memo laughed. "Do politicians like their palms greased? Hell yes, I like beer."

"Come on."

Memo and Rafa followed the Wire to the huge barn outside of his house. Once inside, Memo marveled at the many vehicles partially dismantled all around. There were iron half-moons, apparently used to wrap the drug around a tire rim. Gas tanks were split open.

"The gas tanks are my specialty. I open them at their original seams. I'm very careful to ensure there are no signs of tampering when I put them back."

"What about when they're tapped on?"

"We still haven't perfected that. It makes a *thud* instead of the normal hollow sound a gas tank would have."

"What if you made a box? Something similar to what you've made here for the tire rims. But with thinner walls. Then you could suspend it within the tank."

Rafa and the Wire looked at each other. The Wire ran over to his soldering equipment and went to work. Memo helped the Wire perfect all of his "clavos" or hidden compartments and would continue doing so for an entire year, further securing his place in Rafa's organization.

Chapter 19

Memo turned to Jorge as he drove his brand-new 1999 Ford Lobo up the steep and curvy mountain road to Guachochi, Chihuahua.

"If someone had told me I'd be driving a brand-new truck to pick up a load of marijuana five years ago, I'd never have believed them."

"Yeah, and I'd have never believed that I would be helping my brother-in-law to do that, either."

Gilberto joined in, "And I never thought Memo would be one of the wealthiest drug dealers in Chihuahua. In three years, at that!"

They all laughed, and Memo noted perhaps a touch of anxiousness in their laughs.

Arriving as far as they could go by road, Memo stopped short at a large gulley dark green with vegetation. He turned to his youngest brother-in-law.

"Omar, you stay here in the truck. If we aren't back in three hours, call the Colonel."

"You got it, Memo!"

The Colonel was Colonel Parra, an officer in the Army. He had intercepted one of his marijuana loads once, and after Memo "fixed" things with him, they'd become close allies. If Memo and his brothers-in-law didn't make it back on time, Colonel Parra would have the entire Mexican Army searching the area.

An Apache with three horses waited for them at the bottom of the gulley.

"He waiting."

The Apache spoke Spanish with such a thick accent that Memo could barely understand him. Most of the Apaches in the Chihuahua Mountains still spoke their native language fluently and held on to most of their early customs.

"Okay, Jorge, remember, you just follow to the cave. Gilberto and I will go in alone."

Jorge patted the side of his AK-47 and nodded, smiling.

After riding horseback for about thirty minutes, Jorge stopped short about 50 meters from the cave's entrance. Gilberto and Memo entered with the Indian. Memo rested his hand on the hilt of his .45 automatic, as if to make sure it was still there. Gilberto carried a double-barreled shotgun, mostly for intimidation.

Another Apache, called El Indio, waited deeper inside the cave. He wore boots with a design of two cocks fighting and a matching belt buckle. His gold chain was extravagant, the gold figure of a marijuana leaf hanging from it. He and Memo shook hands without speaking, and Memo laid a metal briefcase in front of him and opened it.

"Fifty dollars a kilo, just like we agreed."

"How much there?"

"Fifty thousand."

El Indio's eyes widened. He looked at the other Apache, and Memo grabbed the hilt of his .45.

"There a problem here?"

"Too much. You take all my supply. Need more money."

Memo tightened his grip on the handgun but still didn't pull it out.

"A deal is a deal. I keep my word, and everyone in Chihuahua knows it. Do you keep your word, Indio?"

The cave was so silent that Memo could hear the water from the river running below the gulley. El Indio looked at the other apache, at Memo, then back at the apache again. Memo nodded to Gilberto, who responded by cocking his shotgun.

"I have word, too, Don Guillermo. Joking." El Indio flashed what passed for him as a smile. Memo returned the smile with sincerity, knowing he had won the battle of nerves. Out of the corner of his eye, he saw Gilberto visibly relax.

With the exchange finished and the delivery details hashed out, the three brothers-in-law traveled down the mountain to where they'd left the truck.

As Memo drove down the mountains back toward Cuauhtémoc, he thought about the way he was getting the marijuana off the mountain. El Indio would deliver the load to a secret runway located close to the caves where he stored the marijuana. Memo would have his pilot pick it up under the careful observation of Gilberto and Jorge, his two older brothers-in-law. The plane would fly the load to Memo's ranch, just outside of Cuauhtémoc, and the marijuana would be stored in a barn and re-distributed in smaller amounts from there. He wished he could do something different; everyone in the business used the same method to transport marijuana from the mountains, and sometimes planes were captured by the military. Memo slowed down as he drove around one of the many hard curves in the road. A large semi-truck carrying several, large pine tree trunks drove slowly in front of him. As Memo was about to pass the truck, a thought suddenly occurred to him, and he stopped in the middle of the road. In his mind he could see these huge trees hollowed out, allowing for hundreds of kilos to be packed within their spaces. The lumber company was located just thirty minutes away, in a small town called Temochic. When Memo turned off onto a dirt road headed for the lumber company, a confused Omar turned to question Memo's action.

"Where are we going?"

"We're going to buy a lumber company."

Jorge, Gilberto, and Omar laughed. They stopped laughing as soon as they realized their brother-in-law was very serious.

Omar asked, "And just why the hell are you buying a lumberyard?"

"We're going to hollow out the pine tree trunks and pack them with marijuana."

The brothers just looked at one another.

"Look, by using the pine trees to move the marijuana, we cut out the plane trip and the storage at the ranch. That means there will be two less chances our loads get intercepted. We can ship the marijuana directly to Juárez using the lumber as a cover business as well. No one will ever think the lumber is being used this way."

Memo parked the Ford directly in front of the factory and walked in like he already owned the business. "Who's in charge here?" he yelled out upon entering.

A man who looked to be in his forties answered. "I am. What do you need?"

"I want to talk to the owner."

"Well, you happen to be in luck. I'm one and the same."

"I want to buy your business."

The man smiled, his wrinkled face wrinkling even more as he did so.

"I'm sorry, young man, but it isn't for sale."

Memo smiled back. "Sure it is. Just name your price."

"Half a million dollars."

"Done. How do you want your money? Dollars or pesos?"

The owner's jaw dropped; his disbelief was evident in every wrinkle of his windblown face.

Memo called Don Rafa and arranged a meeting.

Guillermo and Gilberto left for Ciudad Juárez early the morning after the El Indio exchange. They arrived five hours later and stopped at Guillermo's two-story home. The home was modest compared to the residence he owned in Cuauhtémoc, but Memo wanted to keep a lower profile in Juárez, where the police were even more crooked. He preferred not to share any more of his profits than he already had to with the greedy police and local politicians.

Later in the afternoon, he and Gilberto went to a strip club called Amadeus and met up with a few girls who worked there. After Memo gave him a few hundred dollars to cover the girls' absence, the owner let the girls have the rest of the day off. From there, they went to a nightclub called El Patio, where they danced to live music.

As the four stepped out of the club, Guillermo's stomach knotted with apprehension, and he glanced around them. A gold, newer model Ford Expedition slowly drove by and Guillermo instinctively reached for his .45. Nothing happened. No fireworks, no bullets. He shook his head, wondering if the paranoia would ever go away, or if would simply intensify.

The girl who was with Memo, Yvonne, had an incredible body. Her breasts were obviously not real, way too round and big for her small frame. But she still looked great.

"Do you have any coke? Me and Candi love coke!"

Memo didn't use it, but he knew that much like the way to a man's heart was through his stomach, the way to a stripper's was through her nose. He had brought a half ounce with him. After Memo passed the waiter a fifty-dollar bill, the group of four went to a table in the VIP section of the bar.

Memo handed the girl the baggie of cocaine, and she squealed in delight, much like a little girl would at the sight of her favorite candy. The girls excused themselves and went to the ladies' room to do some unladylike snorting.

Memo turned to Gilberto. "So, what do you think of Candi?"

"I think I might develop a sweet tooth."

"Well, don't. These girls only love us when we've got money or coke."

"I know. Don't worry."

The girls returned to the table, their pupils wide, and their nostrils red with irritation.

Candi grabbed Gilberto by the hand. "That stuff is great. Let's dance!" The two went to the dance floor. Yvonne smiled at Memo, moving her head slightly toward the dance floor. He smiled and nodded, then took her hand and led her to a spot open by Gilberto. They twirled their partners almost in unison, Gilberto having picked up many of his moves from Memo.

Two bottles of Tequila and a few beers later, Memo and Gilberto were ready to retire for the night. Candi and Yvonne went to the bathroom several times, so they were still ready to party.

"Yvonne, let's get a hotel room and continue this there."

"That sounds perverse-I mean, perfect." Everyone laughed.

The two couples continued to party until around five in the morning. Gilberto left with Candi to another room. Guillermo sent Yvonne home in a taxicab, so he could get some sleep. He could never sleep well with any woman other than his wife or Galilea. He knew it was probably just another part of his paranoia and more than likely unfounded. The thought of being dead asleep and at the whim of a stranger who could do whatever they wanted to him was quite unsettling.

After a few hours of hard sleep, Guillermo called the adjoining room to wake up Gilberto.

"Wake up, Cabron! We have to meet Javier at three."

"Bueno," Gilberto growled into the phone, his voice rough with sleep.

Guillermo pulled on his light blue crocodile boots, a matching belt, and his expensive 100x black Stetson, playing the part of a Mexican Mafia drug trafficker to the hilt. The more expensive the clothes, boots, and hat, the higher up on the food chain one appeared. Guillermo always dressed impeccably with the best clothes money could buy. He put on his gold chain with a 14k gold marijuana leaf and slipped on the matching ring. While he professed to being "low profile," Memo enjoyed the extra attention he received from the ladies by dressing up. He and Gilberto drove to the "Baca Blanca" boot company. Gilberto stood watch outside of the office while Memo went in.

Javier and Memo embraced each other, in a masculine way, then shook hands.

"It's been a long time, Javier. Haven't seen you since 'school,'" Memo said, "school" meaning their time in prison.

"It seems like a lifetime ago, doesn't it? Broke, alone, then, out of nowhere, Don Rafa gives us a new life."

Memo thought about what Javier had just said. It was true, Don Rafa had helped them both, but there was a price to pay. "Definitely. Javier, we have a new plan for the shipments."

"Don Rafa didn't tell me anything."

"That's because I haven't seen him yet to tell him. I know he'll go for it, though. You see, I bought a lumber company up in Temochic. We'll be hollowing out pine trees and shipping the marijuana to a lumberyard here in Juárez. Your lumberyard. We'll still be using your boot factory for now, but once I get everything approved through Don Rafa and you buy the lumberyard, it will be the way to go."

Javier smiled. "For a minute, Memo, I thought you were going to cut me out."

Memo frowned. "Don't ever say that again, Javier. Don't even think about it. I'm more loyal to you and Don Rafa than I am to my own wife."

Javier turned slightly red. "Sorry, Memo."

With everything in place, Guillermo and Gilberto went out again, this time just the two of them. They danced, met women, and collected their numbers. Just before the bar closed for the night, Gilberto and Memo met at their table, ordered two shots of tequila and a beer chaser, and counted the numbers they had collected.

"Fuck!" Memo handed over a one-hundred-dollar bill to Gilberto. "This is the third time you got more than me in a row. You must be cheating."

"Cuñado! How dare you suggest such an awful thing. I'm younger and dance better. What do you expect?"

"Cabrón! I taught you everything you know."

"And the student becomes the master-" they both said in unison. They laughed and a pretty girl with a big butt tapped Gilberto on the shoulder. He turned to her and smiled. "Yes, my love?"

The girl smiled and flicked a long, curly bang away from her eye. "My friend," she pointed at another pretty girl sitting just a few tables away from them, "and I were wondering if you two would like to join us?"

Gilberto smiled and looked at Memo who simply nodded approvingly. Gilberto stuck out his hand. "Name's Gilberto, and this is Memo."

"I'm Rachelle, and she is Betty." They all shook hands and went to the table where Betty, all smiles and eyelashes, greeted them. They got more drinks just before the last call. Betty was the shyer of the two girls, but she made it evident that she was a more than willing participant by continuously touching Memo, be it on the hand, the leg, or his broad chest. Memo didn't think it was possible, but he was too weary for sex. Or for another girl. He stood up and Gilberto looked at him, surprised.

"Ladies, Gilberto, I'm out. Have a good night."

Gilberto looked at him quizzically. Betty looked disappointed.

"I'm sure Gilberto can entertain you both tonight. I must be getting old." He threw his keys to the truck and an eight-ball down on the table. Gilberto nodded and grabbed the coke and the keys. The girls' eyes lit up and they smiled. Memo left the bar, hailed a cab, and went home.

Memo laid down in the master bedroom of his two-story Juárez home and closed his eyes. If only Galilea was out of jail, she could be there with him now, and he wouldn't have to be so alone. He picked up his cell and dialed Gilberto.

"Gil, what are you doing?"

"Screwing, until you called anyway. What's up?"

"You go without me tomorrow to Cuauhtémoc," Memo said. "I've got some business to take care of."

"Are you sure you don't need my help?"

"Yeah. Just check on your sister."

"I'll have someone take you the truck tomorrow morning."

"Make it early, Gilberto. I've got plans."

"It's three in the morning. How early do you need it?"

"Just have them get it here by eight. And call me when you get to Cuauhtemoc."

"Will do." They hung up, and Memo rolled onto his side.

All night, Memo thought about how he could get Galilea out of jail. He thought about paying the prison director, the guards, judges, everyone involved. It would cost a lot of money, and many of those involved would probably try to get more from him later. He opted to simply pay the guards off. The guards would have few resources to go after Memo for more money later, and would be easily dismayed because of their relatively little influence within the government. Satisfied with his conclusion, Memo finally slept.

Chapter 20

At nine a.m., Memo was first in line for visitation at the prison. He carried a small gym bag with $10,000 and some clothes for Galilea. After haggling a bit with a guard at the entrance, Memo went straight to the guards who watched the people exiting the visitor's common room.

"I've got something for you."

One of the guards made a sign at the other, turned, and motioned for Memo to follow her. She entered a small office. She was short, unattractive, and had a thick mustache.

"What you got? You need to take something to your girlfriend?"

"No. I need her out."

The guard's eyes widened, and she paused. "That will cost you. There are two of us, you know."

"I brought enough for both of you." He dropped the bag onto the desk the guard stood beside. She opened it up and whistled.

"And how do you know we won't just take it from you. You know, confiscating contraband?"

"Because I'm pretty sure both of you want to live to see tomorrow's sunrise." Memo stared hard into the woman's eyes.

She broke away from his smoldering stare.

"Okay, okay. I get it." She put her hands up in a peaceful gesture. "You plan to just walk her out of here?"

"Yep."

The guard laughed.

"Okay. Go to the visiting room. When I make a sign, you guys leave."

"What will the sign be?"

She smiled, her crooked, yellow teeth glistening. "Oh, trust me, you'll know it when you see it.

As soon as Memo walked into the common area of the women's prison, Galilea made her usual scene so the other women there would know Memo "belonged" to her.

"Gali, remain calm. Act like nothing is going on."

"Okay." Her hands trembled slightly.

"You're getting out of here."

"Really?!?"

"Shhh. Relax. Yes. I paid off the guards. Screw the lawyers, the judges, this stupid system. I'm going to walk you right out of here. We'll get you a new identity, and you can come with me to Cuauhtémoc."

Galilea's eyes lit up, but she remained calm. A few minutes later, a fight broke out in the common area. The guard who had made the deal with Memo was at the doorway while her partner nonchalantly approached the now formed circle of inmates chanting, "Fight! Fight!" Memo squeezed Galilea's hand, and, as they approached the doorway, the guard walked over to help her partner. Since the inmates wore civilian clothes, and Memo had already paid the guard at the entrance, the couple walked out of the prison together, as easily as if they had just walked in. They got into his truck and drove off, Galilea crying out of joy.

They arrived at his house in Juárez that evening.

"Welcome to your new home, for the time being."

"Iaaayyy!" Galilea screamed her approval. "I love you, love you, love you!" She jumped up and wrapped her legs around his waist. He still found her very sexy, even with the small baby-belly that was forming.

"Make love to me."

"My pleasure."

Later that night, Memo laid awake, Galilea's curvy body beside him. She was asleep, but he couldn't seem to get there. Something didn't feel right.

Thump. Thump. Whispers.

Memo turned toward Galilea and placed one hand firmly over her mouth. She awoke, surprised and afraid by his strange action.

"Shh. There's someone outside. I need you to move very quietly to the closet and get in. Lie down on the floor and do not move. No matter what."

Galilea nodded emphatically.

"Go."

Memo went to the bathroom, turned on the light and the water in the shower, and closed the door.

He quietly creeped to the back bedroom. Knowing the most inconspicuous place to break into the home was through the rear door in the patio, Memo went to the window just above it. Two men were at the door: one was providing cover and the other was picking the lock. Memo would have shot the two from above, but, if he didn't get them both, one could get away and bring more help. Maybe there were more waiting in a car nearby. Memo ran back to the master bedroom and looked out at the street. A black Crown Victoria was parked on the curb a few blocks down, but it was too dark to see if anyone was inside it. He would have to assume that the car had reinforcements, so whatever his move was, it would need to be quick and decisive. Memo placed the pillows in the form of bodies and covered them up with a sheet.

The footsteps were inside the house now. Memo positioned himself behind the door. He could barely make out the barrel of the gun held by one of the men who entered the room.

Thwip. Thwip. Thwip. The silencer-muffled shots slammed into the pillows, and the bed vibrated. Pieces of bed innards poofed up and away from the bed.

The shooter kept the gun trained on the bed, and the other man tiptoed across the floor and slowly opened the door to the bathroom. Memo only had a moment to act.

Rolling his body from behind the bedroom door as the other man entered the bathroom, Memo fired off three rounds, two hitting the shooter in the chest. The bathroom man reacted, but too slowly, and Memo emptied the clip into him. Reloading, Memo walked over to the first man. Crouching down, he yanked the shooter's head up and glared into his pain-glazed, panicked eyes. Then, placing the barrel of his weapon against the assassin's skull, he finished him off.

Wiping sweat from his face and some sprinkles of blood from his hands, he got up and opened the closet door. Galilea came running out of the closet and hugged him with all her strength, crying unabashedly.

After a moment, he shoved her away and went to inspect the bodies. They both wore designer jeans, shirts, and expensive boots.

"Dios mío! They're cops!" Galilea pointed at the badge one of them wore on his hip.

"Judiciales. Detectives. They probably work for El Soldado. We gotta get out of here."

The couple grabbed some clothes and shoved them in a go-bag Memo kept in the closet. The go-bag had some money and an AK-47 in it as well. They snuck out the door on the side of the house and Memo instructed Galilea to stay hidden until he returned. After inspecting the AK-47 and preparing it to fire, he snuck around the house and put himself in a corner of the wall near the tall fence that surrounded his home. He noticed that the gate was open, the severed lock lying on the ground. He could see the Crown Victoria but couldn't make out if there was anyone in it. He had no choice but to clear the car before they could escape. Exiting through the gate, he walked briskly on the opposite side of the street from the car, the AK by his side. When he got close enough, he trained the AK on the car and moved quickly to the car. There was no movement, no gunfire, just silence. He saw that the car was empty and after returning to Galilea, Memo called for a ride and some "clean up". They would leave for Cuauhtémoc early in the morning. He didn't want Galilea to be so close to his wife's home, but it was the safest place for her. He practically owned the town.

Chapter 21

Memo stared at the calendar on the wall in the office at the body shop he owned – one of his many legitimate businesses – a little dizzy from the smell of fresh paint that penetrated the building. Curvy women standing by sleek sports cars. Memo particularly liked January, a dark-skinned brunette.

He was startled when one of his underlings, Martin Espino said, "Don Guillermo, a man wants to talk to you about work."

The sound of men buffing and sanding cars forced Memo to almost yell. "Does he come recommended? What do we know about him?"

Espino answered loudly. "He's Socorro Ortiz, Juanito's tío, and a hard worker. Socorro's small grocery store went under about five years ago, after his wife was in a bad car accident and he had to take care of her and the kids. He's been running marijuana from the mountains to Ciudad Juárez for the Mennonites, but he knows there is a better future for him with you. Besides, he doesn't want to be a burro anymore."

Memo had many contacts who were Mennonites. The local culture had affected the local Mennonites in ways that weren't very positive. Many were no longer practicing their religion and had joined the ever-growing drug trade. He shifted in his chair. Not fond of poaching local talent, Memo asked, "what can I use him for?"

"About two weeks ago, he was surrounded by Federales on his way back from the mountains. Someone had put the finger on him, but he didn't give up. He paid these guys protection money, but they wanted his load as well." Espino coughed from the strong odor of the paint being stripped from the vehicles inside.

Memo smiled, remembering the story. "Now I know who he is. I heard he told the Commander he'd kill himself fighting the Federales before he'd turn himself in. The Commander laughed, and that Socorro guy blew his head off with a sawed-off shotgun. The Commander's men were so shocked they didn't react fast enough, and he blew them away with an AK-47 that he had hanging from a strap on his shoulder. Flamboyant, but effective. And ballsy." Memo stood. "I think I'll like him. Send him in and we'll talk."

Socorro came into the office, his cowboy hat in his hands in front of him. His hair was black with a few streaks of gray. He wore a simple white, pearl button western shirt, black jeans, and mule hide boots. He was slender, his long, sinewy muscles evidence that he had worked hard all his life. After a few minutes of silently measuring one another, Memo spoke.

"I hear you got into this business to take care of your kids."

Socorro nodded, looking down at Memo's feet. Memo made a "wait a minute" gesture with his finger and poked his head out of the office door. "Everyone take thirty!"

The workers looked puzzled. Memo smiled, then yelled, "get out of here for thirty minutes, now!" The body shop employees scattered. Memo shut the office door, straightened his shirt and pants, then cleared his throat before speaking again.

"I have a wife and two boys. I love them more than my life. Things have gotten, well, complicated. I need someone who can be around when I'm not and who would be willing to take a bullet or even die for their safety. Anyone can say they would be willing to do it, but very few men would actually go through with it."

Socorro looked Memo in the eyes. "My life is unimportant. I'd give my soul to ensure my wife and children had everything they needed. My life is a small price to pay. When I saw that I was going to be detained by the Federales, the only thing I could think of was the poverty my children would have to endure. My poor wife would die without my assistance. I have no formal education. I have no skills other than farming, and now, killing. If you can assure me that no matter what happens to me my children will be cared for, I'll protect your family with my last breath."

Socorro had arrived at a perfect time. Memo knew he would need full-time protection for his family now more than ever; business was booming and his wealth growing exponentially. El Soldado's recent attempt on his life was only the beginning. The two men came up with both a salary and an agreement as to Socorro Ortiz's duties. Guillermo knew the man needed money for his family, so he gave him a month's salary in advance. He'd seen the hard look of desperation in too many faces not to recognize it. It was as simple as reading a man's face for a request he was too proud to make. Socorro left happily with money in his pocket but anxious to get to work.

With Socorro near his family, Memo drove back to Juárez, stopping to get gas before he left. The attendant immediately cleaned his windows and checked the air in his tires without asking. Memo gave him 500 pesos. The attendant thanked him profusely and Memo continued on his trip, wondering if he would need the same kind of protection for Galilea.

Chapter 22

Smiling, the pleasing smell of tamales cooking in steam, Memo took a bite of a sweet tamale and washed it down with a swig of black coffee. He frequented La Choza, a small tamale shop downtown every morning he was working in Juárez. The grainy texture of the corn meal was a pleasant contrast with the plump raisins and the juicy pieces of pineapple mixed inside. He frowned when he remembered he had killed two would-be assassins in cold blood as well as the strong case of déjà vu he felt afterwards. Memo shivered at the thought of his recent memories. The cell phone on Memo's hip rang, snapping him back to reality.

"Memo, this is Rafa. Have you been trying to get a hold of me?" Memo had left several messages for Rafa at his used car dealership in Albuquerque.

"I sure have. When can I see you? Just tell me when and where," Memo said.

A short pause, then Rafa said, "Today, around one p.m., at the cathedral in Juárez. You're lucky I'm in town."

"I'll be there."

In the central part of the city, within walking distance from the El Paso/Juárez border, was the huge cathedral of Juárez. The old Catholic church, filled with beautiful artwork and statues, was an oasis in the middle of a desert of poverty, drug addicts, and prostitutes: the primary inhabitants of this area of the city. A large Mercado was next door, and the human traffic was incessant. An open market was an easy place to disappear and way too public for someone to kill you.

Memo met Rafa outside the main entrance, and they proceeded to a shrimp cocktail stand down the street. After they ate, they walked down a street filled with men shining shoes for two dollars. Rafa and Memo had their boots shined, carefully avoiding business discussions as they waited. Memo paid both the shoe-shiners, tipping them each $10. Rafa shot Memo a look like maybe he thought Memo was crazy for tipping so much. Memo just smiled; he knew they had plenty, and it was better to have the common man on their side if the proverbial shit ever hit the fan. Memo and Rafa entered the Hotel Continental, where Rafa was staying for the evening.

They settled into chairs in his room, where they could talk undisturbed.

"Rafa, we've got to do something," Memo said. "A couple of his police tried to kill me."

Rafa nodded. "I've been thinking about that, too. El Soldado has an associate named Carlos Medina. So you understand, let me tell you about Medina. He started selling cocaine in the early eighties. He and his wife lived in a dangerous part of Juárez, and he hated to leave her alone when he went to work. At the bar where he worked as a waiter, he began to deal cocaine."

He leaned back in his chair. "At first, he simply made the connections for the bar patrons, buying from a local street dealer named El Soldado, and settling for whatever tip the patron gave him. After a few months, more and more patrons sought him out. El Soldado sold the purest coke available on the streets, and that was hard to find. When others asked where he got it, he would simply tell them his cousin brought it to him from down south." He paused and Memo held up a finger.

"You want something to drink? Beer?" Memo asked.

"Yeah. Have them bring up a six pack of Modelo Negra."

Memo ordered room service to bring up the beers.

Rafa continued. "Medina decided to buy larger quantities from El Soldado. When people began to look for him at his house, his wife confronted him about the visitors. He had no choice but to come clean. Luckily, the money was good, so his wife didn't complain much. After a while, Medina didn't have to leave home to conduct his new business, and he was able to quit his job."

Someone knocked on the door. "That was quick," Memo said, unholstering his .45.

"Who is it?"

"Room service."

Rafa got up and opened the door, Memo on the side, ready to fire if necessary. A pimply, young man handed them the beer. Memo relaxed. He uncapped the bottles and handed one to Rafa. "Go on."

"Every week, Medina bought a half a kilo of cocaine, took it home, and cut it with a milk thistle." Rafa took a swig of the beer.

"Why milk thistle, of all things?"

"Believe it or not, it blends exceptionally well with coke. Anyway, the kilo was converted into a kilo and a half, and he sold it by the ounce. A young neighbor, Yeyo Morales, began selling for Medina, and Carlos could stay out of the limelight. After about a year, Medina and his wife moved to a bigger house in a nicer part of the city. He paid cash for it." Rafa paused again to drink, then went on with his story. "Medina bought a seafood restaurant in a ritzy side of Juárez to justify his steady income and consequently got a visa with the intent of buying a house in El Paso."

Rafa set his empty bottle on the table.

"Meanwhile, El Soldado became the most powerful man in Juárez and took over the Juárez Cartel in a bloody coup d'état," he said. "During the violence, Medina moved to his home in El Paso and began to deal in the U.S. There was a coke shortage in Juárez, so Medina came to me, and I supplied him with marijuana. That turned out to be one of the problems El Soldado had with me. He thought we were trying to cut him out. Actually, we just didn't want to bother him while he was dealing with his little war. And to be honest with you, Memo, we thought at the time that El Soldado wasn't going to make it. A lot of people wanted him dead. We straightened it out by giving El Soldado a huge cut of our profits during our dealings together, but he never was truly satisfied."

Memo jumped when the hotel room's phone rang.

Rafa answered, and as he talked, his expression was troubled.

"I understand. Thanks, Tomas." Rafa hung up the phone. Frowning, Rafa turned to Memo. "Let's get out of here. Tomas is the owner of the hotel, and we've been friends for a long time. Four detectives are outside right now asking about me. I guess El Soldado knows I'm here."

Hotel Continental, not the most luxurious hotel in Juárez, had a distinct advantage over the others in the area – an escape route. Tomas had built an underground tunnel linking the hotel with one of his other businesses, a strip club just a block away. No one but he and a few of his closest friends knew of the tunnel; not even the hotel employees suspected its existence. Rafa and Memo hurried through its cool corridors to the club. Their best bet was just to stay put until the evening. The cops would never know they were there.

The club was still quiet; it was way too early for the strippers. Rafa and Memo sat at a table and ordered more beer. Rafa continued where he had left off in the hotel room, just slightly out of breath from their brisk walk.

"Memo, about a week ago, an El Paso police lieutenant paid me a visit. He said he knew I was involved with drugs, that all my businesses in Albuquerque were just fronts. He said he wasn't there to bust me but to help me. He works with Medina."

"So, he wants to cut out Medina?"

"Exactly. This guy, Barba, doesn't think Medina will be around much longer. I don't know if we can trust Barba, but he has connections in Customs too."

"Well, I've lost more than a few loads at the border. It could be profitable."

"Look, if something happens to Medina, El Soldado will go nuts. He'll forget all about us for a while. In the meantime, we can plan against him. We need to get rid of him."

Memo thought about it and frowned. He really didn't want to wage war with one of México's biggest drug traffickers, but El Soldado started it. Feeling particularly paranoid, Memo called Socorro.

"What's up, boss?"

"Just be extra alert. A lot of shit has gone down."

"Yes sir."

Chapter 23 (Arturo)

El Patio, a hole-in-the-wall bar in downtown Juárez, barely withstood the number of people within its trembling walls, as was the case normally on any given Friday night. Arturo Cereceres watched smoke clouds fill the room, making it even harder to see in the already dimly lit bar.

The entrance on the top floor led to a small bar area in the middle, and tables ran along the side of the walls in a horseshoe shape. The bottom floor was the center of the bar, and the dance floor was set against the back wall toward the middle of the room. Rustic wood tables held beer bottles, mostly the two Mexican brands of Tecate and Carta Blanca half and quarter full bottles of liquors, Tequila and Presidente, and many squeezed limes. Arturo enjoyed the music from a local band, a typical "Norteno," or northern style; the group boasted an accordion, percussion, and both acoustic and bass guitars. Songs about drug trafficking or regional patriotism were always popular at any of the local bars. Lined up in the bathroom for thin, white lines of temporary courage, men bought small papers of cocaine-like first-graders-bought candy. Supposedly the coke would offset the effects of drinking, and they would be able to "last the night."

Arturo laughed to himself, as he observed the drug dealers, obvious by their appearances with their large gold items hanging from their necks and around their wrists and fingers, cellular phones on their hips, and often beepers as well. Among the hands of the drug dealers, bartenders, waitresses, and patrons, the coke and hundred-dollar bills flowed as easily as melted butter. Men haggled over the prices of their vices, and prostitutes over the rents of their bodies.

Arturo would have liked to have been at the bar for pleasure, but his job was about to begin. He had arrived early in the afternoon to observe Yeyo Morales and Paco Amador; they sat at a table in the corner furthest from the entrance. Arturo knew all about them, even though neither of them knew him. Yeyo had dealt drugs since the ripe old age of fifteen; he was now thirty. Paco started out just five years ago with Yeyo, but the two soon became a fast-rising team within the Mexican Mafia. Using farm trucks transporting apples and corn from the mountains of Chihuahua, they trafficked large amounts of cocaine and marijuana to produce stores in Juárez and El Paso.

The head of the operation was "El Soldado." Answering only to El Soldado, the pair pretty much ran the business as they saw fit. Yeyo convinced Paco to join him in the business when Paco's produce business failed. Becoming inseparable compadres, they had baptized each other's children. Neither of the two was accompanied by their wives at that moment, however, and they were definitely not thinking about their children, much less their wives. Paco and Yeyo each had a girl on his arm, both gorgeous and showing a lot of cleavage. Arturo had stealthily moved closer to their table to listen in on their conversation.

Paco swallowed half his beer and set it on the wooden table with a thump.

"Oye, Cabron, don't forget about our meeting with Medina tomorrow. If you keep drinking, you'll be so hung over you won't get up in time," Yeyo reprimanded Paco.

"No, guey, don't worry," Paco assured his friend. "I don't even plan to go to sleep."

"El Soldado wouldn't appreciate you showing up unprepared," Yeyo grumbled. "We'll have to go home sometime."

"I'll be ready." Paco picked up his beer and drained it. "Sleep or no sleep."

The four laughed about the lame joke, the humor enhanced by the alcohol and coke. Yeyo and Paco were very good at what they did, but too many people heard them talking, mentioning important people's names in their conversations. The drug business was for the wary, and above all, for the inconspicuous. Arturo stood up suddenly, pulling the AK-47 he had hidden in his coat and aimed it at the two men.

"El Soldado sends his regards!"

Paco and Yeyo tried for their guns, but Arturo had the element of surprise on his side. As soon as Arturo opened fire on the two men, the thunder of the AK-47 caused panic for the rest of the bar's patrons. People screamed and ran toward the bar's single exit, some trampling over others as they did. The more levelheaded people dove for a covered position under a table or chair. Beer and liquor splattered over everything, glass shattering as bottles broke.

As quickly and as frightfully as the scene had begun, it ended. The gunshots were replaced by an awful silence, almost more deafening than the gunfire itself. Arturo walked briskly out – no one really seeing him – as invisible as a vampire after taking his victims. The images of Yeyo and Paco, eyes rolled back in eternal sleep, seemed to follow him.

Arturo heard distant sirens growing steadily louder. He signaled a nearby taxi and got in, urging the driver to speed into the night. As he left this scene, the Juárez city police and ambulances arrived. Arturo doubted anyone could identify him as the killer, the dimness of the bar making his already very average features even less memorable. People in the city of Juárez were too scared of repercussions from the Mexican Mafia to say anything to the police, regardless. The crime would be added to the already endless list of unsolved crimes in the area.

He lounged back in the taxi, thinking the ten grand he'd just earned for the two dead men would last him several months. He'd finally be able to replace the stereo system in his Dodge Ram pickup with a newer and more powerful model.

He leaned forward to talk to the man driving the taxi, his friend since childhood, Leobardo. "Let's go to the S-Mart off of Lopez Mateos, Leobardo."

S-Mart, a local supermarket, stayed open twenty-four hours. Stopping at a payphone in the parking lot, Arturo called his contact and simply stated "done." They proceeded to a dark alley and parked, talking about girls, trucks, and music as they waited for their rendezvous. They never discussed the work, partly because of superstition and also because of the Mafia's code of secrecy.

Twenty minutes later, an unmarked police car pulled up to the passenger side of the taxi, and both men tensed up. People who dealt with the Judiciales often ended up buried in the surrounding desert to be found months or even years later. Sometimes they were never found; they just disappeared. Most of the police worked for El Soldado, the ex-military man in charge of the entire Juárez Cartel.

Arturo opened the window, taking the paper bag handed to him. As he counted the money, the police car sped off, tires squealing. Both men relaxed, and Leobardo drove the taxi to a local hotel called Le Baron.

The oasis-style hotel rooms had an armed guard at the gateway and were connected by individual parking garages. Arturo and Leobardo's spacious room, with two beds and large mirrors on the ceilings, looked classy, but there was no doubting its purpose. After changing clothes, they left in Arturo's Dodge and proceeded to Norma's, a cabaret that arturo frequented and consequently was treated like royalty.

Leobardo left to go with a young stripper to her place. Arturo placed a call to his main girlfriend, Selene, from his cell phone.

"Hello?" Sleep gave her voice a husky edge.

"It's Arturo," he murmured into the phone. "Can I pick you up?"

"What time is it?" Arturo heard the creaking of her bed springs as she moved. She sounded pleased to hear from him.

"It's late," he told her.

"I'll be waiting."

Arturo drove to Selene's apartment and took her to eat at Posole. Afterwards, they drove to his hotel room. Arturo nearly ripped Selene's clothes off of her curvaceous body. When they were both undressed and on the bed, Selene took control and moved on top. Arturo didn't complain. After all, she was the expert. Selene worked in a "massage" parlor and, like so many attractive women in the big city did, she used her looks and special skills to make money.

Later, Arturo took a long, deep drag from his Marlboro, held it for a moment, and then exhaled. Smoky rings lazily drifted upwards around his face. Lying next to him, Selene's body lay still except for her slight breathing.

He reflected on when they had met. Claudio, Selene's boss, was Arturo's good friend, and the couple met on his first trip to his friend's business. Selene often told Arturo she loved him, but Arturo did not reciprocate the feeling, unable to trust a woman who sold her body. Most of the women he dated were either strippers or prostitutes. It wasn't like he didn't like "nice" women, but he'd only known one decent woman in his life – his mother.

Tall and personable at twenty-two, with a good education, Selene served as Arturo's "official" girlfriend. By no means monogamous, Arturo used her to accompany him to important events and parties. As a hired killer, he was often invited to his various employers' functions. He didn't care for many of his employers but attended their functions to provide a false sense of security around him. One never knew when a prior employer would become a potential mark. Selene had no idea what he did for a living, and she never asked. It was one of the reasons he liked her. As he thought about her and the day's events, Arturo drifted into a disturbed sleep, the type of sleep that assassins with some semblance of a conscience had.

Arturo woke with a start and looked at her again. Selene's body, lifeless beside him, spilled blood across the satin sheets wrapped around them. He grabbed the sheet and pulled, somehow already knowing what he would see, yet powerless to stop himself. Selene was missing her head, and Arturo jumped up, frantically searching for it. Panic overwhelmed him.

He ran outside to search the streets of Juárez. Continually tripping over things, he combed the area for Selene's head. Every time he tripped, though, dead human bodies and open bags of cocaine stared up at him. Suddenly surrounded by malnourished children dressed in rags selling gum, as is customarily seen at Mexico's borders with the United States, Arturo ran madly toward the U.S. border, the Bridge of the Americas.

He reached the bridge and started to cross, but gunshots rang in his ears. His gut felt hot and wet. He fell to his knees, watching a figure from his past walk toward him, a border patrol agent. A shiver ran down his spine, the kind one feels throughout the entire body. Arturo recognized the border patrol agent's decaying face, as a man he killed years ago. He couldn't make out the agent's words because the man's mouth had mostly rotted off his face and, to Arturo's horror, so had his eyes. Arturo knew this was to be his escort straight to the fiery pits of hell.

Literally dripping in sweat, Arturo woke from his nightmare. He hesitantly looked over at Selene again. As if she felt his gaze, she stirred, a sleepy mumble escaping her lips. He pushed the sheets away and went into the bathroom to bathe. After showering, he looked at his scar- and-tattoo-ridden body in the long mirror on the door and laughed. Each one of his scars held a painful memory. Only God knew why he'd narrowly escaped death so many times.

Leaving more than enough money for a cab on the dresser, Arturo took to the streets. He didn't stay at his home often; it was the easiest way for someone to find and kill you. He mostly used his one-bedroom apartment to shower and change. Driving around Juárez, he noticed there was someone selling something – cigarettes, candy, newspapers, or just plain begging – on every corner. Sometimes the streets were like that no matter what hour one was out and about.

Distressed by his haunting dreams, Arturo called his mom. He explained his dream in detail to her and asked her what he should do.

"You need to go and get a spiritual cleansing. Go to downtown Juárez, to any of the shops selling natural medicine and candles, stuff like that. Ask them how much is a cleansing. The cheapest one is the one you go with."

"But mama, I'm okay with money."

"I know, son, thank God, but that is not the reason. The ones who charge the most are usually fakers."

"Okay, Mama, thanks."

Arturo did just what his mother had said. After asking around in five or six shops, Arturo finally found the cheapest. Five dollars. The small store was just outside of the Mercado, full of candles, herbs, and anything else related to magic. A young man ran the shop, but he said his grandma did the ritual cleansings. He led Arturo to a back room connected to the shop. A large altar was in the center of the wall, a statue of a skeletal figure surrounded by various types of candles, booze, and cigars.

"You need a cleansing, young man. Badly. You've done some terrible things. Come here, closer."

Arturo saw the incredibly wrinkled, balding old woman out of his peripheral vision, but he couldn't keep from staring at the altar. Most of the candles around the statue read, "La Santisima Muerte."

"You are scared of that, heh? No need to be. That is Saint Death. She will come to you, as she comes to us all, when it is your time. She is the one thing in life everyone is guaranteed, poor or rich, big or small. She discriminates against no one. Murderers, thieves, holy men, light skin, dark skin, they are all the same to her."

The old lady began the ritual. She took out an egg, and praying, she ran the egg over every part of Arturo's body. When she was finished, she cracked the egg over a glass of water her grandson had prepared. When the egg yolk plopped into the water, dark blood formed all around it.

"You see? You see how much you needed the cleansing?"

Arturo could only nod. Uneasy about the whole magic thing, he handed the lady her five dollars. As he turned to leave, he had an afterthought. If this magic lady was for real, five dollars was hardly enough. He pulled out a hundred and handed it to her. The lady smiled, placing the five-dollar bill he had first given her at the feet of the statue of death. Arturo shivered, wary of the statue, yet fascinated by it as well.

At about two p.m., he stopped at the D'Mazatlan, a fancy seafood restaurant. Being part of the most respected or feared organization in Mexico had its advantages. Arturo was known for being a good tipper and the waiters nearly got into fisticuffs over who would wait on his table. The manager brought six bottles of Dos Equis chilling in ice in a tin pail.

Arturo ordered a fish filet covered in a spicy sauce of tomatoes, chiles, and onions. The fish had been grilled first, with garlic and pepper, and the sauce added afterwards. It was accompanied by white rice with Monterey jack cheese melted over it. Content after the meal, he left a $10 tip for a $20 meal. He stopped outside, and the parking attendant rushed to assist him. He looked familiar to him, so Arturo asked the man his name.

"José Alfredo Cereceres Santiago, Señor, a sus ordenes."

Arturo knew him, all right. His father, who'd left Arturo's mother with seven children over twenty years ago, was now a parking attendant at Arturo's favorite restaurant. Life was just full of surprises. He gave the man a dollar and left, deciding not to tell his father anything. It would have just caused him more pain. Surely his father would want to leech off his good fortune, or worse, maybe Arturo would let his emotions get the best of him and end up doing something he might have regretted.

Arturo believed that some men were actually born evil. Evident in their actions toward other children, and even in their eyes from the time they were small, they did things other kids didn't do. Other men are made evil through a series of events, choices, and other factors that all contribute to the self-destruction of one's soul. Arturo felt he was this latter type of man, born an essentially good person, but after years of perversion and poor choices, he became an evil man. He killed for money, and that, in and of itself, damned him. One day, he would have to answer to God, and no amount of money would save him. Many times, he'd been arrested for suspicious circumstances or for possession of weapons, but he'd always bought his way out. Buying his way out of Hell probably wasn't an option.

When Arturo turned nine years old, his father supposedly left the family and illegally entered the United States to support them. After a year, the family assumed he was dead, and all seven brothers went to work. Arturo worked with three of his older brothers at a mine a few miles east of his hometown, Mapimí, Durango, Mexico. The mine had officially been closed for some twenty years, but people still sometimes would get marble out of it, and the boys' uncle sold the marble in the nearby city of Torreon. After three of his siblings died of work-related causes, Arturo decided to head for the United States. He arrived in Juárez at the age of twelve, without a dime to his name. At night, he slept in the parks on benches, and in the day, he looked for work.

One day, he began at the end of the street called Benito Juárez, named for a famous Mexican president who once said, "Respect for another's rights is peace." It was the main strip for tourists from the United States, everything in easy walking distance from the border. Stopping in front of every store, stand, and restaurant, Arturo swept up all the trash and dust that collected directly in front of them. Some of the owners gave him some spare change; many of them simply shooed him away.

In front of Tenampa, a much-frequented restaurant, someone had just thrown up. It didn't stop Arturo. He found some plastic bags and cleaned the whole area. He asked the owner to provide him with some sort of cleaning agent to get the smell out. The owner watched him diligently clean, and, impressed by the young man's work ethic, hired him to do the dishes and fired the lazy bastard who had the job.

Arturo made the job his priority, arriving early, leaving late, working hard throughout the day, and taking few or no breaks. He soon was making enough money to rent a hotel room on a weekly basis, and after he cleaned up a bit and bought some new clothes, the boss promoted him to waiter, amidst grumblings from the rest of the staff. The other waiters were upset, too, but when Arturo made more money in tips than they did, it enraged them to the point that they wanted to do something about it.

After a late shift on a payday Friday, two of the waiters decided to follow him home. Arturo had grown very streetwise and sensed he was being followed. He broke out in a run and, arriving at his room, locked the door. The waiters following him were bent on hurting him, teaching him a lesson. Paying the Mexican equivalent of twenty dollars to the clerk downstairs, they got a spare room key and let themselves in.

Arturo put up a hell of a fight for a thirteen-year-old, but the waiters were nineteen and twenty-four, and he was no match for them. They left him bruised, with black eyes, broken ribs and nose, and no money. He didn't show up for work for two days because of the pain, but when he finally came in, the owner immediately took him to a doctor. At the clinic, waiting for the doctor, Arturo's boss asked him what happened.

Arturo didn't believe in snitching. "I got mugged after work on Friday."

The boss didn't look convinced but couldn't sway Arturo from his story. When the waiters who'd beat him realized Arturo had not told the boss anything, things calmed down, and they left him alone for a while. After a few weeks had passed, one of the waiters approached Arturo.

"You have huevos, kid," the waiter said, motioning to his testicles with a cupped hand. "Here's the money we took from you."

The experience taught Arturo a valuable lesson about silence and commanding respect, a kind of code he'd follow for the rest of his existence.

At sixteen, Arturo illegally crossed the U.S. border for the first time. Once over, he got a job picking chiles. It was hard work, and there were ways of moving one's hands just right so that a person with skill could do about twice as much work as anyone just starting. Everyone was paid by the number of bags of chiles picked, not by the hour, and even the older folks out-picked Arturo. When the foreman requested volunteers for some special night work at a higher pay, Arturo was the first to volunteer.

A single event in one's life can significantly alter the entire course of it. For Arturo, it was the first evening of the special night job. At two-thirty a.m., six Mexican nationals and one American – Felix, the foreman – set out across the U.S./Mexican border, each carrying a hundred-pound duffel bag full of marijuana. As they crossed the Sierra Mountains on foot, gunfire from men in green uniforms erupted, and two of the seven fell. Felix and one of the other men pulled out handguns and blindly returned fire, hitting only dirt.

The fear of the border patrol agents and the gunfire that they were taking only fueled a bubbling anger within him. Observing the gunfire between the BP agents and Felix, Arturo maintained his position behind a large rock. Only three agents were left, but they had Felix pinned in a depression on the side of the hill.

Arturo crawled across the ground toward one of the fallen traffickers and picked up the gun next to his body. Only he and Felix were left; the others were either dead, wounded, or had simply run off. Felix managed to wound one of the three agents and now only two fired on him. Knowing that probably within a few minutes more agents would be upon them, Arturo made a decision that would both haunt and change his life forever.

He took careful aim at one of the agents and fired. Surely it was pure luck; he had never fired a firearm before that day, but it was the kind of thing that made someone a legend, albeit an infamous one. The BP agent went down immediately, a bullet in his eye. Arturo took aim at the other, but Felix finished the job for him. The two ran off, each with a duffle bag, and escaped back over the Mexican border. That night, Arturo crossed the line between good and evil, and whatever childhood innocence he once had disappeared.

Within two years, Arturo became a highly sought-after hitman. At first, his targets often did not suspect that he was an assassin because of his youth. He spent all of his waking moments target practicing and learning everything to know about the tools of his trade. As he aged, his appearance remained deceiving; he was tall, thin, and had a slight overbite. His two front teeth were very large, and more than one man had made the lethal mistake of calling him Bugs Bunny until his reputation finally began to precede him. Years of serious acne had scarred his face forever, and the beard he wore was patchy and irregularly colored.

An unattractive man, he dressed in nondescript clothing – an older, regular Western style shirt, old Wrangler jeans, a pair of leather sandals or mule-skin boots, and a straw cowboy hat were his typical attire. Upon first sight, most people would mistake him for a common ranch hand. If any of those falsely assuming people looked a little closer, right into his eyes, they would see he was a man who had seen death; he'd made a pact with her, cursed to serve her until the day he died.

As Arturo's workload increased, he was finding that travel to and from jobs was increasingly riskier. He was having to change vehicles constantly. Not trusting just anyone, he decided to call upon his childhood friend, Leobardo, for help. Having little experience in anything but ranch work, Leobardo would primarily drive him to and from the hit locations. After changing vehicles three or four times, Leobardo made the suggestion of using a taxi. Instead of changing cars, they could change license plates and numbers on the car. Arturo did even better. He bought a series of ten taxis, all of the cars actually in service.

Whenever Arturo and Leobardo made a hit, they would change taxis. Five of the ten vehicles would always be in service. Not only was it an excellent cover, but it was also a good business investment. Even if it meant losing potential business, Arturo made it a steadfast rule to never divulge his modus operandi to potential employers.

One never knew in the assassination business when one would become the prey instead of the predator.

When the cell phone rang loudly, a startled Arturo dropped his just lit cigarette, his reminiscing over abruptly. "Shit! Bueno?" Arturo was in his apartment's living room, the television barely audible.

"I have a job for you," answered El Soldado. "That piece of shit Godinez has been sharing information about the company with an El Paso pig. I'll give you ten thousand reasons to ensure he never makes that mistake again."

El Soldado was a man of few words and hung up immediately without even waiting for an answer from Arturo. No one ever really said no to El Soldado. Godinez was a go-between, having more connections than AT&T, and primarily united people and services that couldn't be found in the Yellow Pages. Most drug dealers put up with his mouth, but El Soldado had a strict policy about discussing company business with non-company people.

Arturo was in the process of lighting his cigarette again when the cell rang again. "Yeah, what is it?"

"Hey, Arturo, Godinez here. I need to see you about a job."

Arturo laughed to himself, thinking how ironic it was that his next mark was calling to see him. Usually, he had to go out of his way to find his victims. Godinez obviously had no idea he was out of El Soldado's favor.

"Meet me at the Noa Noa." Arturo loved the bar where Juan Gabriel, a poor and humble singer/composer made his first steps toward the fame and fortune he now had. The Noa Noa wasn't exactly a high-class joint, but it was right smack in the middle of downtown Juárez, and just a few minutes' drive to an arroyo where Arturo could shoot him and dispose of his body. Arturo re-lit the cigarette and took a long drag, as if it was really providing his lungs with the oxygen he really needed. He called Leobardo and they drove downtown.

Including Arturo, Godinez and the employees, all of ten people were at the Noa Noa on a Wednesday at one in the morning. Prey and predator drank several beers, and Arturo set his trap by giving Godinez the one lure he could not resist – food.

"You know, Godinez, I know of this place just around the corner that serves the best Menudo. They put lots of meat in it, and the toasted bread with butter is incredible."

Godinez licked the saliva now oozing out of the corners of his mouth. "You want to go?"

"But we haven't even discussed the job."

"We'll think better with a full stomach."

Godinez nodded in emphatic agreement, as if he had shared the same thought. Arturo paid the bill and strolled out of the bar with his arm draped casually around Godinez' shoulder. Leobardo was waiting as instructed and drove up when he saw the two men exit the bar.

"What luck! A taxi at this hour?" Godinez exclaimed. Luckily for Arturo Godinez didn't see the smirk that appeared on his face.

"El Arroyo Restaurant," Arturo said to the "cab driver" and they drove up a steep hill on a road that would eventually lead them to a dead end that became an arroyo.

"Umm, Arturo, I didn't know there were any restaurants up in this area. As a matter of fact, I've never even been in this area." Godinez peered at Arturo, nervously.

"Don't worry, Godinez, I'll protect you."

"I'm sure. Where is this place, anyway?"

"It's a little hole in the wall just up a little farther. You know, a lot of times the smaller mom and pop type places have the best food." As if the mere mentioning the word "food" had a tranquilizing effect on the obese Godinez, he seemed to relax again.

"Well, let me tell you about the mark."

"Sure. Go ahead."

"He is a cop for the El Paso police. He has been snooping around in company business, and some members are getting nervous-" Godinez stopped suddenly when he realized the road had ended and the two were now in an arroyo.

Arturo placed one hand already on his .44 Magnum he had tucked in his waistband.

"Get out of the truck, Godinez."

"Please Arturo, don't kill me! I'll double whatever they offered you." Tears rolled out the sides of his eyes.

"Get out, Godinez, or I'll beat you until you do."

Godinez, whimpering, got out of the truck. "Please, please, I beg you. I'll triple the offer! I'll do anything!"

"Godinez, you know I don't work like that." Arturo aimed the pistol, centering the barrel to Godinez' forehead, then pulled the trigger. Blood and brain matter shot out the back of Godinez' head, and he fell forward, landing with a thud. Blood oozed out of the quarter-sized hole in his forehead, painting the desert sand. Lighting a Marlboro, Arturo boarded the cab and they drove off in silence, recognizing that one day he too would be on the receiving end of the gun. He decided to call Selene, perhaps in need of some semblance of consolation, or maybe it was just the way the moonlight reflected off the pool of blood that made him feel a little romantic. He called her cell phone, and when she didn't answer, he decided to drive to her apartment to surprise her after Leobardo dropped him back off at his apartment. On the way, he stopped at a convenience store to buy her a small chocolate rose.

Selene lived in a neighborhood called the Galeana, a poor but livable area of Juárez where apartments crowded together like frightened children. Her white Sabre caught his eye in the parking lot, and he noticed the lights were on in the apartment. Suspicious, he parked the truck around the corner and quietly approached her front door. He heard Selene's voice, then a male voice talking, laughing, and whispering.

Arturo was never jealous of Selene's clients in the massage parlor. This, however, outside of work, seemed more like a date. For some reason, the thought infuriated him. He hurried back to his truck and pulled out a crowbar he carried behind the seat of his pickup, then made his way back to the apartment. Rather than assassinate the man with her, Arturo would give him a beating. It was the only way to restore his honor. A beating for Selene would also be in order, though Arturo was not accustomed to hitting women.

Arturo slowly turned the key in the door of the apartment he had rented for her. He gently pushed the door open. What he saw enraged him more than he would have ever dreamed. Selene and her "friend" embraced passionately, both naked and on the living room floor; Selene made noises she never made when she was with him.

"You puta! What makes you think it's okay to bring any cabrón to fuck in the apartment I rented for you?"

"Arturo!" Selene's eyes were wide with fear and her hands trembled.

The man was attractive and well-built, and Arturo decided he would change that. The man started to say something, but Arturo, crowbar in hand, swung the crowbar into his handsome face. Selene screamed.

"Shut up, bitch!" Arturo hit her in the chest, directly in her operated breast. She curled up in pain. "Oh, Arturo, please…don't…"

"Now, my good-looking young friend, it is time to pay. Selene never told you anything about me?"

The man emphatically shook his head no, unable to speak, his jaw broken.

"If she did, you're lying. If she didn't, you're just a poor bastard. Either way, I'm going to fuck you up!"

Much like when he had seen a news report of the way sailors beat upon seals without mercy, somewhere in the North Pole area, Arturo repeatedly whacked the man about the face, and his hands and arms when they covered his face. Blood spurted all over him, the floor, the furniture, and the walls. Arturo knew the guy wouldn't last much longer, so he turned his anger on Selene. The beaten man slumped down on the floor, barely conscious. She begged for forgiveness.

"Arturo, please, it was just a job! I needed money, and I didn't know where you were. Please stop!"

Arturo smiled sarcastically, his crooked, yellow smoker's teeth shining in the moonlight that entered the window of the apartment. Selene was good; her lies were as quick as his bullets from the .44 magnum that he carried. He threw the crowbar down, then began to pound Selene in the face, stomach, arms, legs, and wherever else he could. When she finally fainted, Arturo pulled a large hunting knife from the sheath he carried on his side.

"You know, it's amazing the things one can do with a sharp knife."

Selene awoke for a moment as Arturo cut out the first implant from her right breast. She looked at her open breasts and screamed.

"Bitch, I paid for these things!"

Blood streamed freely across Selene's chest and stomach, dripping down onto the cement floor of her apartment, and she passed out again. Not wanting her to die, Arturo wrapped her chest tightly with the sheets from the bed, blood quickly staining their off-white color. Arturo took a long shower and changed his clothes. He took the few items he owned out of the apartment and left. They'd never denounce him to the authorities, though; Selene knew she'd be as good as dead if she ever did. Suddenly too tired to drive back home, Arturo stopped and rented a motel room. He sat down on the bed and lit a cigarette, studying his acne-scarred face. No woman would ever love him for his looks. He wondered if any woman other than his mother would love him at all.

The violence of the night penetrated his dreams. He dreamed of being in his hometown of Mapimí, at someone's funeral. His mother cried loudly, other women consoling her. He was dirty, with bloodstains on his pants and shirt, and he had a strange need to see who the deceased was, so strong that he felt he no longer had a will of his own. He recognized people in the shadows – his dead brothers, people he'd assassinated, and a Border Patrol officer.

He finally reached the open coffin, but it was empty. Then, he was no longer looking into the coffin, but rather in the coffin looking out from inside. The Immigration officer smiled and closed the coffin lid. Arturo could hear the dirt being thrown over the coffin, and he couldn't breathe. He tried to scream, but there wasn't enough air. He awoke from the nightmare, drenched in sweat, face down on his pillow.

He sat up and punched his pillow, muttering obscenities to the empty room. Arturo missed the times when he actually slept well. Why couldn't he find a nice girl like his mother? Thinking of her, Arturo called her up.

"Bueno?" his mother answered in a sleepy voice.

"Mama, sorry to wake you. I miss you."

"Ayyy, mijo. Me too. But did you have to call me at four in the morning to tell me that?"

"No mama. Sorry."

"Ahh, it's okay. Is everything okay, Arturo?"

"Yeah, everything is fine. I just wanted to hear your voice. I love you, mama."

"Me too, hijito."

Arturo got up and lit a cigarette. He remembered the way he had felt when he had been "cleansed." Santa Muerte was perfect for someone like him. After all, didn't he help do her job? He had sent many men to see her over the years. Arturo decided he would build her an altar.

Chapter 24 (Memo)

Don Rafa and Memo didn't want control over drug trafficking in Juárez. They just wanted to be able to conduct business without having to fight El Soldado's people. Being in charge of the Cartel in Juárez was too dangerous for their families, and they would have to adapt to a new way of life. Memo and Don Rafa sat in the living room of Memo's spacious Cuauhtémoc home, the fireplace blazing. The constant howling of the wind outside was a reminder of the extreme mountain cold outside of the warm interior.

"Memo, after we get El Soldado out of the picture, all of the local factions, as well as outside cartels will fight for control."

"It will be a regular anarchy. If we can stay organized, then we could deal more than any other group out there."

"El Soldado can barely keep up with the orders he has now that Medina's dead. He seems to be too busy even to notice us. We need to take him and his top men out at the same time so none of them has time to get away." The fire flickered, seemingly in agreement. "Next week, we'll meet up with Captain Barba. He knows the ins and outs of El Soldado's operation now that he can't rely upon Medina."

"I don't trust that man."

"I don't either, son, but he needs us even more than we need him. He told me that ever since Medina's death he's been losing men left and right."

"Cops?"

"Cops, customs agents, lawyers, you name it. It appears someone is taking out everyone within his little crooked organization, and he thinks it is El Soldado."

Memo got up and put another log onto the fire. He stared at the fire, mesmerized as it sneakily began to burn the fresh log from the bottom, then suddenly spread to the side and top as well. Soon the log was consumed by the flame, and Memo thought it was similar to how he and Don Rafa planned to get rid of El Soldado and his organization.

A week after Memo and Rafa had discussed their plans, Memo and Barba sat in silence high on a desert hill in Ciudad Juárez, the heater on full blast. Barba pulled out a cigarette and began to light it.

"No smoking in my truck, Barba."

The EPPD captain gave Memo a dirty look and left the warm confines of Memo's Ford Lobo. Shivering, Barba made three futile attempts to light his cigarette in the bitter cold wind. After the third failure, Barba gave up and got back in the truck. Memo smirked, holding back a laugh. While he didn't like the smoking; he really just wanted to make sure Barba knew his place.

"El Soldado should be arriving any minute. He always supervises his cocaine loads that come up from Durango."

Memo remembered when he had been a sheriff, the way he used to get excited at seeing an eighth of an ounce of cocaine. Now he was dealing with tons.

"Look, Memo. There he is." Barba handed Memo a pair of binoculars.

Memo watched as El Soldado arrived in the backseat of a Lexus. His driver and bodyguard got out first, scanning the immediate area.

"So, do you still work for El Soldado, Barba, or do you work for us? Or are you playing both sides of the field?"

"I've never worked for El Soldado. I worked *with* Medina, and Medina kept his side of the operation secret, just in case El Soldado got more ambitious than he already was. El Soldado and I have never even spoken."

Memo nodded. Men unloaded crates from a semi parked in the middle of the crossroads in the desert outskirts. "Why don't you tell me whatever you know about El Soldado."

"I only know what Medina told me about him. He was an orphan and at sixteen, he joined the military, only to be discharged a few years later. He'd risen quickly to the rank of sergeant but was so bloody and ruthless in his treatment of the Indian guerillas that he intimidated even the top-ranking officials. His men's loyalty to him was unequivocal, so they released him from service, along with two of his most loyal men, German Prieto and Mario Quintero. El Soldado began his business in downtown Juárez, later teaming up with Medina. The other two buddies from the service went their own ways, but they apparently stayed in touch. One is an ex-wrestler from Mexico City and the other is a tranny. El Greñas and El Joto."

Memo was surprised. "A tranny? So, let me get this straight, after the military, one of his buddies became a wrestler and the other a tranny?"

"Yep. A prostitute. From what I've heard he looks just like a chick. Was even in a porn movie."

As Memo digested the rather outlandish information, Barba continued. El Soldado had primarily dealt cocaine, but he did get a lot of orders for marijuana, and he only dealt the best quality of drugs. The Father was his third partner and primary supplier. The Father, a Catholic priest in the mountains of Chihuahua, came from a family with a long tradition of the third born having to dedicate his life to God.

Forced into priesthood, Giorgio was literally caught with his pants down in a rather compromising position with the church secretary. Church officials punished him by banishing him to a small town in the mountains of Chihuahua.

The town's Apache Indian population knew very little about the church, and most didn't even speak Spanish. The poverty level encouraged the Father to help the people there begin cultivating marijuana to improve their economic situation. His family's wine-growing affinity gave him a green thumb, and his marijuana quickly gained the reputation as being the best in Mexico.

Memo was surprised by how much Barba really knew about El Soldado. Barba picked up the binoculars and watched the desert rendezvous. Memo picked up his pair and did the same. One of the bodyguards began pointing toward them, yelling frantically.

"Shit, Barba, they've seen us!" Memo put the truck in drive and drove as fast as the dirt road's condition would allow him to. Luckily, they had been parked a good distance from the rendezvous point, so they had a good head start. Within just a few minutes, they had hit the highway and soon were lost within the heavy Juárez traffic, safe from anyone who may have attempted to follow them.

Months passed after the meeting with Barba, and Don Rafa and Memo sat in the hotel Camino Real in Juárez, each man with a cold beer in hand and the dark bottles of Negra Modelo sweating despite the hotel room's excellent air conditioning. They had been planning their prospective assassinations that each man would have to carry out when Don Rafa's cell phone rang.

"Bueno? Really? That is good news." Rafa closed up the phone and turned to face Memo. "We are in luck. El Greñas died of a cocaine-induced heart attack last night. Looks like we only have three to take out now."

"Rafa, I've been thinking about that. Do we really need to take out the priest? I bet after El Soldado and the Joto are dead he won't be much trouble out in the mountains. Hell, we could probably do business with him. I hear he has the best marijuana around."

Don Rafa nodded. "Funny, I was thinking the same thing. Well, when do you want to do the deed?"

"Barba and I followed that bastard around for three months. He is well protected, and I haven't seen him let his guard down even once. Last year when you and I started planning this, I followed him to a cemetery in Puebla. Barba says he goes there every Día De Los Muertos to see his family that he lost in a car accident."

"That's true. When I worked with him it was the same. Me, El Greñas, and El Soldado were all pretty tight for a while. Until of course El Greñas got jealous and started shit for me with El Soldado."

"Was that how it all started?" Memo recalled the long talks he and Rafa had when they were in prison.

"Jealousy causes a lot of destruction. Neighbors are perfectly compatible until one has more than the other, or at least it is perceived that one has more than the other. Then the problems start. Me dealing with Medina directly was the straw that broke the camel's back."

"November 2nd is just a month away. I'm going to have to go to the cemetery and do some planning."

"You just tell me what you need. How many men will you take?"

"Me. That's it. El Soldado is very powerful. No one but you and I should know about this. You never know who might get greedy, another problematic emotion."

"Is greed an emotion?"

"If it isn't, then it should be. An emotion is a person's state of mind deriving from their mood or circumstances or reaction to others. Broke mother fuckers are gettin' awfully greedy while we're just getting' rich."

Rafa and Memo laughed.

Memo drove a Durango from his Puebla hotel to the local cemetery early on November 2nd. He had several handguns and an AR-15, only an arm's length away in the back seat, covered by a blanket. A Kawasaki in a trailer pulled behind.

The idea was to look like someone that was going four-wheeling, and he carried fake identification, as well as the vehicle being registered in someone else's name.

About ten miles outside of town, a federal patrol car stopped him for speeding. Memo pulled out a hundred-dollar bill and handed it to the officer, a short man with a thick, dark mustache who appeared at his window a few minutes later.

The officer gave him a long look. "I'll be right back."

Memo watched the officer climb back into his unit with his partner, and, after a brief conversation, both officers disembarked the patrol car and began walking toward him. Obviously, they'd decided there was more money to be made. Memo reached for the AR-15 on the back seat. As they approached the SUV, Memo shot them both, the automatic rifle vibrating in his hands, shooting as he got out of the vehicle. He moved the rifle up and down as he shot, hitting the officers in their legs, stomach, and chest area. Memo looked around. No one drove by, and the sun was just barely peeking over the green hills. Walking over to the officer who'd first approached him, he leaned down and placed his hand on his neck to feel for a heartbeat.

"Greedy piglets," he growled, after confirming the officer was still alive. "If you and your partner hadn't been so greedy, you'd still be alive to enjoy the hundred dollars I gave you. You won't need it now, though. Not where you guys are headed."

The officer's response was a gurgling in his throat. The other man lying on the roadway moved slightly, but the amount of blood seeping onto the pavement let Memo know he wouldn't last long.

Memo took back his hundred-dollar bill from the first officer's breast pocket. He placed the muzzle of the AR-15 to the forehead of the officer, made the sign of the cross and pulled the trigger. The bullet passed straight through his cranium and ricocheted on the asphalt from the road making a terrible pinging noise. The other man was now quite obviously dead, so Memo didn't bother to shoot him again. He dragged the bodies back to the patrol car and propped them up in the seats. It would probably be several hours before anyone radioed them, and probably several more hours before they were found. Memo figured that civilian driving by wouldn't look at them twice for fear of being stopped. The sun warmed up the dew that had settled on the flowers on the side of the highway, making for a strange mix of scents with the gunfire.

Memo arrived at the empty cemetery about a half hour later. Parking the Durango at the rear, Memo entered the cemetery through the exit. When Memo had planned the hit, he'd donated a large sum of money to have the bathroom renovated, and the bathroom was rebuilt to his specifications. Part of the money went to the manager of the cemetery as well, of course, for his discretion.

Memo had specified the bathroom must be kept sanitary at all times, a huge feat, but necessary, as he would have a five-hour wait to spend in it. Another specification he had made was that a hatch, leading to the back of the cemetery, be installed in the broom closet of both the men's and women's bathroom. Memo reasoned, if the door was locked on the outside, he could get out through the hatch. Only he and the builders knew of the hatches.

The door was constructed of thick metal, and the walls were cement blocks with a brick façade. It was not unlike a little fortress. Memo wanted to be sure he could hold up under fire for a while in the bathroom if needed. After having observed El Soldado from daybreak to sunset on the last Day of the Dead, Memo had spent the past year creating his plan.

Memo planned to hide in the closet until El Soldado entered. If anything about El Soldado was regular, it was his regularity. Like clockwork, between ten and ten-thirty a.m., he would hit the john, his bodyguards waiting outside. Memo wondered if the military had taught him that. *"Shit on time, soldier!* "Memo laughed.

Memo had chosen a 9mm Beretta with a silencer for his tool of death. If all went well, he could escape through the hatch before El Soldado's bodyguards checked up on him. El Soldado normally took about twenty minutes to take care of business, so Memo had plenty of time. Contingency plans were indispensable when there was a possibility of "Plan A" going astray, and Memo had one of those as well. Memo had a motorcycle for a quick getaway and an airport ticket to Chihuahua.

In the broom closet, Memo prepared his weapon. The silencer fit perfectly on the barrel. The clip held fifteen rounds, and Memo had four extra clips already loaded. Almost falling asleep, Memo's adrenalin spiked when he heard El Soldado and his bodyguards approaching. El Soldado entered the bathroom, and Memo waited for him to take his position on the "throne."

Hearing El Soldado's pants' zipper followed by the man settling on the toilet seat, Memo exited the broom closet stealthily. The stalls were open, as Memo had specified that they be installed without doors. Memo shot the kingpin several times in the chest, blood splattering all about the toilet and wall. El Soldado looked definitely surprised, but his eyes lacked the usual terror Memo was accustomed to seeing whenever he shot someone at close range. He was still able to get up from the toilet seat and fall, crashing on the floor and alerting the guards. As Memo secured El Soldado's .45, one of the bodyguards entered the bathroom. *So much for plan "A".*

Memo quickly dispatched the bodyguard with a shot to the head and a second to the throat. He pushed the man out of the bathroom into the other bodyguard, then slammed the metal door shut with his foot.

As Memo bent over to lock the door, El Soldado, seemingly back from the dead, grabbed him from behind in an airtight chokehold. Memo's vision wavered as the hold on his neck tightened, so he reached behind himself with both his 9 mm and his newly acquired .45, trying to aim into the man on his back without shooting himself in the process. He emptied his clips into El Soldado, one of the bullets grazing his own back. The grip of the soldier loosened and Memo freed himself in time to react to another bodyguard who stuck his .44 into the bathroom and began firing blindly. Bullets ricocheted all around Memo. As Memo dove towards the door, a bullet grazed his right arm. Memo slammed into the floor behind the door. He stood up and kicked the door as hard as he could, knocking the gun out of the bodyguard's hand. Picking up the bodyguard's gun as he ran, Memo made his way to the escape hatch and slipped out of the bathroom. Circling around to the front, he found the bodyguard praying silently. He shot the bodyguard several times, thinking about Yosemite Sam and his famous line, "Say your prayers, varmint!"

Laughing crazily, he ran to his motorcycle and took off toward the airport. The assassination hadn't gone as planned, but the outcome had still worked out for Memo. He remembered seeing an abandoned adobe house along the way and stopped there to change clothes. He was a bloody mess, but luckily, he had planned for that as well. In the motorcycle's saddlebag he had gauze, tape and a change of clothes. After patching up his arm, he put his dirty clothes and pistols in the saddlebag after removing the money he had stashed there as well. He dropped the saddlebag into a rather deep crevasse that he had seen on the side of the building. Arriving at the airport parking lot, Memo parked the bike, wiping it down the best he could to remove fingerprints. He'd never return for it, nor did he plan to ever return to Puebla.

Chapter 25

After the hit, Memo and Don Rafa met up in Chihuahua. Memo loved the richly decorated, triple-nave stone cathedral and the city buildings still representing their 18th century origins. Cowboy-dressed men filled the streets, ladies in richly colored dresses accompanying them, or simply walking together. Rarely was a lady in Chihuahua unaccompanied by another lady or a gentleman. The plaza near the city hall held a bullhorn-toting man in the gazebo shouting out the righteousness of God's path and meagerly dressed men with shoe-shining kits working on shoes and boots for men of a distinctly higher economic class.

Sitting at a table in a restaurant serving typical Mexican dishes, Memo and Rafa ordered up Menudo, a spicy combination of beef tripe and hominy with toasted bakery bread and butter on the side. Rafa ate while Memo related El Soldado's murder.

Finishing his Menudo, Don Rafa went into his tale of how he took out Mario, the transexual drug dealer.

"El Joto had an appointment for hair removal at his favorite salon on the Day of the Dead. I hired three men outside of our organization to work with. We entered the salon, tied up and gagged the three stylists and two other clients. El Joto was in the back room, naked, with some young fag taking the hair off his legs with hot wax. I opened the door and El Joto turned around. You should have seen his fake breasts bouncing!"

Don Rafa paused for a moment. "I couldn't believe how much like a woman he really looked. If it weren't for the pelotas he had…I shot him six times in a line from his belly to his head."

He mimicked how the tied-up women sobbed in terror.

"I told them," Don Rafa said with a menacing smile, "When the law asks you what happened, you tell them three men in masks robbed you, and you can't identify them. You tell them it sounded like the men were from Mexico City by their accents. I don't plan to ever return to Durango, so none of you should ever see me again. But, if I have to return because of one of you, it will be the last thing you ever see."

Rafa and Memo laughed heartily. Changing the subject, Memo asked how Don Rafa's family was doing.

"Good," the other man said with a smile. "My old lady is happy, my mistress even happier, and the five kids, well, they're in school learning English."

Memo nodded. "And you, how's your English doing?"

"Who needs to speak English in Albuquerque? Almost everyone speaks Spanish, and those who don't, I really don't have any use for them."

Rafa took another bite, before adding, "But I really miss Chihuahua. Sometimes I envy you, Memo, living here. With El Soldado gone, you might be the new number one guy here."

Memo recognized immediately what Rafa meant. After being betrayed by his boss and spending some time in jail, Rafa probably felt he really couldn't trust anyone completely. Memo wanted to assure the other man he had no intention of trying to oust Rafa from his position in their small organization.

"No, Don Rafa, you'll be the number one. I'm here to help you." Memo met the other man's eyes squarely. "Don't think even for one minute that I want to be in charge, or that I'll forget what you did for me in El Cereso. You're like a second father for me."

Don Rafa smiled and gave Memo a fatherly slap on the shoulder.

"And you've been like a son to me." He looked around the restaurant. "I wonder what they have for dessert."

Returning home, Memo was greeted with hugs and kisses from his wife and two sons. Lucia was wearing designer jeans, a hunter-green sweater and matching boots, her long, black hair flowing around her face and neck. The boys were dressed like their father, ostrich boots and straw Stetsons. Later that night, after Memo marinated some T-bones with a mixture of soy sauce, lime, and tequila, he played with his boys for a few hours, letting the coals burn until they glowed bright red. He put on the meat and closed the iron grill. When the house was being constructed, he had specified that a grill be made within one of the patio's brick walls. The normality of cooking on the grill made the recent events seem like part of someone else's life, and Memo forgot, if only for a little while, that he'd just taken out one of the most powerful drug leaders in Mexico. The smell of the cooking beef brought him back to the present, and his stomach growled.

Guillermo's end of the business ran quite smoothly. With the reigning cartel no longer in business, Memo and Don Rafa struggled to keep up with all the orders for coke. The profit margin on coke exceeded marijuana, making coke the number one priority.

A few weeks later Memo was back in El Paso, in a strip club called the Naked Harem. Memo and Barba met to discuss some problems occurring in Memo's system. Every couple of weeks, Memo lost a load of coke at the border to U.S. Customs agents. Such losses were too expensive to tolerate.

"Hey Memo. How's it going?"

"Fine. Sit down. We've got a lot of business to discuss."

"Yeah, I figured as much. At least we have a decent view here."

Memo looked up and saw a busty blonde twirling around a metal pole, and she smiled at him. Memo smiled back and resumed the meeting.

"First problem. We don't have enough Customs on the payroll. I'm losing too much. I'm only going to use your man when we have something really important to pass."

"Well, uh, one problem there, though. He was found murdered last night in his apartment. His throat was slit from ear to ear."

"That is a problem. Oye, Barba, aren't you worried about this? It's getting awful close to you, isn't it?"

"I'll deal with it. But finding new people may take some time."

"Understood, but that needs to be a priority if you want to get paid. My next problem is the storage of loads we get here. The houses we have been renting for storage are not secure enough. Between random burglaries and greedy tenants, I've been losing several hundred thousand dollars a month."

"I can only beef up security so much with these recent losses of my people."

"That's why I decided to make some changes." Memo looked up and noticed that Barba had a worried look on his face. "Don't worry, you're still included. But I was thinking about another way to protect our loads. The Italian Mafia used thugs to extort locals to pay protection. Why can't we use thugs to take care of the storage houses and to keep the tenants honest? What gang in El Paso is the most powerful?"

"Los Aztecas. For the most part, they're unorganized and untrustworthy, and many of them cross the U.S./Mexico border on a regular basis, so they often have problems with the law on both sides. You could use your influence and money to help them with their legal problems in return for their help."

"I like it. I can hire out a certain number of gang members to protect my warehouses and pay them a monthly salary. They could also be used to deliver justice to those who betray me. Arrange a meeting."

Roberto "Chito" Sandoval was about 5'8" and 250 pounds of solid muscle. His shaved head, goatee, and tattoos made him look even more menacing than his physique already did. Memo had killed three men just like him in El Cereso, so he wasn't particularly intimidated, but he was alert. Chito led the Aztecas in El Paso, and nothing important happened without his approval or his cut of the business negotiated first. Thirty-seven years old, he held the respect of both young and old. He was a veterano who'd lived past the expected age for a full-time gangster and his connections to the underworld were innumerable.

"So, you're the Mexican badass who wants to run my gang, eh?"

"No, I'm the Mexican badass who wants to hire your gang."

"Sorry bro, but I'm not interested. This meeting is over. Guard!"

Memo left the prison disturbed. He hated dealing with people who were too insecure and small-minded to take advantage of opportunities. He understood in a way why Chito wouldn't want Memo involved, though. Probably Chito's only reason for living was his power; it was all he had, in or out of jail. Without his power, he was just another thug.

Memo called up Barba. "That piece of shit didn't even want to hear the deal."

"I've got another guy, then. He coordinates the activities outside of prison for the gang."

"This time, I'll try a different approach. I can't afford for him to tell me no, too."

Memo paid for information about the gang's second-in-command. Alex Garcia, a twenty-two-year-old man who had been born in Juárez of a Mexican-American father and a Mexican mother, crossed the border regularly, and had done so since he was ten. Both his parents were cholos and heroin addicts.

Because he knew no life other than drugs and violence, Alex was doomed to follow in the footsteps of his parents. He started with spray paint and glue, then progressed to coke and meth. Robbery, assault, and murder were daily activities, and Alex found he had talent for those acts. Women came and went, proving Alex incapable of love for anyone. Memo thought he would probably have less of a problem convincing him to work for his organization. Barba arranged for Chito's death in jail, and five-thousand dollars later, Chito was no more.

Memo watched as Alex and three of his friends exited one of the many strip bars in downtown El Paso. Barba used his cell to call a patrol car to stop them just a few blocks away from the bar. The patrol car took the men with Alex away and left Alex with Barba and Memo. Although Alex was handcuffed, he remained defiant. He started to stand up from the curb and Barba pushed him back down.

"Fucking pigs. I didn't do a thing!"

Barba responded. "You may not have, but two of your three friends have warrants, and you were carrying a concealed deadly weapon."

"El Paso is a dangerous city."

"You're right," Barba said, as he opened the back of his unmarked unit where Memo was already seated. He scooted over and Barba lifted Alex back up. "Now get your ass in before I beat it in."

Alex spit on the ground in front of him. "It would take you both and then some if I didn't have these cuffs on."

Barba grabbed the much thinner Alex and shoved him in the car. "Don't worry, Alex, you'll have your chance soon enough."

Barba drove out toward the highway leading to Alamogordo. Alex had been cussing the whole way, but when he saw they were long out of any city cop's jurisdiction, he fell silent.

"What the fuck is going on? Those other guys are my friends, you know. They're witnesses."

Memo spoke without looking at Alex.. "I don't give a fuck about witnesses. I brought you out here for a business proposition. If I wanted you dead, you'd already be so. I offered Chito the same deal, but he wasn't much of a businessman."

Alex frowned, obviously aware that Chito had been murdered in prison just a few days earlier.

"Alex, I certainly hope you're smarter than Chito." Barba stopped the car and Memo continued. "Now, the first thing I'll do is remove these cuffs. No one should have to do business with handcuffs on."

Memo and Barba got out of the car and helped Alex out. Barba removed the cuffs, and Alex rubbed his wrists.

"Now, we are all free men. I want you to understand something, Alex. I want to hire you and Los Aztecas to work with me. The jobs will be well paid. I want you to be the leader, not me. I just want to hire you."

Alex said nothing.

"You can tell me no. You can tell me to go to Hell. You're a free man."

Alex laughed a cynical laugh. "Yeah right. I say no, I'm dead. It's you two and me, and you both have guns."

Memo motioned and Barba got into his car and left. Memo showed Alex he was unarmed.

"Just you and me. Do what you need to."

"The minute I do anything your friend will be back to put a bullet in me."

Memo shook his head. "No, he won't. For one, he's not my friend. As a matter of fact, he doesn't like me much. And I sure as fuck don't like him."

"Either way, I'm screwed. You can't fuck with pigs."

"Wrong again. I'm not a cop. My name is Memo, and I'm a businessman in Juárez."

Alex took a moment to decide whether to fight and run or stay and listen. He had heard of Memo and knew he was deadly serious. He moved toward Memo, arms flailing in an effort to hit him.

Laughing, Memo easily evaded Alex' wild punches. Alex, breathing hard, stopped for a moment.

"What the fu-"

Memo stopped Alex's words when he hit him with a left hook to the liver. Alex swayed a moment, then fell to his knees.

"Listen Alex, we can do this the hard way, or the really hard way. Either way, you will be wasting our time." Memo pulled out a pack of one-hundred-dollar bills from his left breast pocket and threw it down in front of Alex. "Or you can start making more money than you've ever dreamed possible."

Alex's eyes widened, and he slowly got onto his feet, picking up the money as he did.

"That's five-thousand dollars, just the start. Listen Alex, Chito was afraid he would lose control of Los Aztecas. And he was right but only because he didn't look at the big picture. I'm not a gangster, nor do I wish to be. I'm a businessman. The gang and the power don't interest me in the least."

"Ok, I get the point. What do you need from me?"

"I need safe passage for my product and safe storage. In return, I'll pay you directly. How you disburse the money, I don't care. If your people get in legal jams with police on either side of the border, I can help. In Juárez, Los Aztecas will be untouchable. Guns and ammunition will be as plentiful as sand on the beach. If you or any of your people are fucked with, I'll ensure whoever causes the problems, be it rival gangs or otherwise, don't live to repeat it."

Alex was smiling.

"I'll be faithful to you and your people. But Alex, if you or any of your people betray me, I'll kill you and the people closest to you. Don't ever doubt that."

A cold breeze whipped by the two men, almost as if it was there to reinforce Memo's words. Stars sparkled in the El Paso desert sky. Memo broke the silence with his cell phone, calling Barba to pick them up.

Chapter 26

Over the next year, Alex and Memo controlled El Paso. No one dared cross them, having learned from the sudden disappearances of those who had. Not one load of contraband could pass through the border or from El Paso to other cities, without prior authorization. Los Aztecas were under strict orders not to kill anyone in El Paso without prior authorization and, in return, Captain Barba promised EPPD wouldn't go out of their way to arrest gang members. Any business involving homicide was taken to Juárez. In Juárez, gang members were given fake factory-worker identifications that, when shown to the police, were used like get-out-of-jail-free cards.

Memo met with some of the burros who transported his drugs to go over the rules he played by. He rented a salon, normally used for birthday parties, in the nicest neighborhood in Juárez. Eleven people – six women and five men – sat at long metal tables.

"You eleven are the best I have. None of you have gotten caught, and each of you have at least crossed over a minimum of fifteen loads." Memo looked at each one of his workers, making eye contact with each one.

"Business has grown; I need more from each of you, and I need you to be even better. I will pay you more per load, but certain rules must be followed. After I go over the rules, if any of you want out, I will give you one chance. Afterwards, my rules must be followed to the letter, or there will be serious consequences. By consequences, I mean death."

"I've hired many burros over the last three years, and you all are the best. The eleven of you are American citizens, and all of you speak English fluently. After studying U.S. Customs' habits, I've devised a plan to ensure the loads make it through. The rules are simple. Do exactly as I direct you to do, every time, following every detail, or you will be killed. If you get caught and don't follow my instructions, I will take out your friends and family. If you are unprepared for these consequences or think that you might not want to follow my instructions, leave now." No one left, so he continued. "I bought each of you a new car."

The burros applauded, and Memo raised a hand to quiet them. "You must register and insure the cars under your real names. Use the cars for everything. We'll use them to pass over merchandise. Customs looks for anything out of the ordinary, so we want to be very 'ordinary.' Each of you has to have at least a part-time job."

Some of the burros whined at the thought of regular work.

"You will cross the border every day at the same time, ensuring you enter a line where the Customs agent is on the driver's side of the vehicle. You will have your ID ready, seatbelt on. Men need to be clean-shaven, and the women dressed properly, with very light makeup. You must remain employed if you want to continue working for me."

Two or three of the ladies smiled when Memo made eye contact with them.

"When you're passing over a load, you will park in a lot designated by me. You will take a taxi to work, and if anyone asks, say the cars in the shop. By the time you get back from work, your car will be back in place and ready to go."

Memo let his words sink in before continuing, "Now, before we go over a few more details, I just want to make one thing quite clear. I will pay you well, get you out of jail, and keep you safe from harm. But, as I said, if any of you ever fuck with me, I will... well, let me just show you. Get up, Sergio."

Sergio Martinez jumped. About twenty-five, he always dressed like a nerd – cotton shirt, khaki slacks, and short hair. He stood, trembling. "M-m-me?" The other burros stepped away from Sergio.

"Who else, Sergio? Or was there another of my employees named Sergio recently caught by the DEA and forgot to mention it to me?" Memo looked around at the group. Many faces paled, as his eyes passed over them. *Good*, he thought. They should worry, because he would show them what fucking up got them. The two men who'd been sitting nearest Sergio moved away from him. Sweat dripped off of Sergio's forehead, and poured down from under his arms.

"Do you think I don't watch my assets? Or my ass? You fucked up, Sergio."

Sergio held his hands out, palms up, stuttering, "I-I didn't tell them anything they could use, Memo. I swear."

"Yeah, that's why you're here and not in the county jail right now." Memo sighed. "You won't have another chance to lie to me."

With that, Memo pulled out his Glock. He remembered that very moment taking place before, but he couldn't place just when or how. One of the women fainted. One of the men who had been sitting next to Sergio sobbed quietly, trembling with each teardrop. Although Memo had killed before, it didn't make this any easier. As if time had slowed down almost to a complete stop, Memo could actually see the drops of sweat in mid-air as they fell from Sergio's brow. He placed the pistol to Sergio's temple, and Sergio's begging became an incoherent blur. As Memo pulled the trigger, another lady screamed, and the gun's roar deafened all in the echoic warehouse. Memo had chosen not to use a silencer for emphasis. His ears rung as he took a good look at the remaining burros. He knew every one of them would remember this day if they were ever caught by law enforcement. Sure, they'd known this would probably be the consequence, but seeing the consequence first-hand was far more powerful than mere conjecture.

After everyone left the room, Memo vomited profusely, the image of Sergio's head exploding repeating itself in his mind like some demonically possessed VCR tape.

Chapter 27

A week after the meeting with his burros, Memo asked Rafa to come down to Juárez to watch them work. Don Rafa and Memo remained in the line to cross the border to El Paso in Rafa's new Escalade, waiting several cars behind two of their "loads" destined for Albuquerque. The first car sported a false floorboard, and the front passenger-side tire held about eighty-seven pounds of marijuana and two kilos of cocaine. Memo heard Rafa's sigh of relief as the car made it through without problems. Memo excelled at details, like positioning the contraband.

The burro, Yvette, a young Mexican-American lady, followed his instructions exactly, lining up so the customs agent was on the left side of the car. The agent checked all the vehicles by banging a hammer on the left side's tires, not bothering to cross over and check the other side of the vehicle, the agent never even suspecting the car carried a sizeable load within, including sixty pounds within the tires on the right side of the car.

Yvette was less than five-feet tall, and the agent didn't seem to notice the floorboard was higher than usual. Memo would never use the floorboard as a hiding place for his taller burros. Their knees up in their chests would tip customs agents off.

The second car passed through even more easily, as the agent recognized the driver as a regular and waved her through.

It had been a successful day, and Memo went home happy.

The cell phone rang. The screen said Galilea.

"Domino's Pizza, would you like to try one of our specials today?"

"Only if it includes a double order of Memo."

"That costs extra, but we can probably fill your order ma'am. I'll see you tonight, baby."

After Rafa crossed back to the United States, Memo drove back as fast as he could to Cuauhtémoc. Lucia didn't expect him until the next day, so he had time to spend with Galilea and their two-year-old daughter, Miriam. All of the lights went out, as Memo pulled into the driveway of Galilea's modest five-bedroom home located in a guarded community. Memo approached the home silently, his gun in hand. As he slowly opened the door, the lights went on and Galilea and Miriam popped up, Galilea yelling "surprise," as she did. Kneeling down, Memo quickly placed his gun between his waistband and the small of his back, hugging Miriam with his free hand. If Galilea had noticed the gun, she certainly didn't demonstrate it.

"Papi, papi, look." Miriam led him by the hand to her room. It was decorated in a Winnie the Pooh motif.

"We spent all weekend working on her room. What do you think?"

Memo smiled. "It looks great."

While Galilea prepared dinner, Memo spent time playing with Miriam. He did his best impressions of Pooh, Tigger, and Rabbit, as they played with her stuffed animals. After dinner, Miriam fell asleep in his arms. He tucked her in bed, kissing her on the forehead. "Good night, my princess."

Galilea and Memo drank tequila and talked until very late, and they went to the main bedroom, clothes coming off before they hit the bed. After they made love, Galilea laid her head onto Memo's chest.

"I wish you were here more, Memo."

"I know. You knew my situation when we got together."

"I know, I know. That doesn't change the fact that we miss you. I told you I would always respect your marriage. I've never interfered, and I won't, that hasn't changed. But it doesn't make it easy."

They talked for a while longer, mostly, Galilea doing the talking, and Memo soon fell into a deep sleep. His sleep was restless.

Although it was daytime, the interior of the church was dark. The typical cross with Jesus nailed to it was not at the back where it normally would be. The statues weren't saints, either. They were naked men and women, forever entwined together in a seemingly eternal orgasm. A priest came out of nowhere, three naked women with him. They all held guns. The priest seemed to be very angry, and he yelled at Memo in Latin. Memo reached for his gun, but it wasn't on him. The priest and his women laughed at Memo's effort, and they all pointed their guns at him.

Memo awoke drenched in sweat, Galilea's hand on his shoulder gently shaking him back and forth to wake him.

"Are you okay, baby?"

"Yeah. Just a dream."

Returning to Juárez, Memo studied drug trafficking diligently, driving through the border frequently to check customs agents' habits and methods. Walking over the border several times, Memo realized the burros didn't have to use vehicles exclusively. Tons of contraband could be crossed over, little by little, with pedestrians. Memo called Barba and arranged a meeting in Juárez. "Bring your man in Customs with you."

Carnitas Don Epi was a restaurant that primarily served smoked pork. Memo sat at a table by himself, his bodyguards situated at other tables nearby him to not draw attention to himself. The restaurant was made up of large palapas, palm thatched-shelters; it was not a good place to go on a windy day, and Memo wondered how they did any business when it was. Barba showed up with Frank Pacheco, a robust man with a short graying beard that matched his thick hair. Barba wore his typical lawyer-type suit, and Frank had jeans and a black T-shirt. When they shook hands, Memo liked the fact that Frank had a strong grip. It made him feel like the man was trustworthy.

"I ordered us carnitas. Have a beer," Memo said, pointing at the tin bucket filled with ice and beer. "Corona is all they have here."

Frank looked puzzled. "What are carnitas?"

"At Don Epi's, it is pork sent straight from the Gods. Smoked and then braised in its own fat."

"Mmmm. Sounds good. It sounds like a heart attack, but one hell of a way to go."

No one discussed business. As they drank beer and ate, the men talked small talk, girls they had met and fornicated, and great places to eat out in El Paso. Memo loved to hear the small talk. It was just as important as when they talked business; he kept all that information locked away in a special place in his mind. If he ever needed to find someone, knowing their habits and favorite spots was a good way to do so. After they ate, Memo started the business part of the conversation.

"Frank, I was walking over the border the other day, and I realized something. All the times I've crossed over walking, I never see any dogs, yet I see them where the vehicles cross almost daily. Can you explain this to me?"

"Sure. First of all, the U.S. Customs' primary objective isn't to find dope, but to detect illegal aliens before they get through. Consequently, drug dogs are used sparingly, and the majority of the agents' efforts are spent on finding illegals, and half the time it is too hot for the dogs around here. Also, how much dope can a person cross over in comparison to a vehicle?" Frank paused as he took a swig of his beer.

Noting there were only two beers left in the bucket, Memo motioned for the waiter to bring more.

"Second, there are two types of dope dogs, aggressive and passive. Passive dogs alert when they smell dope by sitting and aggressive alert by barking, scratching, biting, or a combination. No matter how much it annoys some agents, public safety has to come first, and since the passive dogs aren't nearly as good as the aggressive ones, not too many of them are bought."

After the meeting, Memo called Alex. "We've got some work to do. Meet me at the office at seven."

Alex and Memo called Club Panama, a local strip club, the office. Alex arrived just after seven in the evening. Memo had been there since six. After years of working in Mexico, he was accustomed to people arriving "fashionably" late. He shook Alex's hand when he approached the table and motioned for him to sit down.

"Alex, this is my plan."

A lovely lady suddenly sat on Memo's lap, interrupting their conversation, and Alex smiled.

"Buy me a drink?"

"Not now, honey."

The young lady left, an overpronounced look of disappointment on her face.

"I'll offer $800 per half of a kilo to pedestrian burros." Alex's eyes widened. "I know it is far more than the normal amount of money paid for this kind of thing. Loyalty can never truly be bought, but money helps."

Alex nodded.

"You and your enforcers can deal with anyone who gets greedy. Imagine hundreds of burros walking across the El Paso/Juárez border bridges, small packages worth thousands strapped to their legs, or between their thighs, under breasts, bellies, etc. delivered to designated points, like a rest area in a McDonald's or something similar. Once the dope makes it to an outdoor garbage can, a gang member picks it up. Money will be delivered the next day in Juárez. That way if any cops get into our organization, they'll have a hard time prosecuting us." Memo paused to make sure that Alex was understanding. "The packages will be gathered at the various homes used as warehouses. Once enough is pooled together, the cocaine will be repackaged and sent to other parts of the country in semi-trucks with false walls." He paused again, and stared at Alex until he got a nod from him.

"I'll hire young, clean, good-looking men and women with American I.D.s. Your gang will watch them closely as they make deliveries. All I need is someone to recruit these people."

Alex smiled. "I know someone who can do that."

Memo stood. "Let's go then."

They drove in Memo's vehicle to a place in an area known as the Zona Pronaf. Alex motioned for Memo to stop and he got out.

Alex stood outside of Vertigo, a club primarily frequented by young people between the ages of 18 and 24, talking to the bouncer. Memo sat in his newest vehicle, an Expedition, the Eddie Bauer edition. After a brief conversation, Alex brought the bouncer to Memo. He was short, probably about 5'7", and his head was shaved. He was dressed in very baggy blue jeans with his boxers showing and a wifebeater.

Alex said, "Memo, this is the guy I had talked to you about, Cameron. His Spanish isn't all that great."

"No problem. We'll talk in English. Alex says you know a lot of young Americans who cross over the border to go to this club. I need you to recruit the ones who need money and can be trusted. Preferably girls, but not necessarily. If they are under 18, even better. Everyone I contract gets you $500 dollars. If I don't contract, you don't get anything, no matter what my reasoning is. You're not to question me, ever."

"And how do I know you won't contract them but cut me out?"

Alex slapped Cameron on the back of the head. "Stupid, what Memo says, he does. Don't ever question his word again."

"Sorry."

After dropping Alex off at "the office", Memo had been in Juárez for about a month without going home, so he decided it was time for a rest. Always on the go, having to be aware of his surroundings all the time with possible enemies on every street corner took a toll on him. As he drove to Cuauhtémoc, he felt the joy one feels when they've been gone from home for a long while. Juárez was hot as hell in August anyway, and Memo was sick of the heat and dust. He remembered the simple life he had lived before he had gone to jail. He missed it. Having wealth and power definitely had its perks, but sometimes the cost seemed too high. Sergio, the young burro he had shot in the head, and the nightmare that he had years before that basically foretold the event, intertwined into a single moment, and, as he drove, he relived it. A single tear dripped from the corner of his eye, ran down the side of his nose, and landed on his mustached upper lip. He wiped it with the back of his hand and took a swig of the cold Carta Blanca that he had in his cup holder. His mind returned to the present and as he drove around the curvy road and up the hill before reaching the town, Memo was happy to see rain clouds formed above it.

When he arrived home, his boys and wife were overjoyed to see him. He played with the boys all afternoon and cooked out on the grill, as was customary. When the boys finally tired themselves out, Memo tucked them into bed.

"They should really bathe before they go to bed, my love."

"I know, Lucia, but they're so tired. And you and I have some business to attend to!" Memo grabbed Lucia in his arms and lifted her up. She play-fought him, and they wrestled all the way to bed.

After Memo and Lucia finished making love, Lucia laid her head on Memo's broad chest, hugging him tightly.

"I love you, querida," he whispered against her hair. "You've made my life heaven on earth."

She twisted in his arms to look up at him, her dark eyes shining. "Really, Memo? You really mean that?"

"Of course, I do." He tweaked her nose gently. "You and the kids are the best that's ever happened in my life."

She settled against him again, and after several long moments murmured, "Memo, I'm scared."

He tightened his arms around her protectively. "Why, mija?"

"We have so much," she said, stroking her hand across his naked belly. "I never dreamed that one day we would live in a mansion, have bodyguards, and ranches here and there. It's frightening. I know we never talk about what you do, but it scares me. I don't want to lose you or one of the kids one day to enemies or police or —"

Memo laid a big hand on her cheek to silence her. "I know this wasn't exactly what we had in mind. Believe me, I'd like nothing better than to just get away from it all."

"Then let's do it." She looked up at him again, pleading in her gaze. "I don't care about these things we have. I'd rather have you and the kids safe."

"I wish it were that easy," he answered sadly. "You don't understand. With all the power and money that I've fought for, I can't just leave. I have powerful enemies now, and if they knew I was out, they'd hunt us down and kill us. All of us. It is like a great big cage constructed with bars made of gold."

Lucia began to cry, and Memo held her tightly.

"This whole thing has been like a dream, like I have no control over it. When Don Rafa and I got rid of El Soldado, we thought someone else would take over. Instead, people started coming to us for protection, for guidance, and the next thing we knew, we were the new leaders of the Cartel."

"What can we do, Memo?" she sobbed against his chest.

"I don't know," Memo said, genuinely feeling powerless. He didn't know how to calm her fears when he had so many of his own. "I didn't want this, but it's like some kind of virus that just grows and grows."

He stroked her hair, and Lucia finally fell asleep, her sobs quieted. Memo stared into the darkness, contemplating the fate of his family. Having been in law enforcement, Memo knew he could never truly relax. As the business grew, more and more people wanted to work for him, while even more people were anxious to get their share of the pie. The drug business was a lot of work, and it often became messy. Competition, law enforcement, and even associates often had to be "adjusted," by whatever means. Memo liked to use a sharp object to drive the point home. "Messy and in public," he'd heard somewhere, and the idea had stuck.

It kept normally honest people honest, and the dishonest thought twice before they crossed him. But it was a hard way to live everyday life. And he knew that the chances were better than not that he would eventually "die by the sword".

Chapter 28 (Lalo)

Lalo smirked, as he re-read the article in the months-old El Paso Times that he had happened upon while taking out another of God's enemies. In the article, an inmate named Chito Sandoval had been killed by other inmates in an apparent gang war. Lalo had never forgotten that name, the man who had probably killed his cousins many years before. How satisfying, Lalo thought, is life when one does God's work. He stretched, his body a fine-tuned machine, readying himself for his daily run. He had to be in better shape than any of his enemies could ever be.

Smiling, Lalo ran around Chamizal Park near downtown El Paso, his body there but his mind far away. As he watched the children play, he could almost see Isela and Manuela there too. Day or night, Lalo was constantly tortured by the images and memories of his lost family. His sweaty, chiseled abs glistened in the sun and some girls whistled as he passed them by.

After his two-hour run, Lalo did a long series of exercises he had learned as a Marine. He shadow-boxed and jumped rope for another hour and finally, depleted, took a long, hot shower. The constant pounding of the water on his shoulders helped him to relax, and he shut his eyes. He was transported back to his bathtub right before the explosion, and Lalo's body tensed up. In his mind, he passed through the explosion again; he didn't bother to open his eyes because he knew these constant reminders were part of God's plan for him, contrition for his sins.

Normally Lalo didn't go out to eat, not wanting anyone to recognize him, although he didn't look much like the Lalo before the explosion. When he saw there was nothing to eat in the apartment at all, he opted for some fast food. A burrito shop wasn't too far away from the apartment.

Lalo entered cautiously. He kept his head low, avoiding eye contact with anyone. In doing so, Lalo bumped into a young man, thin, dressed in khakis and a wifebeater. He had short, black hair, a mustache, and a matching goatee.

"Hey motherfucker, watch it."

Lalo's fists clenched.

"Alex, relax, it was an accident. Sorry about that, sir."

The man who spoke on Alex's behalf was Guillermo Smith. Lalo recognized him after a moment of rifling through his memories, even though the was a bit older and had obviously gained some weight. Lalo had never forgotten Smith; he was the one man who had knocked him out. And twice, at that.

Lalo mumbled something barely audible to the effect of no problem and walked away. He felt a heavy hand on his shoulder and turned slightly, ready to react within violence. Smith seemed to feel Lalo's reaction and stepped back a step, ever so slightly positioning his body to be ready for an attack.

"Hey friend, don't I know you? You look awfully familiar," Smith told him.

Mumbling again, Lalo answered, giving his best crazy man act as he could, "No. No. Not me. No one knows me. No. No. Not me."

Memo smiled and let him go. Lalo relaxed some, no longer having to react drastically. He ordered up a foot-long burrito and left. The young man with Smith called Alex stared at Lalo the entire time he had been in the shop.

Lalo wondered what the connection was. The last time he had seen Guillermo Smith he was a deputy in Las Cruces. What was his connection with this Alex character? Maybe he was working as an undercover officer now. Lalo had no real way of checking, and it wasn't something that needed to be in his immediate plans. God had other tasks for him to complete. He needed to stay focused, no matter how much he would have liked to have another chance to fight Smith.

Back in his apartment, Lalo ate his burrito mechanically, careful not to enjoy it, also part of his contrition. Lalo went over what would soon be his next hit in his mind, easily the hundredth time doing so.

Lalo had been planning seven months on how John Barba's time would finally come. Barba's visits to his mother were predictable; the last day of his visit, he would pack up his Grand Marquis, put the coals on, and grill chicken. Lalo could almost imagine Barba's mother telling him to be careful, that she loved him, giving him her blessings, etc. How disappointed would she be to know her little Johnny was really a murderer and drug dealer hiding behind the façade of a police captain?

Just after the sunset, the man known as "Rafa" would show up, driving in from the alley and the two would have a brief exchange, just as he had the last eight times Lalo had observed them. Lalo, God's avenging angel, would rid the world of two more of Satan's pawns in one fell swoop. Or that was his plan anyway.

Chapter 29 (Memo)

After Memo had been running his business for about two years, he hired a young man, Jaime Garcia, who'd begged him for work. Memo used him as a burro to drive loads from the mountains of Chihuahua to Juárez. When Jaime called Memo's cell phone from jail, Memo didn't think twice about getting him out. After Memo paid off a few public officials, Jaime was released.

Something about the situation felt wrong to Memo, though; the load was supposedly lost, and Jaime was unhurt. It wasn't like the police in Mexico not to beat some information out of someone to get to the bigger fish. Jaime had not been himself of late, either. All his suspicions were justified when he got a call from Galilea. She worked at a local bank now, a job Memo had arranged for her to have after she had their baby. Their daughter was now three.

"Hey mi amor." She sounded happy to hear his voice. "How are you?"

"Good, thank the Lord," Memo responded with warm sincerity. He took care of Galilea and their daughter well. Galilea did what she could to help him. "And you? What's going on?"

She paused. "I wanted to talk to you about a recent deposit made to Jaime Garcia's mom."

Memo's hand tightened on the phone. "How much?"

"Exactly 200,000 pesos."

"Almost 20,000 dollars?" Memo's breath came out harshly. "What an idiot Jaime is, having the money deposited to a bank. He thought he was somehow being smart by depositing it under his mom's name. Greed and stupidity are man's enemies, and if you don't overcome them, they get the best of you." Memo, remembering that Galilea was at work and wouldn't be able to be on the phone with him all day, cut the conversation short. "Sorry, babe. I'll see you later."

With a tight feeling in the pit of his stomach, the one he always got when someone betrayed him, Memo drove to Jaime's home, formulating a plan of action along the way. He called Socorro, the family's bodyguard and general task doer, and went over the plan with him. Grabbing a few beers on the way to Jaime's house, Memo drank one, trying to relax before he arrived.

When Jaime stepped outside to meet Memo, he looked worried but not afraid. After seeing the beer, he relaxed. Memo's workers knew he didn't drink on business. Jaime eagerly climbed into the truck with Memo and accepted one of the beers.

"Jaime, how are you? Those pigs didn't hurt you, did they?'

"N-no, Don Guillermo. I was very lucky." He popped the top of his beer and took a long sip, then wiped his mouth on his sleeve. "The Judiciales are scared of you, and they know I work for you."

"They can't be that scared," Memo said. "They stole one of my loads, didn't they?"

Jaime took another sip, remaining silent, as if he wasn't sure where his boss was going with that comment. Memo finished his beer, smiled at Jaime, and turned up the stereo. They drove through town, drinking beer and talking about nothing in particular. Memo could see Jaime relax with every mile they drove.

Memo stopped at a restaurant specializing in grilled chicken. The chickens were being cooked on a long barbecue grill. The aroma of grilled chicken and mesquite smoke outside was far more effective than any advertisement would be.

Jaime followed Memo inside, laughing about some joke they'd just shared. Gilberto and Jorge, two of Memo's brothers-in-law, walked in and sat down with them. Jaime didn't seem to notice anything unusual. After a good meal of grilled chicken, pickled onions, and an exquisite salsa with handmade corn tortillas, the quartet left for Memo's ranch, a few miles northwest of Cuauhtémoc.

Jaime sat between Jorge and Gilberto on the way to the ranch. When they arrived, Gilberto put a pistol to Jaime's head and ordered him out with his hands up. Jaime climbed out of the truck, and Jorge seized the snub-nosed .32 caliber, concealed in the back of Jaime's waist.

The brothers-in-law dragged Jaime into an abandoned barn behind the main building, and Memo stepped up.

"Everything I did for you, for your family, and this is how you repay me," he spat at the younger man. "You know how we deal with traitors in this organization. How dare you insult me this way."

Memo drove his fist into Jaime's liver. Jaime doubled over in pain, all of the strength in his legs gone. Memo and his brothers-in-law duct-taped Jaime to a chair.

"I'm going to kill you, Jaime, but before I do, you're going to make reparation for the wrong you committed against the organization and me. Socorro went to pick up your sister from work. He's a very loyal man. He'll do anything I ask him to. You know that, right?"

Jaime nodded, his brown eyes wide with fear and disbelief.

"Get Socorro on the phone, Jorge."

Jorge called the bodyguard/assassin, and Jaime talked to Linda.

"Are you okay, Linda?"

"Sure Jaime, why wouldn't-"

Memo grabbed the phone before anything else could be said and hung up.

"Jaime, you stupid piece of shit. What the hell were you thinking? Did you think you would get away with betraying me?"

Jaime sobbed.

"I'm going to explain how this is going to happen. If anything doesn't go just as I plan it, I'm going to bring in your sister, your mother, and your father. Then, I will kill each and every one of them…while you will watch."

Memo didn't like going to these extremes, but he knew if he showed weakness, his men would lose respect for him. And his enemies would lose even more.

About two in the afternoon, Jaime's mother got to the bank and withdrew the $50,000 that belonged to Memo. It was about a fourth of what he would have made had the load arrived at its original destination, but he had to show the others these types of occurrences would have severe consequences.

After about an hour, Jaime's mom arrived at the rendezvous location with the money. Jorge picked the money up and called Memo, who in turn called Socorro and ordered him to return Linda home safely.

Only partly satisfied with getting the money, Memo jabbed Jaime in the chest with a one-two punch. The force of the blow knocked his chair over.

In the silence, Memo could hear the fallen man wheezing for breath. He nodded to Gilberto, and they righted the chair, placing it squarely in front of Memo again.

He drove a fist into the man's kidneys several times, each time Jaime answering with a grunt and a heave. Memo continued to punish him until Jaime began coughing up blood.

"Just kill me, dammit!" The young man glared up at Memo, lines of pain drawn across his features.

"Don't worry Jaime, I will. But you'll talk first." Memo tilted his neck to one side, feeling the tension in the corded muscles. "Tell me everything. Unless you want someone else in your family to pay for your betrayal, too."

Like a repenting sinner in the confessional, Jaime breathlessly related the events leading up to his imminent demise.

After picking up a two-hundred-pound load of marijuana in a Chevrolet Dually, Jaime headed back toward town. The Judiciales stopped him on a lonely stretch of highway. It was almost two in the morning, no sign of other drivers on the road, and Jaime knew he was in danger. The windy, narrow stretch of road was notorious for banditos with makeshift roadblocks stopping vehicles, robbing the drivers and passengers, and killing them. Not allowing himself to panic, he rolled down his window and smiled into the flashlight being pointed in his face.

"How can I help you, officers?"

"Don't fuck around and get out of the god damn truck," one of the officers yelled.

There were five officers, three with AR-15s pointed right at him. One of them grabbed him hard and threw him down on the blacktop highway.

The officer said, "I'm Julio Cesar Rocha, head investigating officer here. I don't bullshit around. If you fuck with me, I'll torture you, kill you, and rape your sister, then kill your family. I know who your boss is, and I am going to take this load you just picked up. If you're smart, I'll make you a hell of a deal."

Either he could accept the money, not say anything, and continue losing loads once in a while, or he could die. Jaime opted for the former. Twenty thousand dollars would be deposited to the account of his choice, and with just a few more lost loads in the future, his family would be set for several years. All in all, it wasn't a bad deal, he blubbered, and Don Guillermo had more than enough to spare. Two or three loads wouldn't hurt his business, and the only time Jaime would be directly involved would be this one. He would provide the information on the other loads and they would get other drivers, relieving some of the suspicion on him. Or so he thought at the time.

Memo looked at Jaime, duct-taped to a chair by his ankles, wrists, chest, and head, and almost felt sorry for him. Almost.

"Please forgive me, Don Guillermo," the bound man begged. "I'll do anything you want, just don't kill me."

Memo grabbed the gun he had in his shoulder holster. "I'm truly sorry that you did this, Jaime."

Memo trained the pistol's barrel at Jaime's head. Jaime pissed his pants, the wet spot getting larger and larger around his groin and upper legs. Ignoring the pain in his soul, Memo pulled the trigger, splattering brain matter and fractured skull bone across the barn.

Memo ordered the body be taken to the brickmaker, who had a kiln where a constant fire burned, fueled by tires, plastic refuse, wood chippings, and manure. For quite a reasonable fee, he also burned human bodies.

Memo drove back to his three-story home in Cuauhtémoc, just in time to put some coals on the fire and play with his two boys, now four and two years old. No one at his house would ever suspect this man, a loving father and husband, of killing a young man and leaving his body to burn in a kiln.

Memo told Socorro they would have an emergency meeting soon and to gather everyone up. Retribution was due, and since the cops stole his load, cops would be the next targets. He knew Socorro loved to kill cops, and Memo understood his logic. Police in Mexico were the biggest hypocrites. At least mafia was mafia; there were no masks involved. Cops were supposedly upholding the law, enforcing it, but instead they used that cover to commit the most intense criminal acts while on the job. To Socorro, killing a few cops would be like exterminating roaches.

After arranging a meeting with the most dangerous members of his cartel Memo stopped at a liquor store for some expensive tequila. He drove for about fifteen minutes, just out of town, in a shady area known as the "Zona Rosa". A meeting like this in town would surely draw unwanted attention. He drove into the entrance was a dirt road bordered by an old barbwire fence. There were several dilapidated buildings and the only people there now were the whores that worked the bars at night and a few caretakers. Memo stopped at one of the bars and opened it with a key he had on his keychain. The bar was an old ranch-type building, the paint on the walls chipping and the smell of piss, smoke and beer a permanent fixture. He set the bottle of tequila on a table in the center of the bar and lined up five shot glasses from behind the bar. The bar had plenty of cheap tequila available for the patrons, but Memo didn't serve cheap tequila any more. One by one, Memo's people arrived.

Socorro and the three other men were an interesting bunch. The other men were hired hands, their eyes lifeless, their dark smiles and laughter an unfriendly reminder to Memo of what he would possibly become. Socorro was different; he killed, but his eyes still held some compassion. Memo poured tequila into each of the glasses.

"Due to the indiscretion of a particular pig, we lost a man in our organization. That is only the beginning, as he is a dangerous cop with plans to bring us down. We need to make a statement to all the other cops and competition wanting to steal our business. I put ten-thousand dollars on the head of Julio Cesar Rocha, literally. I also will be hunting him, so it's every man for himself. May the best man win. Salud!"

Everyone picked up the shot glasses and downed the tequila. After bullshitting

Julio Cesar…the mere thought of the name brought up anger and resentment in Memo. As he drove back to his body shop, he thought about how the man must have had a serious obsession for Lucia to do something as outrageous as what he had done. Finally alone in his office, he remembered when he had fought with Lucia over him finding out about her pregnancy first. His fist clenched, Memo slammed it on the desk, and Socorro ran in, gun drawn.

"Boss, everything okay?"

"Yeah, don't worry. Go home, now. I'll be alright."

Socorro started to leave but turned back, a look of concern on his face.

"Memo, you did what you had to do. Betrayal is the worst thing someone can do. You treated him like a friend, like you do with all of us. You're generous with us as well. Some take that as a sign of weakness, but I know better. If you hadn't treated the situation just as you did, you'd have lost all respect from your people and your business, as well as your life, would be in danger."

"You know I wouldn't have had you kill that girl."

"I know. It isn't like you."

"Sometimes, Socorro, appearances can be just as powerful as reality."

"You're right boss. Take care, okay? I'll drive by your house and make sure everything is in order."

"Thanks." Socorro gently shut the door behind him as he exited.

Although that wasn't what he had been thinking about, now Memo's mind returned to the day's events. As he replayed Jaime's death in his mind, Memo felt suddenly very sick. Tears formed at the corners of his eyes, trickling down his cheeks, epitomes of the remorse he felt for the heinous act.

It wasn't long after the meeting when someone let Julio Cesar know of his impending execution. Knowing that Memo would be looking for any of his vehicles, Julio Cesar contacted a good friend who transported illegal immigrants across the border, then packed a backpack and left for the bus station to travel to his friend's house in Palomas, Chihuahua, an excellent place to cross over the border.

Palomas was a desert area with limited immigration coverage and many clandestine routes along the ranches on the U.S. side. Once Julio Cesar reached it, Memo would have very little time to act. He called Socorro but he was too far away. Memo got a hold of two of the hired hands that had been at the meeting. They waited at the bus station in town until Julio Cesar arrived. From inside the bus station, he watched the hired hands step into place, ready for the cop.

They opened fire on Julio Cesar as he walked towards the bus, careful not to hit the other potential passengers. One of the things that made Memo such a powerful and popular man was his respect for innocents, unlike other Mexican Mafia hits that would carelessly take the lives of people who were simply at the wrong place at the wrong time. Julio took advantage of Memo's rule, grabbing a young woman hostage. An excellent shot, Julio Cesar annihilated the two hit men in two shots from a gun he pulled from his shoulder holster. Commandeering a passing car with the gun and hostage, Julio made off for Palomas, dumping the woman to the ground before spinning out of the gravel lot.

Memo called someone to come pick up the bodies of his men and arrange the best funerals and support for their families before setting his mind to tracking Julio. He could not let him get far. He offered a generous reward for any information that led to Julio Cesar's whereabouts, sending a message to both local authorities as well as people who, directly or indirectly, worked for his cartel.

Julio Cesar contacted an old friend for help in Palomas, Flaco, who also happened been a business partner of Memo's for a several years. Memo got the information from Flaco almost simultaneously and smiled because Palomas was the perfect place to commit the execution; the so-called lawmen were few and far between and cheaply bought. Memo would take his most trustworthy man, Socorro, as back up.

In the middle of the desert, full of dust, indigents, drug users, and the people who tried to eke out a living with their restaurants and hotels, the town was built by drug dealers and polleros who illegally crossed the border. Palomas, Chihuahua, was a town of about ten-thousand and about another ten-thousand in visitors with dreams of work in the United States – easy money via drugs or other types of illegal contraband. Faces changed constantly here, and it was a great place to get in and out quickly, without any real witnesses being able or even willing to talk.

The residents were long accustomed to mafia happenings, and they knew better than to speak about anything they saw. If they were to ever talk about the illegal events witnessed, they probably wouldn't know where to start. Palomas existed because of its prime location on a hard-to-watch part of the Mexican-American border, the lack of law enforcement, and the overall catering to crime that was the town's norm.

Two main roads connected Cuauhtémoc, Chihuahua, to Palomas. Memo and Socorro left in a red Chevy Suburban with weapons hidden in a space below the back seat. Only one roadblock blocked their path, but the soldiers didn't look carefully enough to find the weapons.

Once in Palomas, the two retrieved these weapons, an AK-47, an AR-15, and a .40 caliber Glock. Memo took the Glock and the AR-15, Socorro the AK. Julio Cesar was booked into Hotel Palomas, and the homicidal pair parked just a few blocks away from the scruffy hotel.

One of Memo's attributes was an uncanny instinct, an ability to comprehend its signals, and suddenly it screamed at him.

"Socorro, watch out!" he shouted.

Just as he said the words, several men from different angles opened fire on them. The thunderous rain of bullets upon them, Socorro shoved Memo down and returned their fire. Finding cover behind a Lincoln parked in front of the hotel, Memo returned fire. Despite various bullets penetrating Socorro's body, he managed to take out two of the assassins with his AK before he fell.

Down to just two attackers now, Memo took careful aim with the AR-15 and shot the leg of one ambusher behind an old Ford pickup, then ran and rolled behind another car to get a better angle. As the man struggled to bring his gun back up, Memo shot him in the head.

"It's just you and me, Julio Cesar," Memo called across the open area. "Fight like a man. Come out and defend yourself with your hands, not your guns."

In the silence following his words, Memo heard Socorro's heavy breathing and risked a glance at him.

"Wait. I'm coming out."

Julio Cesar's words brought his attention back to the front. Memo stood then, and the two walked toward each other, much like two gunfighters of the Old West. As soon as Memo was within his range, Julio Cesar tried to hit him with a roundhouse kick to the head. Memo blocked the kick, absorbing it with his left arm and hand, and countered by moving in and hooking Julio Cesar to the liver and the head, following up with a straight right. Fighting for his life, Julio Cesar tried punching his way out, but Memo kept close to him, Julio Cesar's kick most effective at a distance, and continued with hooks to the head and body in a merciless assault. Memo smiled with every punch that landed, Julio's blood and teeth flying from his now badly swollen mouth.

Down on his back, Julio Cesar managed to kick Memo in the solar plexus as he bore down on him with his fists, but it did little to stop him. Realizing Julio Cesar was incapacitated, Memo stood up, lifted his booted foot, and said to his rival, "Lights out," stomping down to crush Julio's skull. After several tries his head finally flattened, the human skull being much harder than Memo had imagined. Whatever skills Julio Cesar had as a several-degree black-belt instructor in Taekwondo had been no match for Memo's skills as a boxer.

He looked back across the dirt to where Socorro laid, his chest still and head lolled to one side. Socorro had become more than a bodyguard to Memo, but also a friend and confidant. He realized that this was most likely just one of what could be many losses in the future.

A week later, Memo gave Socorro a funeral any dead man would envy. Mariachis played as the coffin was lowered and dirt poured over it, and they continued for almost an hour. A small altar with Socorro's photo, a painting of Socorro's weapon of choice, the AK-47, and another of the Virgin Mary was placed over the grave. Quite drunk by the end of the ceremony, Memo placed a bottle of the best Tequila money could buy on the altar.

Socorro's five daughters held each other in a tight circle, crying along with their grandmother. Memo cried with them, too, his heart broken at the sight. They would be well taken care of with a sum of money large enough for all the daughters to attend the best schools and universities in Mexico, and Socorro's mother would never have to worry about any material needs. No amount of money could ever replace the man that Socorro was, and that was a fact that Memo was painfully aware of.

"I know this can't make up for what you've lost," Memo said, as he gave Socorro's mother the cash, "but it is the best I can do for the moment. Anything you ever need – I mean anything – you just call."

The old woman accepted the money without looking Memo in the face, and Memo felt a coldness from her. He was not offended because he understood that it was often easier for people to cope with loss if they had someone to blame. Socorro had made his choice to live by the sword, as had Memo.

After days of analyzing the Palomas fiasco, Memo decided the only way that Julio Cesar was able to put together the ambush, or even know for a fact that Memo was headed there to kill him, was the very man that had alerted Memo of Julio Cesar's presence there, Flaco. Perhaps Flaco felt remorse for his friend and had a change of heart at the last minute. Memo was without time and out of good assassins now, and he would need the best to take out a powerful and well-protected man like Flaco.

How he still remembered him was a mystery, but Arturo the assassin came to mind. If he were still alive, the man he'd briefly encountered six years earlier while incarcerated would be perfect for the job. Ciudad Juárez was his stomping grounds and only thirty minutes away from Palomas. Before he could complete his next thought, the cellular rang.

"Bueno? Who is it?"

"This is Rafa," a familiar voice said. "I'm having some problems. Big problems. When can you and I get together?"

Memo sighed. "No rest for the wicked. I'm headed to Juárez tomorrow."

Rafa laughed. "You're right about that, we are definitely wicked, and for us, no rest. I'll meet you at the same hotel as always. Hasta manana."

"Until tomorrow," Memo repeated and made his way back to his vehicle.

The cold wind blew hard against the roof, which made tumultuous, ominous sounds. Lucia was feeling particularly frisky and had gotten on top of Memo, grinding on one of his thick legs. Memo was tired, but Lucia's movement and, feeling her wet vagina on his leg, made him ready for action. Lucia took off her blouse and began playing with her nipples. Memo sat up and licked each of them, hard, brown and round. Lucia giggled and became even wetter. A sudden knocking on the door ripped the couple back to reality.

"Mami! Papi! We're scared!" Both Miguel and Guillermo Junior were pounding the door incessantly. Lucia covered herself up, and Memo threw on a pair of boxers, the soldier still saluting. He covered himself with a blanket as well.

"Come on in, boys." So much for their night of passion, thought a disappointed Memo.

He left for Juárez at about five in the morning. Despite his speeding, no cops stopped him, and he arrived in a record four hours. Hotels were abundant in Juárez, but Memo usually stayed at the Holiday Inn, one of the more luxurious and by far safer hotels in the city. A bellboy who recognized the Mafioso ran up to Memo and took the bags he carried to the front desk. Memo didn't donate a lot of money to the church, but he tipped the working man very well, feeling it a more "direct" donation to the poor. Unlike a $50 tip for bellboys and waiters, church donations   rarely caused much fervor. Being generous was a key to his level of popularity in the community, and he planned to keep it that way.

Rafa was waiting for him in the lobby, and, after shaking hands and exchanging brief pleasantries, the two went to Memo's room for their meeting. Rafa recounted the past few months' events, having lost all but one of his police contacts in El Paso to Mafia-style hits, which didn't make sense to either of them. Their competition couldn't know of all the ties they had with the El Paso police and immigration. No one else had contact with them. In fact, the only cop they'd ever had direct contact was with Captain Barba. Maybe Barba was tying up loose ends in the event of a DEA investigation, in which case Barba would come after them as well. The only logical conclusion they could come up with was that Barba had to be the culprit and needed to die.

Neither Rafa nor Memo wanted to risk getting caught for murdering Barba, so they agreed to hire a professional. Memo decided to talk to Rafa about Arturo. Remembering the man from before he moved his operation to the United States, Rafa's had a loose connection to Arturo was through some Juárez detectives. Memo would go to the detective's office in the state building later that day, but first, they would have a good lunch at Los Canarios, a taco joint that served the best flautas in the world.

Not having been to the state building since he'd been incarcerated, Memo wasn't thrilled to go, especially to see a couple of dirty cops. Rafa had long lost their numbers, so it was only logical to contact them at their last known place of work. Of the two detectives, only one, Juan Guerrero, still worked there, according to the secretary that coldly attended Memo. Her long, black hair was up in a tight bun, and she wore light makeup and glasses. Memo noted that she was actually quite attractive as he watched her go to the back offices to advise Guerrero of the visitor.

A tall man with a light complexion returned, and Memo recognized him as one of the officers who'd interrogated him at his arrest. Guerrero didn't recognize Memo, though, and after Memo told him it was a private issue, the two proceeded to his office. After a quick check for wires and other surveillance devices, Guerrero motioned for Memo to sit down.

Guerrero lit up a Marlboro, dragged in deeply, and exhaled. "How can I help you?"

Memo, uncomfortable with the smoke, coughed. "Don Rafa said you might be able to help me."

Guerrero peered over his wooden desk, waiting for Memo to continue.

"I need a number or location, something, for a guy I met in jail a few years ago. He may not even be around anymore."

"How much is this information worth to you?"

Memo counted out five-hundred dollars onto Guerrero's desk. "His name is Arturo. He 'cleans up' for people in Rafa's type of business."

Guerrero smiled and took the money. "I'll give you a number." He wrote the number down and slid it over to him. "Pleasure doing business with you. What did you say your name was?" Guerrero studied Memo's face. Memo was sure that he would remember him.

"Guillermo."

"Guillermo what?"

Memo got up. "Just Guillermo."

The man nodded as if it were the expected answer. "Anytime, then, Guillermo, just Guillermo."

Memo hated dealing with the police. They were a bunch of sarcastic pricks, and in Mexico, they were killers, unpredictable and dangerous.

Memo called the number the detective gave him from his cellphone. Arturo answered and the two agreed to meet at the hotel where Memo was staying. When Arturo arrived at the hotel, he was exactly as Memo remembered him. Tall, dark skin, and slim; Arturo had an aura of maleficence about him. He wore a non-descript western-style shirt, faded jeans, and scuffed mule-skin boots.

Memo said, "Let's go for a spin."

"Sure."

Memo's gold Dodge Durango was parked in front of the hotel. Memo and Arturo got in and, driving through town, they discussed the marks, the money, and the payoff. They stopped at a drive-thru convenience store to pick up some beer, Carta Blanca. At one of the stoplights, a blue Ford Expedition cut in front of them, causing Memo to brake hard and spill his beer.

Highly irritated, Memo pulled up beside the SUV and rolled his window down. The man on the passenger side rolled his down as well and motioned with his head as if saying, "What the hell do you want?" About six men with shaven heads and enough tattoos to cover a billboard filled the seats of the vehicle.

Memo gave them the one finger salute and sped up. The other SUV took pursuit behind them.

Slowing down, Memo turned to Arturo. "We'll turn into that gas station." Arturo pulled out his handgun.

"You won't need that."

Arturo holstered his weapon. Memo needed Arturo to know just what kind of a man he was, so he had to make an impression. Opening the door, he slid out of the vehicle. A gas station attendant asked him how much gas to put in, and Memo waved him off.

"I'll fill my tank, friend. You just stay out of the way."

The blue Expedition pulled up alongside their Durango, and the attendant ran inside of the station, his eyes wide and frightened.

"Hey, pinché Guero, fuck you," one of the tattooed men yelled.

"You faggots think you can? Good luck with that," Memo taunted them, gas nozzle in hand.

Infuriated by Memo's comments and attitude, the driver and two backseat passengers got out, yelling profanities and making gang signs. Thinking better of it, Arturo unholstered his handgun and had it ready while Memo waited until they got closer to him. When the men were just a few feet away, Memo sprayed the three men and their vehicle with gas. All three men ran back to the vehicle, climbing in, as they called him a crazy fucker. Memo jumped in the Durango and followed them. A red light and congested traffic detained the Expedition, and Memo pulled up beside them. The idiots had their windows down, screaming at each other about the gas burning and what a crazy bastard he was. Arturo lit a cigarette and Memo motioned for Arturo to hand it to him. Memo slipped it between his lips, squinting his eyes at the smoke. He rolled his window all the way down and pinched the cigarette between his fingers.

The passenger saw Memo and screamed at the driver to go, but it was too late. Memo flicked the cigarette into the Expedition and drove off as the light turned green. The Expedition and the men inside burst into flames, and the Cholos erupted from the SUV to roll on the asphalt.

Memo drove back to the gas station laughing. Arturo laughed as well, causing phlegm to fill his throat. He coughed the cough of a lifetime smoker and spit out the window.

Memo looked over at Arturo as he filled the tank and said, "I never did like Cholos anyway."

He paid the attendant and got back in the truck.

"Okay, back to business." Memo placed a photograph in Arturo's hand. "This guy's name is Flaco. His address is on the back. His problem is he's still alive."

Arturo smiled a crooked, yellow-toothed grin. "I have a cure for that."

Memo grinned. "I thought you would."

Chapter 30 (Arturo)

Arturo waited outside Flaco's highly guarded residence for about two days. Tired of waiting, Arturo called Leobardo and asked him to bring his Israeli .50 caliber. It was perfect for the job. Arturo found a good spot to fire the rifle from a hill about a thousand meters away from Flaco's home. Never having been professionally trained to be an assassin, Arturo was not known for his delicacy. People who hired him usually wanted a high profile and messy execution. Training the weapon's sight on Flaco's wide chest, Arturo fired. A gaping hole replaced part of the mark's chest and belly, and from the look on his face, Flaco never knew what hit him.

Suddenly, the house was full of movement, armed men running outside to scan the area for the shooter.

Arturo smiled. Let them look; he was well hidden and had plenty of time to get away before they figured out where he was. He packed up his weapons and left. It was an easy ten-thousand dollars, but he had one more kill to take care of, worth two times Flaco's, and he was eager to finish the job. Using back roads only known to ranchers and drug traffickers and that the police didn't dare use, Arturo returned to Juárez, dropping off his .50 caliber. With all of the random roadblocks by numerous law enforcement and military units in the area, driving around with a military-grade weapon was a bad idea.

Arturo felt that Mexico was a country full of hypocrisy and double standards. Prostitution was illegal, yet in certain areas working women paraded the street at all hours of the day and night while marked police vehicles drove by all the time. Guns were illegal, but you could have a small handgun in the home. If you used it on the street directly in front of your home, however, that was a federal crime. But the system worked perfectly for him.

Arturo always carried a handgun with him. If he got caught, the crime was fairly minor, and he would just lose the gun and a few hundred dollars. A .50 caliber was a totally different story and would carry a serious penalty, or he would have to put up some heavy cash to get out of jail, at least twenty-grand.

Whenever Arturo took a trip to the "otro lado," the United States or other side, he took out one of his speakers mounted behind his seat in the truck and placed the handgun he would be using behind it, this time a Glock .40 with clips holding extra capacity. Arturo planned to buy extra ammo in El Paso, then drive to Albuquerque after that to settle in and find his target. If the police stopped him along the way or on his way back, his cover story was simple but believable – he was on his way to the auto auction in Albuquerque to buy a used American car, and he carried enough cash to back up the story.

Crossing the border at four a.m. to avoid the long early morning lines, Arturo ate breakfast at a truck stop on the north side of El Paso. When the gun shop he normally visited opened, he bought two boxes of hollow-point rounds for his Glock and headed north on I-25 to Albuquerque, about a four-hour trip. He arrived around three in the afternoon. He didn't worry too much about being seen; it would back up his cover story.

Rafa and Memo set it up to where Rafa's usual meeting with Barba at Barba's mother's house would happen in the early evening the same day as the auction.

Memo planned most of the hit himself, leaving the minor details for Arturo. Arturo was impressed with Memo's extensive plan. It was clearly designed for success, with contingency plans for every scenario.

It seemed Memo wanted to use him for future jobs, and Arturo wasn't sure how he felt about that. Arturo had never even considered working solely for one person or organization until now, but he was impressed with Memo's generosity, charisma, and intelligence. Memo was able to look ahead and see the various different scenarios and prepare for each, all off the top of his head. Arturo respected that and decided he wouldn't mind working for a man like Memo, who was honest, yet cunning, keen and wise beyond his years.

The hotel offered nothing but a place to sleep, barely, and after preparing his weapon and taking a hot shower, Arturo settled in for the night. He set the alarm for five a.m. so he could take an early morning run to burn off any adrenalin and keep his aim steady.

The following morning, he attended the auto auction and bought a Nissan Sentra in nice shape for a few hundred dollars. He hooked it onto a tow bar onto his truck and drove to his motel. About seven that evening, he unhooked the Sentra and attached license plates from another vehicle Memo had in Juárez. The plates were New Mexico and current, so he'd just have to be careful to not be stopped by the police. If he was stopped, the hit was off, and he'd have to try again somewhere else.

Ever since someone had been killing off Barba's people, Barba wouldn't go to Juárez like before and was hardly seen in public in El Paso. A hit anywhere else would be difficult, so Arturo would have to make this one count. He drove to a grocery store in the area of the hit and waited at the corner. Rafa drove up in a Ford Aerostar minivan and Arturo climbed in.

The plan was fairly simple – Arturo would be dropped off at the end of the alley behind Barba's mother's house. As Barba and Rafa made their usual exchange of info, Arturo would come up from behind and put a bullet into Barba's head, then one in the back and one in the heart. He and Rafa would leave in the van, and Rafa would drop Arturo at the same corner where he'd picked him up. They hoped to leave quickly before anyone knew Barba was hit.

Chapter 31 (Lalo)

Punctual as ever, Rafa drove up to the gate and parked next to the trash cans in the alley. After putting the silencer on his 9 mm, Lalo took a few breaths, crossed himself, and sprang out from behind the trash cans, as Barba opened the gate. The smell of grilled chicken permeated the alley.

Lalo shot Rafa in the back and Barba in the liver. He didn't have the luxury of time to stretch out their deaths being in such a public place. Dark blood seeped into Barba's Hawaiian-style shirt, and he slid down the gate. A blood stain followed him down the fence, as if he painted it with his back. Rafa lay face down, a pool of blood staining the pristine green grass that was Barba's family's lawn.

"Remember me, perro?" Lalo liked the man's expression when he called him a dog, better than he deserved. "Yeah, I can tell by your eyes that you do."

Barba tried for his .357 magnum, but Lalo snatched it away from him, his gloved hand faster than the dying police captain.

"You don't need that, not where you're going. Tell Satan when you see him, I'll be sending more of his pawns to him later. Remember my daughter and my wife, you bastard? I had you over for dinner once, and you met them. How could you?"

Barba coughed up some blood and grinned. "A means to an end. It was never personal. You were too damn difficult. You just had to know the truth, didn't you, no matter what the cost? You're just as much to blame."

"I know," said Lalo, as he took careful aim and shot Barba point blank in the forehead. He heard Rafa mumbling something. It sounded like "Memo." Lalo turned quickly around and turned Rafa over onto his back.

"What did you say?"

Rafa coughed up blood and his eyes rolled back.

"Who did you ask for? Who do you want?"

"Memo…" and Rafa died.

A familiar wash of release filled him, such as he'd felt the last several times he'd executed Satan's pawns, but footsteps in the alley roused him from his dream-like state. Bullets pierced his right thigh and foot as he jumped behind the fence, returning fire. A skinny, dark-skinned man walked up the alley, placing deliberate shots through the wood fence protecting Lalo but getting closer with each blast. Lalo dropped to the ground, his leg burning, and fired into the fence, but his ammo didn't penetrate very well, the shots missing his target.

A woman screamed, and neighbors appeared at the doors and windows of their homes to view the grizzly scene. The skinny man paused to look around, then turned and ran back the way he'd come. As the wail of sirens screeched in the distance, Lalo struggled to his feet while keeping his face away from any light so he could not be identified. A motorcycle awaited him just a block away. Mustering all of his remaining strength, Lalo loped to his motorcycle and drove off.

Weakened by loss of blood, Lalo stopped several streets away in a dark corner and tied his cotton shirt around the wound in his leg. It helped a little, but he was starting to feel faint, and he wracked his brain trying to figure out what to do.

As if he were drunk, the loss of blood taking its toll, Lalo drove slowly and weaved all about the road until he reached the county hospital. Lalo waited in the parking area to find someone who worked there leaving for the night.

A good-looking nurse with long, blonde hair and fair skin came through the emergency entrance and walked to her car, keys in hand. Lalo trailed her on his motorcycle all the way to an apartment complex on the northeast side of town. Barely able to keep the bike on the road, Lalo followed the attractive nurse to an apartment, hoping she lived alone, and he wouldn't have to hurt anyone else tonight.

God would help him continue on, if his mission wasn't completed, and he would look for this tall man who had come from out of nowhere. He watched her fumble for her keys and slide them into the lock before moving up quietly behind her.

"I need your help."

She opened her mouth to scream, but he stumbled against the wall and her nurse's mode overtook her fear and she moved to help him.

"My God, what happened to you?"

She pulled his arm across her shoulders and pulled him inside, dropping him onto the couch just inside the door.

"I'm shot," he mumbled, unable to see anything. His eyes refused to stay open. "Please, help me. And don't call and ambulance. If you do, or if the police are involved, it will be the end of me and the mission."

"Let me see," she muttered, wondering what the hell she was doing helping this mysterious and possibly dangerous stranger, but the sincerity in his eyes when he said *mission* won over her better judgment. "This is going to hurt."

With both hands, she hooked fingers into the tear in his pants where the bullet went through and ripped. He groaned as the fabric gave way, pain searing across his skin.

"This is bad." She had a knack for understatement, but Lalo didn't care; his leg hurt too badly for his brain to function well.

"I'll get my first-aid kit."

She got up and slammed her front door closed, then hurried further into the apartment. He heard her rummaging around, and then she came back with towels and a big white box with a red cross emblazoned on it.

He looked up at her, as she busied herself laying out what she would need, but before she could get to work, he stopped her with a hand on her arm. She stared at the gun he held out to her, then gingerly took it and laid it on the floor. She dressed his wound efficiently.

"I have to pull the bullet out," she said flatly. "Can you take it?"

Lalo nodded, but he needed her to understand his situation. Cool hydrogen peroxide burned across his skin and he saw her reach for the scissors.

"Please, don't call an ambulance or the police," he murmured, his head swimming. "Let me explain…"

Sharp pain shot up his leg as she probed the wound, and darkness took him.

Lalo awoke the next day in a queen-sized bed, his head hurting like hell. He took a moment to remember how he got there and vaguely recalled following a nurse from the hospital to a nearby apartment complex. For whatever reason, she hadn't called the police, or he would be in a hospital instead, an armed police officer outside of his door.

He looked around a room full of pretty trinkets, butterflies, unicorns, and ribbons of every color. The curtains were a light shade of pink, and the bed coverings matched. As if she'd heard him awaken, the woman who'd helped him last night opened the door and smiled.

"Good, you're awake."

She pushed the door open further and brought in a tray, setting it on the bedside table. Then, she sat in the chair beside the bed and handed him a cup of hot tea.

"My name is Sara White."

Lalo stopped with the cup halfway to his mouth. "I'm Eduardo, but people call me Lalo."

"I made a difficult decision last night, Lalo," she said, watching him sip his tea. "But something in your eyes convinced me you were telling me the truth. Now, you owe me an explanation."

Lalo took a deep breath and began to tell his story, swallowing his tears, hands sweating when recounting details of his wife and daughter's death. He told her how he began to exact vengeance on the people responsible for their deaths, leaving out the part about becoming God's avenging angel. He didn't want her to think he was crazy. The nurse listened intently, crying, surprisingly understanding about his killings.

When he was done, she hugged him. Crying, he hugged her back, not having felt the comforting touch of another human being since his family had been taken from him.

Over the next few days, they became friends. After some prompting from Lalo, Sara told her story, almost with the same passion.

"I lost my husband eight years ago. We both drank and used drugs, but it affected him more, and he lost control," she told him, tears streaming down her face.

"He never mistreated me; he loved me, and the only thing that really ever separated us was the alcohol and drugs."

She looked at Lalo, expecting him to give her a disapproving look since he felt so strongly against drugs, but he was looking at her with sad eyes, compassion pouring out of his stare.

"We were drunk almost all the time, but he started to use crack, and it was really screwing him up. I never tried it; I just stuck with my weed and wine. One day we were both high, and we decided to cruise to the park and drink while we watched the sunset. We had an argument because I really didn't like him smoking crack, and he drove off. He had a fatal accident and killed three innocent people. Two of them were small children."

She paused, overcome with guilt and shame. "I've held myself partially responsible since. I decided to clean up, and I went to nursing school. So here I am, a lonely mess who misses her first love, no matter how messed up he was."

Lalo reached for her hand, squeezing it tightly while she cried. He felt helpless, wanting to help her, but he didn't know what else to do. She smiled at him, wiping her wet cheeks. "Your leg is going to be okay, but you'll need several days of rest." Sara indicated by looking at the bandages tightly wrapped around his thigh. Pink showed through in some spots on the top layer.

He struggled to get up, but she leaned over to stop him.

"What are you doing?" she asked with a frown.

"I've got to find somewhere to stay." He tried to move again, but she kept him down without much effort. "Please help me."

"Lalo, you don't need to go anywhere." She looked him straight in the eye. "I trust you. You can stay here until you're better."

Lalo stayed a few weeks, he and Sara spending a lot of time talking about their pasts. He woke one morning, knowing it was time to move on. Sara didn't get off work late in the evening, so he waited, not wanting to leave without saying goodbye. When she returned, she somehow sensed he was leaving and she reached over and touched his cheek.

Neither of them said a word, but their loneliness took over, and they began to kiss. He knew he might never see Sara again, yet he couldn't resist her tender passion, responding out of a need to touch someone after such a long time of being alone. Lalo stayed the night.

The next morning, while Sara slept, he placed five-thousand dollars in her purse and left for El Paso. A few more of Satan's pawns were awaiting Lalo, their final days soon coming to an abrupt end.

Chapter 32

Moving his long black hair out of his eyes, Lalo watched Alex, the gangbanging partner of the drug lord called Memo – the man he knew as Guillermo Smith. He knew who he was now that he had seen the two together, making exchanges, scheming, doing the things drug dealers do. Lalo laughed, once again affirming God had a plan for him. After all, he never did like that Smith guy anyway. Lalo remembered the tension he had felt when he had seen the two at the burrito stand. He never would have thought he would be killing the both of them later.

The 1992 red Ford Tempo Lalo was in was inconspicuous enough that no one bothered to take a second look at him. Alex had been visiting one of his many girlfriends in town, as was customary for him. The dusty wind common in October for El Paso forced Alex to shut his eyes. The whistling sound of the wind hitting the side of the Tempo, forcing its way over the roof reminded Lalo of when he and

Manuela had been dating, sitting in the car talking about nothing and everything simultaneously, oblivious to whatever conditions were outside, be it rain, wind, or snow. The memory was so powerful he could smell her perfume, as if she had been sitting right beside him. A tear formed at the far corner of his left eye, and it made him angry she was not there with him. Shaking his head violently to clear his mind, Lalo got out of his car and walked purposefully toward Alex's Hummer, his .45 in hand.

"Move over, now!" Lalo yelled, as he shoved the gun's barrel into Alex's temple.

Alex obeyed, sliding over to the passenger seat as Lalo got in.

"I just need to know one thing, Alex; where and when is the next money drop?"

"Y-you a cop?"

Lalo's answer was a hard slam to the head, the butt of his .45 cutting Alex just over his eye.

"I'll ask again, and your answer better not be another question. Where and when?"

Alex took a deep breath and spit into Lalo's face. Lalo burst out in anger, repeatedly hitting Alex in the head with the butt of the gun. When he realized Alex was no longer moving, Lalo stopped and checked his pulse. Dead. Shrugging, Lalo searched Alex's pockets and the Hummer for some kind of clue. He found an address and time on the back of a parking receipt. It could be anything, thought Lalo, from a drug shipment to a date with a girl. With nothing better than an address, Lalo started the Hummer and drove away. As he drove, the strange power he had been feeling after he terminated anyone came over him. Visions of his wife and child dancing about in white dresses clouded his vision. Breathing slowly and steadily, Lalo eventually took control of himself before he had an accident. He stopped on the side of the road, sweat rolling down from under his arms.

After he recovered, Lalo drove the Hummer over the border. Once in Juárez, Lalo relaxed some because he knew he was unlikely to be stopped by police, and even if he was, something could be done to remedy the situation. He drove past downtown, the neighborhoods declining progressively, as he moved on. In the northernmost outskirt of Juárez, called Anapra, Lalo parked the Hummer and walked to a nearby bus stop.

The people in Anapra would strip the Hummer of anything with the least bit valuable before they would call any cops. *If they even did call the cops*, he thought. He got the next bus heading back to town. Once downtown, Lalo walked back over the border and took a cab back to his apartment. The date on the paper was for tomorrow, so he'd have to wait.

Sleep was never an easy feat for Lalo. As soon as he closed his eyes, his troubled mind would immediately wander back to when he still had a family, and after luring him into a series of loving memories, it would then meticulously guide him back to the night his wife and child died, dragging him painstakingly through every horrendous detail. This night was no exception, and he awoke with a start.

Blackness was all he could see. The motel room wasn't just dark; it was as if he had been teleported deep into outer space, a black hole looming over him. The silence was broken by a terrible ringing sound in his ears. He frantically searched for the remote control of the room's television. Like a blind man, yet certainly much less proficient, Lalo systematically searched the bed, fingertips replacing his eyes. The incessant ringing worsened with every minute that passed. His hand glided under a pillow and stopped suddenly, the feel of cold steel pulsing from his fingers to his brain. Lalo picked up his .357, contemplating the simplicity of the gun, and its utter deadliness.

One pull of the trigger, he thought, and the ringing stops, the loneliness ends, the suffering over. One tiny movement of one finger, a simple series of electric pulses from the nerves to the brain, and it ends. No, that would be too easy. My girls didn't die in vain. I must go on. I can't go on.

The ringing became more insistent, the blackness somehow darker. The explosion at his home played out over and over before his mind's eye. Lalo placed the barrel of the .357 in his mouth, took a deep breath, and pulled the trigger.

Click! Lalo laughed, a short cynical wheeze. Of course, he thought, that was way too easy. God had plans for him. Who was he to think he could get out of his mission so easily? What a pussy he had been. Finally, the ringing in his ears stopped. Lalo lied down, thinking about how he was not quite sure he had the real address for the money drop. He knew God would not let him down, though, and with that he fell asleep.

The morning of the drop seemed more like a dream than reality to Lalo. In fact, he wondered if he wasn't actually asleep still in his motel room, even as he shot the gangster who carried the backpack up the stairs of the address that had been written on the paper he had found. The gangster fell backwards, a look of total disbelief on his face as he went down. It seemed as if it was all happening in slow motion for Lalo, and he shot the man three more times as he fell. A shirtless man opened the door of the home, tattoos over every part of his skin, including his head. Lalo shot him three times before the guy even knew what had hit him, placing a shot dead center of the eight-ball tattooed on top of his head. Lalo felt the strength God gave him after killing bad men, and he shuddered, the power seemingly electrifying him. Police sirens wailed in the distance, but it didn't bother Lalo. He simply walked away, the backpack swinging with every step, bouncing happily on his back. Lalo smiled as he thought of a happy backpack.

Chapter 33 (Memo)

Memo was in serious trouble financially. In just a few years, he'd amassed a fortune, but in order to maintain his resources, he needed a continuous flow of money. Rafa's murder had been just the beginning. Rafa's killer had been tipping off the police, stealing Memo's cash, and destroying the drugs. Arturo was doing his best to find him, but the man was like a ghost.

The gang connection Memo had worked so hard to make to protect his safe houses had been annihilated. After losing most of his best men to firefights with the police, Mexican military, or incarceration, Memo changed his tactics and ran his drug loads from the mountains to the border himself. After successfully running several loads with his brother-in-law Omar, their luck ran out.

Memo drove a red Bronco loaded with seventy kilos of cocaine they'd picked up in Durango for about five-grand a kilo. Denver, Colorado, was its final destination, where it would sell at wholesale for fifteen-grand a kilo. Memo had run primarily marijuana until recently, the risks outweighing the profit margin. Seven-hundred-thousand dollars of profit was a load worth running, and he needed it.

Just outside of Guachochic, in the mountains, was the first of five Mexican army blockades Memo and Omar would have to pass. Memo smiled at the soldier who greeted them.

"Where you headed? Oh –" The soldier recognized Memo. "Sorry, I didn't recognize you, Don Guillermo."

"No sweat. See ya." Memo turned to Omar. "I wish all the blockades were this friendly."

Omar smiled nervously. "Yeah, that'd be great."

The second blockade was past Cuauhtémoc, just before Chihuahua.

"Where are you going?" asked a somber-faced soldier.

"Chihuahua."

"And your business?"

Memo smiled and said, "To find us some women."

"Yeah," Omar chimed in.

The soldier laughed. "Be on your way, then."

Omar and Memo chatted about what their plans would be once they crossed the border and joked about the "Gringas" they would be with at the local strip clubs in Denver. Their laughter was abruptly interrupted by the ring of Memo's cellular.

He flipped it open. "Bueno."

"Don Memo?" a familiar voice whispered. "Be careful with the blockade outside of Chihuahua. They've been tipped to watch for you."

It was an old friend and partner, Colonel Parra, who worked several years in Cuauhtémoc before being moved to Mexicali, clear on the other side of Mexico. Memo looked out the window and his chest tightened.

The blockade was just ahead, and there would be no evading it.

"Get out your Cuerno, Omar. They know we're coming."

Omar pulled out his AK-47 and a hand grenade, pulled the pin, and handed the grenade to Memo. Memo held it in his right hand while driving with his left, holding the lever down to keep it stable. It was Israeli and had a three- to five-second delay. The soldiers gathered into two groups on either side of the Bronco; Memo and Omar smiled as they drove up, their weapons in their laps.

"Where are you headed?" the soldier asked, and Memo stifled a laugh. This was only the third time that day he had been asked the same question. An officer approached the soldiers near their vehicle and whispered something to them. They immediately tensed up, confirming what Parra had told him earlier. Memo smiled. "We're going to Chihuahua to see our girlfriends."

The soldier nodded and directed them to park. Memo had already released a grenade's lever as they had driven up to the checkpoint. He swerved as if he was headed to the side like he had been instructed, then he tossed out the grenade and floored the gas pedal.

"Now!" Memo yelled, and Omar fired on the soldiers to the right of their vehicle as the grenade Memo had thrown exploded on their left. Some of the soldiers, barely shaking off the effects of the surprise bombing, began to fire back. Realizing that survivors would certainly alert the Mexican military, Memo pulled the emergency brake to flip the vehicle around. The Bronco did a 180, and he floored it.

"Omar, make sure there are no witnesses."

Another grenade and several rounds from the AK later, only a few wounded soldiers were still alive. Memo and Omar used their handguns to finish what they started, putting a bullet in each soldier's head. Memo paused for a moment, waiting for the usual nausea that followed when he killed, but it never came.

Neither Memo nor Omar were so much as scratched by the soldiers' fire. They drove off in their bullet-ridden Bronco, heading toward a Mennonite colony just outside of Rubio, a small town forty minutes from Cuauhtémoc. The Mennonite nicknamed "the Wire" had worked with Memo many times in the past, devising secret compartments for his vehicles.

"I'm glad you are here, Guillermo. Everything okay?"

"Nein. Someone blew the whistle on us and we had some problems. We really need another vehicle."

"Okay, no problem. Let's go to the barn. I probably have something that can get you safely out of here."

Memo and Omar were led to the warehouse in back. Memo chose a Mercury Sable, one of five vehicles in the warehouse; the merchandise was transferred to the car from the Bronco. Memo and Omar slept while the Wire worked.

The operation took about ten hours, but it was an impeccable job. Memo and Omar were off to Colorado again. Memo decided his operation was no longer safe in Chihuahua, and once this load was delivered, he would move his operation to another border. He would play one last card in his hand, though, before he moved to another location. Too much time and money had been invested in Chihuahua for him to move that easily.

Chapter 34 (Arturo)

Six months had passed since Albuquerque, and Arturo still had made no real headway on the identity of the mystery-man. Now, Arturo and Leobardo waited outside a house in a fairly nice neighborhood.

Arturo lit a cigarette and inhaled. He spoke to Leobardo as he exhaled. "See that walking tub of lard standing at that window?"

"Yeah. Is he our mark?"

Arturo took another drag, exhaled, and spoke again. "Yeah. He's a police sergeant. He was with El Soldado's crew. Now that the police are pretty much owned by Don Guillermo, the other guys don't like the Sarge anymore."

When the round sergeant came out of the house, Arturo motioned for Leobardo to go toward him. Leobardo floored the taxi and made a screeching stop right beside the man. Arturo opened the back door of the taxi and pointed his AK-47 at the sergeant.

"Get in, fat boy, or I'll turn you into a dead man."

The short, round man with a thick, dark mustache seemed like he was going to run. Arturo shook his head ominously, and the man changed his mind. As soon as he got in the cab, Arturo hit the man in the head with the butt of the AK, knocking him out.

Arturo laughed. "This is going to be fun. I hate cops."

Leobardo nodded in agreement with Arturo.

After they drove a short distance, Arturo grabbed some smelling salts. "Let's wake this pig up."

They had driven to the middle of the desert, just outside of Juárez. The sergeant was sweating profusely in the awful heat. Leobardo had handcuffed him so tightly that his hands were already purple. He coughed as he woke up.

"Hola, stupid pig. Must have really pissed someone off," Arturo said as he smiled his sick smile.

"Pl-please, don't harm me. I have money. I have properties. I can make you rich men."

Leobardo smiled, "We already are." He hit the sergeant hard in the face, causing him to turn his head and spit blood.

Arturo pulled out his knife. "You would be amazed at what a good, sharp knife can do."

The sergeant began to cry. Arturo stabbed him in the gut with the knife, and the man squealed, kicking and flopping around like a fish in its final death throws.

Arturo and Leobardo laughed. Arturo didn't normally like to prolong people's deaths, but this was an exception.

"Did you hear the man squeal, Leobardo? Why, he's not a man, he's a human pig! Squeal, pig, squeal!" Leobardo and Arturo laughed while Arturo repeatedly stabbed the man in the stomach. The Sarge's stomach was apparently so large that Arturo's knife didn't seem to penetrate any major organs. The Sarge just kept flopping his round body all about the van, smearing blood and other bodily fluids around the van's floorboard and walls.

"I'm tiring of this sport, Leobardo."

"End it then."

Arturo finished the job by gutting the policeman. As he pulled out his victim's entrails, he showed them to the sergeant, running them across the sergeant's face. He was still not quite dead when Arturo pulled out his liver.

They torched the van with the sarge in it and decided it would be best to leave town for a while, not wanting to risk attracting the attention of other police who may have been friends with the deceased Sergeant Piggy.

"Where are you going to go, Juan?"

"Mapimí."

Just the sound of their hometown's name brought Arturo powerful memories, smells of a mother's cooking, laughter of children playing, oblivious to life's complexities. Arturo left for the state's capital city, Chihuahua. On the way out of Juárez, Arturo stopped at a Capilla, or altar. The Santisima Muerte stood tall, a globe in her left hand and a staff in her right. Arturo took off his straw Resistol, opened a beer, and placed it nearby some candles that were in front of the statue.

"Drink up, Death, and thanks for another successful job."

On the way to Chihuahua, he stopped in a small town called Villa Ahumada to get some sleep. Arturo didn't bother to get a hotel; he knew his sleep wouldn't be peaceful. After a few hours of light sleep, Arturo bought some truck driver-style coffee, lit a cigarette, and continued on his way. He ate breakfast when he finally arrived, over-easy eggs with salsa served on fried tortillas.

As Arturo was cruising the main streets, admiring the beautiful women everywhere, he received a call from Don Guillermo.

"Arturo, the Mystery Man is here," Memo's voice sounded strained. "Several times now he's intercepted my loads."

"I'll be there in half an hour." Arturo hung up and went to fill up his gas tank.

Chapter 35

Arturo met at Memo's ranch to discuss how to trap the killer. Arturo would be the passenger on the next load of marijuana, and Memo would be the driver. Memo would pay a few Federales to follow them for back up. They agreed it wasn't the most ingenious plan, but it was the only one Memo could come up with to trap this man who was slowly destroying his business.

Memo and Arturo picked up a red Jeep Cherokee from Memo's marijuana supplier in Guachochic, a small mountain town about four hours from Cuauhtémoc. Exportation of marijuana was the primary basis of the local economy, but it was so unknown and difficult to get to that the Mexican government didn't really work to enforce its laws there. Memo had called ahead to have the vehicle ready for them.

The Jeep wasn't loaded with marijuana. Instead, it was packed with various high-caliber weapons. They set off down the long, winding road, barely wide enough for two vehicles. Both were tense with the anticipation of a firefight with this ghost-like man who killed Memo's men and escaped unscathed. Reputations and legends went hand in hand in Mexico, and no one was willing to be a hired gun for Memo until he fixed this problem.

"Arturo, you ever think about, you know, good and evil, Hell and Heaven, all that?"

"Sure. Not a lot. Sometimes."

Memo smiled; his friend was obviously flustered by the question.

"What do you think about it?

"I think Heaven and Hell are right here on Earth. When the smoke clears, there isn't any good or evil. All that is left is the living or the dead. And the living write the history books."

Arturo laughed.

Six hours into the trip, a gray Dodge Ram with a large push bumper appeared on the highway behind them, driving dangerously fast on the down slope of the mountain and around a curve. Arturo and Memo prepared themselves for a fight.

When the modified Ram with oversize tires and a roll bar hit the back end of the Cherokee, Memo and Arturo jolted forward hard, even though they were expecting it. The shove caused many of the weapons and ammo in the back to shift forward, some of them hitting the two men. When the Ram struck them again, Memo lost control of the Cherokee, and they drove off the side of a hill, rolling several times until they came to a rest near some trees at the bottom.

With only a few fractured ribs and fingers, Arturo climbed out immediately, and then went to the driver's side to help his boss. Memo was no longer in the vehicle. After noticing the shattered windshield, Arturo thought Memo had been thrown out of the Jeep during the roll.

The Mystery Man fired from a small hill above them, his Glock .40 blazing, disrupting Arturo's train of thought. Bullets slammed into the vehicle and the ground around Arturo, way too close for comfort, and he jumped behind the Cherokee for cover.

His broken fingers throbbing with pain, Arturo pulled his back-up .38 revolver from his shoulder holster and fired back. The anonymous figure above moved like a panther, darting back and forth behind trees and rocks as he slowly closed the distance on Arturo. For the first time in many years, Arturo's heart sped with fear.

Shots from an AK-47 rang out, shutting out the sound of the Mystery Man's .40 and Arturo's .38 as Memo fired back. One of the bullets from the burst hit the man in the leg. How Don Guillermo ended up where he did with the AK was a mystery to Arturo, but he had not become one of the biggest suppliers of marijuana to the United States in just a few short years for nothing.

The man crawled behind some trees, and Arturo and Memo closed in on his position, maintaining constant gunfire. Arriving at the spot where the man disappeared, the two were surprised to hear his Dodge Ram roar to life and drive off. The man was brave but not stupid, and he knew he was outgunned that day. And then the Federales arrived like usual, a day late and a dollar short. All Memo and Arturo could do was laugh helplessly at the irony of it.

Memo drove to Galilea's house in order to tend to his wounds. Their daughter ran and embraced him, her shiny black curls bouncing around her heart-shaped face.

"Papi, what happened?" she cried, clutching his arm. "How come you have blood on you?"

Memo laid a hand on his daughter's head. "Papi was in a little accident at work. But don't worry; I'm okay."

As Galilea tended his cuts, young Rosita chattered about all of the things she'd seen and done for the past week. She only saw her daddy once a week, so it was normal for her to talk Memo's ear off for the first hour. She was Memo's only girl, and he treated her like a princess. His other three children with Lucia were all boys, and he was proud of them, but Rosita held a special place in his heart.

Still, he loved them all and often thought it a shame their father was a drug dealer. He wished now he could change his life, but it was too late, and now a ghost haunted him, one he'd managed to shoot. But the ghost would be back, of that he was certain.

"Are you going to stay the night?" Rosita asked, her tiny face alight with excitement.

Memo looked up at Galilea. "Is it okay?"

"Of course, my love," she answered with a smile. "I wish it could be every night. Now, when Rosita goes to sleep, I expect you to tell me everything that happened."

She made them a fine dinner of grilled chicken and vegetables, with a huge bowl of rice, and Memo and Rosita teased each other throughout the meal and into the evening, as they relaxed in the living room. Soon, the little girl got sleepy, and Memo carried her to bed.

"Good night, Papi," she whispered against his cheek, her arms tight around his neck.

He kissed her, then brushed a strand of dark hair from her face. "Good night, mija."

Galilea waited for him in their bed, her eyes shining with pleasure at his company.

"Come, my love," she invited, patting his side of the bed. "Talk to me."

After Memo related the story to her, Galilea fell silent. He leaned to kiss her, and she snuggled against him, holding him tightly.

"What's the matter?" he asked.

She sighed. "I hope we don't ever lose Rosita to this damn drug war."

Memo held her away far enough to look down into her worried face. "My God, don't even say that."

Galilea shook her head. "My cousin Manuela grew up in El Paso. I hardly knew her. She married some cop who was hard core against drug dealers. They had a beautiful little girl, and a couple of years later they were all killed when someone bombed their house."

"Really?" Memo murmured, barely paying attention.

"They found most of the bones of Manuela and her daughter, but all they found of the cop were a few teeth. It was weird."

"Mmm hmmm."

Memo had only been half-listening, but an idea suddenly occurred. How hard would it be to pull a few teeth and leave them scattered around if one survived the explosion? It would take some nerve to do that, right after losing his loved ones, but the Mystery Man was definitely that type. The more Memo thought about it, the more it made sense to him.

He sat up abruptly, and Galilea looked up at him in confusion.

"What is it, Memo?" she asked, holding the sheet to her chest.

"Tell me more about your cousin and her cop husband," he said.

"Well, they met at a quinceanera. I was only six at the time, and I was there with my mom and dad. It was awful because someone shot his cousins there."

"Someone shot his cousins at a quinceanera?"

"Yeah. Terrible, huh? Some kind of gang drive-by. Anyway, they met again like fifteen years later. I really don't know much about the rest of their story. Manuela quit talking to me after I got into trouble."

"What was her husband's name?"

"I don't remember. All I know is that one day my aunt told me about the explosion."

Chapter 36

"Memo, I don't think that guy survived. I know he must have taken at least a few bullets. It's been months since anyone has had any 'Mystery Man' problems." The two men sat in Memo's office in his body shop. Arturo lit a cigarette.

"I don't know. That man had a mission. He might be recuperating, planning. I want you to go all out and find that man. Some doctor somewhere had to have fixed him."

"Okay. It's your money." Arturo turned to leave.

"Hey, hold on a minute. I need something else. You ever hear of the priest who sells weed up in the mountains?"

"Sure, who hasn't?"

"Well, he's got the best weed anywhere as far as I'm concerned. I've got an order for two tons of the best to San Diego. You up for it?"

Arturo smiled, exhaling smoke through his yellow teeth.

"I already spoke with the Father. We'll meet at his church, high in the Chihuahua Mountains, in a small town called San Juanito. He made it pretty clear only I would be allowed in the church, and I should not have anyone else try to enter or no deal will be made. It was a weird conversation."

"How do you mean?"

"I don't know that I can explain it. We just need to be on our toes."

After a six-hour drive, the two entered the town, and Memo stopped the truck. "Arturo," he asked, "do you have a problem with killing people inside a church? Not everyday churchgoers. A bunch of well-armed Apaches."

Arturo thought for a moment. "No."

"Okay," Memo said. "Here's the plan. After you drop me off in front of the church, take off as fast as you can to that hill." Memo paused to point to a nearby hill with a perfect view of the front of the church. "If I don't come out in fifteen minutes, come in with guns blazing. Kill anyone who isn't me."

Arturo nodded. "Got it."

Wearing a bulletproof vest, with handguns stuck in every space, Memo entered the small, luxurious church. A few Apache men inside the door of the church grabbed Memo when he entered and searched him for weapons, their hands squeezing his testicles hard. Memo minced, but he kept quiet. He didn't dare show any signs of weakness before the Apache. After finding five of his seven guns, they allowed him to proceed. One of the two Indians who searched Memo told him something in Apache and began walking away. Memo looked at the other man, not understanding, and the man pointed at the other man as if to follow him. The other Indian stopped at the door of the church office and knocked. Another Apache answered and beckoned Memo into the office.

Half-dressed in his priest's garb, the Father smiled and invited Memo to sit down. Three lovely naked Indian women accompanied the Father. The Father noticed Memo's reaction. "God's most beautiful creation, wouldn't you agree, Guillermo?"

"Of course," Memo said with a polite smile. "I've always loved women."

"I hear. When I was banished to this town twenty years ago, I didn't even know their language. Now, because of God's grace, not only do I share the love of these three beautiful women, I also share the love of the entire town. God is good to those who truly appreciate His works. I must admit, though, it is nice to speak with someone who knows Spanish. I really miss speaking Italian, though."

He nodded to one of the women, and she offered Memo a drink. He shook his head, returning his attention to the Father.

The priest smiled. "I hear you also have a beautiful wife and an equally attractive mistress."

Memo inclined his head. "I see you've done your homework."

"I would be a fool not to investigate the man who took down the Juárez Cartel," the other man said slyly.

"I wish I could take all the credit, but I'm afraid that was Don Rafa's idea, may he rest in peace."

Memo made the sign of the cross as he said Rafa's name.

"I don't believe that for a minute. As a matter of fact, I am offended you would tell lies in the house of God."

Memo shifted uncomfortably in his seat, wondering what the priest meant. A half-naked priest, living with three women in the church office, was not one to pass judgement, certainly not in regard to an offense as insignificant as lying. Besides, Memo hadn't lied about anything yet.

"I'm not sure I know what you're talking about, Father."

The Father spoke to a man in Apache, and the Indian hit Memo in the jaw with the butt of his rifle, knocking him back in his chair. Shaking off dizziness, Memo began to appraise the situation. He'd seen more or less about twenty armed men throughout various parts of the church, and three more in the office with the Father. Assuming the women were probably equally dangerous, he had seven enemies within a ten-foot by ten-foot space.

"Forgive me, Guillermo," the Father said in a less-than-sincere tone. "Lying is not permitted here. Please don't mistake me for a fool. After you and Rafael killed the main players in the Juárez Cartel, your end of the business flourished. Then suddenly your business partner dies, leaving you the most powerful man in Juárez.

And now you're here, ready to take out the only man in Chihuahua who doesn't already do business with you."

Still tasting blood in his mouth, Memo knew there would be no reasoning with the paranoid priest, so he said nothing.

"You have made a dreadful mistake in underestimating God's power," the Father continued. "He gave me the foresight to keep anyone from abandoning his children here, in the mountains. And I assure you, many have tried and failed. As you have, today. By now, the friend you came with should be dead, and you are all alone."

Memo thought about Arturo being dead, and he decided he didn't want to risk the same fate. Pulling out his trusty .380, Memo shot the Father in the head. Three screaming Apache women grabbed rifles, and Memo ran for cover, shooting as he went. Hiding behind a beautiful statue of San Judas Tadeo, Memo took out two of the three women and one of the men. Bullets sprayed all around Memo, pieces of statue and dust particles flying through the air. One penetrated his shoulder, a wet, burning sensation running up and down his arm.

A sudden crashing sound erupted over the sound of the gunfire, and the entire church trembled, as Arturo drove the truck right through the church doors. Arturo tossed a grenade that took out the altar in the middle-rear of the church, destroying the cover for about ten men hunkered down behind the structure.

Out of ammunition, Memo yelled at Arturo to toss him a weapon.

Like a highly trained military team, Memo and Arturo took out each and every man and woman in the church.

Memo suddenly became aware of the church bell clanging, and he knew he and Arturo were in trouble when he smelled smoke. Somebody outside had set the building on fire.

"Arturo, let's get out of here!"

They ran to the pickup. Arturo started it up. The engine roared, and the assassin muscled the vehicle through heavy black smoke out the ruined church doors. Memo fired an AK-47 back at the church as Arturo drove, running over anyone who got in the way.

Arturo drove like a madman, and they reached the outskirts of the town in record time, leaving a trail of swirling dust and broken bodies behind them. As the town disappeared in the distance behind them, Memo passed out, the bullet wounds finally taking their toll on his muscular body.

Arturo stopped along the way; Memo was a pasty white color, his left sleeve drenched in blood. Arturo ripped off the sleeve with his pocketknife. Finding a jacket in the backseat, Arturo did his best to bandage the wound and stop the blood flow. He made Memo drink some water, waking him up just enough to respond. When he felt Memo was out of danger, Arturo headed for Chihuahua.

About an hour later, Memo awoke.

"Where are we?" Memo asked in a sleepy voice.

"About forty minutes outside of Chihuahua."

"Shit man, I'm not ready to die."

"You won't die, man. I'll make sure of it. I'll even light a candle. I need to get paid."

Memo passed out again.

Chapter 37

Memo awoke, the smell of medicine and hospital sheets filling his nostrils. A small altar was in the corner of the room, a skeletal figure on the candle that burned in the middle of it. Bodyguards and policemen hovered everywhere, just in case someone tried to assassinate him. A nurse came in, smiling when she saw he was awake.

"Welcome back, Mr. Smith. A lot of people have been interested in your recovery."

"How long have I been out?"

"Three days."

Memo's eyes widened. "You mean that a bullet to my shoulder put me out for three days?"

The nurse smiled again. "Nope. A bullet to your belly did that."

Memo lifted up his shirt to verify what the nurse had just told him. Gauze and tape covered an area just below his liver.

"Damn. You're right. I guess I'm not such a wuss after all."

"I'd say you're not. The doctor wasn't sure you'd make it. You had lost a ton of blood. I'll get the doctor. He'll want to talk to you. Also, it might not be my place to say anything, but…"

"But?"

"There are two ladies waiting for you. There seems to be some sort of confusion as to which one is your wife. We decided neither would be allowed in until you came to. But neither wanted to leave, either. I'll get the doctor now." The nurse turned to leave, stopped and turned to look back at Memo, smiling, then left.

Memo's heart sunk. There was no way Lucia would believe any stories he could come up with about Galilea's identity.

The doctor entered and spoke with Memo briefly about his wounds, the operation, and how delicate his situation was. Memo only heard about half of what the doctor said, worried about his love triangle being discovered.

As the doctor took his leave, he asked Memo, "By the way, which girl do you want to see first? There are two of them out there."

"Lucia. She's my wife."

"Okay. I hope you don't mind me saying it, but you're a lucky man."

Memo thought maybe he wasn't quite so lucky, after all. Lucia opened the door, peering in first, as if she didn't believe the doctor who said he was better. Her long, black hair looked as if she had just walked out of a shampoo commercial. She was radiant. Memo thought he would really hate to see her with another man after she divorced him.

"Mi amor, thank God you're okay!" she said while hugging and kissing him, a tear running down her face.

They talked for a while, about the kids; her mother was sick. Nothing about the other woman was ever mentioned. She left after a few hours.

"Hey baby, you gave me quite a scare! Glad you're back with the living." Galilea gave Memo a passionate kiss, taking his breath away, literally.

"I'm glad to be back. I'm a little confused though."

Galilea laughed. "You remember when we met? I told you I'd always respect your marriage."

"But how? I mean, what–"

"When I saw your wife, I immediately presented myself to her as your half-sister. I even gave her a hug."

"But she knows I don't have any sisters."

"Yeah, I thought of that. I told her that the day you went and got yourself shot, I had just found you."

"I can't believe she bought that."

Galilea smirked. "If she wants to believe it, she will."

After Galilea left, Arturo entered.

"You feel better?"

"Yeah. Thanks. Did you make the little altar?"

"You needed all the help you could get."

"Well thanks."

"It was nothing. Like I said, I needed to get my paycheck."

"Arturo, I want you to find the Mystery Man. I don't believe he's dead. As a matter of fact, I think I know who he is. Galilea told me about a cousin of hers who was killed in an explosion meant for her cousin's husband. He was a cop and they never found his body, just those of his wife and daughter."

"I've already checked all the way to Torreon. But I'll do it again."

"No expense is too great. Find him."

Chapter 38

With an enemy as dangerous and astute as the Mystery Man, Arturo wondered if he'd ever see his mother again, so he decided to visit her before the impending encounter. A straight drive from Chihuahua to Torreon, the main and only highway connecting the cities, his only detour came in Vermejillo, a thirty-minute drive to the west.

Mapimí was the same as he remembered it from his childhood, the only real change being a handful more cars, telephones, and houses than thirty years earlier.

Large new trucks drove around the local plaza with U.S. plates, townsfolk who immigrated and made their living either working in construction of some type or drug trafficking. Many did both. Everyone in town knew Arturo was Mexican Mafia, but they didn't care or, if they did, they didn't dare say anything to his face.

After stopping to buy some flowers from a young girl on the corner, Arturo happily sped over the dirt roads to the house he'd built for his mother, Maria. As he turned the corner, he repeatedly hit the horn, his custom whenever he arrived. Already two years since he'd been home, he felt elated to be there again. She ran outside to greet him, giving him a big hug. He hugged and kissed his mama on the cheek, then on her hand, also his custom. She made the sign of the cross on him, and he kissed her thumb and forefinger when she put them to his lips.

"Thank God you're finally home, Arturo," she cried. "I've been worried about you."

Arturo smiled down at her, lightly touching her lined cheek. "Ah, mama, you're always worried about me."

"Yes, but I had a terrible dream last night about you," she told him, taking his arm to guide him into the house. "You were getting married."

"Ohh," he teased. "That does sound horrible!"

She looked at him, her face somber. "Mijo, you know that weddings in dreams mean death."

Silenced by his mother's last statement, Arturo waved it off, as if by merely waving his hand he could dismiss any possibility of death with it. She'd told him many times that weddings meant death when he was younger.

Mother and son chatted, laughed and cried together, and she made him a simple dinner of Carne con Chile and frijoles. The corn tortillas she made were better than any other tortillas he'd ever eaten, and he gobbled them up as if he'd just been rescued from a deserted island.

After a brief walk to the small store on the corner, Arturo and his mother shared a bottle of Presidente Brandy before they retired to bed. It was a beautiful evening, and Arturo relished every moment. His mother was the only person he truly trusted and loved, and she was also the only one who'd ever showed him real affection. He'd lived a difficult and dangerous life, and he was thankful to have a loving mother.

Arturo went to his bed, and he tossed and turned. Sleep did not come easy, as his mother's words of a wedding still rang in his ears.

Arturo dreamt he walked the streets of Mapimí. People he'd grown up with pointed and stared at him. Arturo was unable to wake himself up. Wondering why everyone was staring and pointing at him, he looked down and saw a gaping hole in his middle. Blood-covered intestines hung out of the wound, and his fingers pushed frantically at them, trying to shove them back into the cavity. He knew he was dying.

He fell to his knees, and a terrible feeling of dread washed over him. He knew that if he looked up, he would see the horrible figure of his past, the one who always came to him in these nightmares. As if he no longer controlled them, his eyes opened and gazed up. The border patrol agent, about three-quarters decomposed, smiled a toothless smile, and extended a bony hand toward him, beckoning Arturo toward him. No one in his right mind would go with a decaying corpse anywhere, but Arturo was no longer in control, so he stood and followed the dead man to the local cemetery.

The cemetery was behind a small mountain, just west of the town. Typical of Mexican cemeteries, it was not well planned. It grew haphazardly in all different directions. When the last available land for burials met up with the mountains bordering it, older unmarked graves were re-dug, and newer corpses placed over them.

Arturo knew in his soul this was hell. With no good concept of what Hell really was, his subconscious drew on movies and descriptions by the priests at church when his mama used to drag him to church with her on Sundays. From a gaping hole in the middle of the cemetery, he heard what seemed like screams and moans of excruciating pain coming from within its bowels. Peering into the hole, Arturo swallowed hard, feeling faint. As he watched, the corpse took a position behind him and abruptly pushed him in. He could hear the dead border patrol agent laughing, as he fell into the bottomless hole, and it still echoed in his mind as he awoke from the nightmare.

Arturo's mother called him from his door, rousing him from his dream. "Arturo, someone's here to see you. A friend."

Many months had passed since Arturo had seen Leobardo, back when they had terminated the fat cop outside Juárez. He gave him a sincere hug. Maria served coffee while she warmed up tortillas and beans. The two men caught up on events, and Arturo told Leobardo about the large quantity of cash offered for the Mystery Man. Leobardo's eyes lit up.

Leobardo asked Arturo to describe the man. After Arturo provided the description, he asked Leobardo why he wanted to know.

"I've been here for the last six months courting this girl," Leobardo said. "About that time, a stranger came to town. He'd been badly wounded in the leg, and Dr. Baeza cured him. He's been recovering here ever since, and he matches your description exactly. He goes to the cantina every afternoon, and he stays 'til the old man closes."

"It has to be him," Arturo blurted out. "This can't be coincidence, Leobardo; this is destiny. You want a piece of the pie?"

Juan nodded enthusiastically. "You know I do. Let's go get him."

"No, he's not that easy. We need one more man and a lot of firepower. Can we get some grenades?"

"Not right now." Leobardo frowned. "The military has checkpoints all over. Some kind of a crackdown operation or something. I'll get what I can. Who will you get for help?"

"Manuel."

Manuel Santiago Serrano was Arturo's cousin, wanted by the Federales for several murders and bank robberies throughout Mexico. A treacherous area of the mountains was now his home, accessible only by foot or horse.

Manuel was three years older, and Arturo knew his brother wouldn't be afraid to help. When Arturo was about fifteen, the two went to a local dance, and after the band didn't play the song Manuel requested, he grabbed the microphone and used the cord to choke the singer, almost killing him. Everyone in town feared Manuel, and Arturo had always looked up to him.

After giving his mama a kiss and receiving her blessing, Arturo, Leobardo, and Manuel drove off to make plans. They decided to wear long, leather coats to conceal their hardware, and they joked about how they looked like gunfighters from an old western scene. The plan was simple – they would walk in and, if Arturo positively identified the man, he would pull out his shotgun, and the other two men would follow suit.

Arturo emphasized their prey was very quick and dangerous. The terrible threesome made its way to the local cantina. As he drove, Arturo remembered Porfirio, the owner of the cantina, from his childhood. Arturo had once asked for work there, and Porfirio had laughed and kicked him in the rear as he left. Years later, Arturo returned and gave the man a serious beating, scarring Porfirio's right cheek with a pocketknife.

The three men entered the cantina at about six in the evening. Arturo remembered he had not lit a candle to La Santa Muerte, and he frowned. No time now, he thought. The sun was just on its way down, and their eyes had to adjust to the dim light of the bar. The Mystery Man moved like lightning, pulling out a .380 and shooting Leobardo twice, then taking cover behind the bar. After overturning some metal tables for cover, Arturo and Manuel fired upon the bar, Manuel's AK-47 raining bullets upon it. The wood splintered as the bullets hit, and liquor bottles shattered, showering the bartender and Mystery Man with glass slivers and alcohol.

Suddenly Manuel's firing stopped. Arturo glanced over to see him splayed in a pool of his own blood, part of his head missing.

The Mystery Man peered out from behind the bar. Moving with the speed of a striking snake, Arturo fired his shotgun, hitting the man before he could get back to cover.

Arturo swore. He looked down at Manuel and Leobardo and surged to his feet in a rage. He started toward the bar to finish the job, to kill this man once and for all before any more of his compadres lost their lives.

The Mystery Man flew from behind the bar, firing two weapons simultaneously, hitting Arturo in the stomach and left arm. Arturo dropped his shotgun as he fell to the ground. After a moment of shock, he yanked his .38 from the shoulder holster and got back up.

The Mystery Man had his back turned to him, and Arturo took advantage of the situation, firing several rounds into the man's back. The man turned as he fell, and Arturo smiled grimly at the surprise on his face.

A split second passed from when Arturo realized that Porfirio had picked up the shotgun he'd dropped to the moment Porfirio fired it. Arturo knew now that, just like an old western, he was one of the bad guys, destined to die. Fear penetrated every cell in his body, and he felt the border patrol agent's presence when he fell to the ground, hearing the corpse's cold, dead laugh echoing in his head as he exhaled his last breath.

Chapter 39

Voices woke Lalo, but he couldn't open his eyes.

"I can't believe this man is even alive, much less conscious. Five bullets and a shotgun blast to the face. Incredible."

"Lucio," Jose, Mapimí's sole doctor told his colleague, his voice holding urgency. "It's imperative your employees do not mention this man's presence to anyone. If they do, he's a dead man."

Lalo tried to move, speak, but nothing worked. His body felt like a log, even as he continued to listen to the conversation.

"I imagine so, Jose. But why do you care about this man so much?"

"When he showed up in my town several months ago with a bullet wound in his leg, I thought he was just another narco. After I gained his confidence, he told me what happened to his wife and daughter as a direct result of drug traffickers, and I understood why this man was in my clinic with a bullet in him. He's a good man. Crazy, but good."

"Your word is as good as gold with me, Jose. You helped me through med school when we were students, and for that, I'll never forget."

"It was a favor, Lucio, and favors should never be asked to be repaid. Besides, I always knew you'd be a great doctor. You've always had the knack for knowing what's wrong with someone without a medical book. Studying was really your only weakness."

Both men laughed, and then Jose spoke again, a more serious tone.

"Lucio, be careful. Explain to your employees the danger of anyone having knowledge of this man's presence. It could be their deaths."

"Don't worry, Jose. I have him in the quarantined section of my clinic. Two nurses and I will be the only ones to attend him, and the cleaning lady – well, I have complete confidence in her."

"Okay. Don't worry about the expenses. I am sure this man has money somewhere."

"We can deal with that later." A shuffle of movement and Lalo felt pressure against his pulse. After several seconds, the doctor named Lucio spoke once more.

"Lunch?"

The two men moved away, still talking, but only about where to eat and the weather. Lalo didn't want to let them go because any human contact at this point helped, but his face hurt so badly he couldn't move his mouth. The smell of antiseptic tickled his nostrils.

He didn't know how long he'd lain like this, his body frozen and unable to move. Every day was longer than the last, and Lalo's condition didn't change. He spent every waking moment concentrating on moving a finger, a toe, something – anything.

One day, his finger moved. A week later, he could move his hand. The nurses and doctors seemed overjoyed that he could finally move. Every day was a struggle, but Lalo battled on, the images of his dead wife and daughter spurring him on. After a year of intensive physical therapy, Lalo was ready for the next step.

The doctors told Lalo his chances of ever walking again were very slim. But Lalo knew God had a mission for him to complete: to kill Memo. Lalo was sure he would recuperate fully. Why else would he still be on the Earth?

Dr. Baeza had been a real godsend. Lalo knew he was covering the expenses of the clinic out of his own pocket. Lalo planned to return to El Paso to recover the money he'd been collecting from interrupting Memo's business transactions, and he would return to repay the doctor for his kindness. He had just met the man a half a year earlier, after the almost final shootout with Memo and his hired gun.

Lalo knew he had to hide out for a while. Memo would surely be looking for him. After a haphazard bandaging of his wounds, he drove south, not knowing where he was going, but knowing he had to get out of there. He drove past the capital city, Chihuahua, then Delicias, Camargo, and numerous other towns south of Chihuahua.

At a town named Vermejillo, Lalo stopped and asked for the local doctor. The doctor was on vacation, an older man told Lalo, his dirty straw hat tilted on his wrinkled forehead. He pointed down the road. To the west, the doctor at Mapimí might be available. Lalo drove for nine hours, losing blood all the way. By the time he made it to the doctor's office, it didn't take long for him to lose consciousness.

Dr. Baeza came from a wealthy family in nearby Torreon, a city 40 miles from Mapimí. He often didn't charge for his services, and he had been practically disowned by his family when he left Torreon and married a local girl from a poor family. When a car accident ended the lives of his parents, Jose became a wealthy man, but his wealth meant little to him, especially now, with his mission to save life.

The doctor immediately went to work on him, not questioning the circumstances that brought Lalo to him in his condition. When he was done, he and the nurse cleaned Lalo up and put him in a bed in a small room in the tiny clinic. After Lalo rested for a few days, the doctor only charged him the equivalent of a hundred dollars. Lalo paid the man then gave the nurse a hundred as well, knowing he probably wouldn't be alive much longer to spend money anyway.

Spent, Lalo decided to stay a few weeks in Mapimí. It was peaceful, and the people were friendly. Dr. Baeza let him stay in a small adobe house used as a guest home, not because he was broke but because Mapimí didn't have a hotel.

Lalo spent the next several weeks there, then months. His wounds healed slowly, and he would need to be at full capacity to accomplish his final mission: to kill Don Guillermo.

He'd never gotten a very good look at the man with him, but Memo's face etched itself forever in his memory. The day he met up with the other man in the bar had almost been his last. God kept him alive, and Lalo knew he had to recover somehow.

After Dr. Lucio Barrera started injecting Lalo with steroids and growth hormone, Lalo knew he finally had the key, not only for total recuperation, but also to defeat his enemy. He spent day after painful day in the gym; every movement completed a new lesson in the course of agony. Another year passed, and Lalo was walking normally and even began running. Torreon had a great gym, where he began to seriously weight train, and a boxing gym with numerous sparring partners.

Four years passed since the ambush and his near-death experience in the small bar in Mapimí, and Lalo felt it was almost time for him to return to action. After the length of time passed, surely Memo thought him dead. As he'd done once before, Lalo planned to return from the dead. The last time he'd confronted Memo, Lalo started by destroying his business. This time, Lalo would strike only once and with one objective. Memo had to die.

Lalo couldn't find anyone to spar with him at the local gym. Daily injections of the hormone, combined with bi-weekly injections of testosterone, assisted him in incredible muscle gains, as well as his recovery from the injuries he had sustained. Stronger than ever in his life, Lalo didn't care about any possible long-term effects of his abuse of the drugs; one mission remained to complete, and nothing would matter after that.

Lalo only had one man he felt truly indebted to, Dr. Baeza, so he visited the clinic before he left.

"Lalo!" The doctor smiled broadly with sincere joy. "How are you? You look great."

Lalo leaned against the doorjamb of Dr. Baeza's office, smiling. "I've been working out."

"I can see that." Baeza nodded. "No one could have made me believe you'd have recovered so much after that last shootout. It was a miracle you survived."

"You don't know the half of it."

Lalo wanted to tell the doctor about becoming an archangel of God, but he couldn't confide that in anyone, not even this kind-hearted man. It was his cross to bear alone.

The doctor looked up sternly. "Revenge is very dangerous. I hope you can find peace someday, and I mean while you are still alive."

Lalo laughed, but it sounded forced, even to him.

"I mean it, Lalo," Dr. Baeza went on. "It's obvious to me fate likes you, or you'd be dead by now. I wish you'd reconsider the gift of life you've been re-given and look for a new path. I'd hate to not be able to patch you up the next time."

"I appreciate your concern, doctor," Lalo said, reaching for the doctor's hand to shake it firmly. "I came to see you before I left for the last time. You won't be patching me up again. I have something to take care of, and I'm sure it's why I am still around."

"You're a grown man," the doctor said, rising to embrace Lalo. "Whatever it is you are set on doing, I certainly hope it's worth the price of your life."

"It is, doctor," Lalo said, returning his brief hug. "It is. Have a good life, and may the Lord bless you and keep you well. You are the best man I've ever known."

He turned and walked away, feeling the older man watch him leave.

Chapter 40

Driving on the long stretch of Highway 5 toward Cuauhtémoc, Lalo couldn't help but reminisce about his youth, his wife, and his little girl. Soon he would be joining them in the afterlife; of that, he had no doubt. Death hung over Lalo, present ever since he'd nearly died in Mapimí, and he had no intention of trying to cheat her. Rest from his constant mental anguish was what he needed, and the only way to achieve it was through death.

But rest was not to be his until he carried out God's final mission. A monumental billboard penetrated Lalo's thoughts and carried him swiftly back to his mental torture, his momentary glimpse of eternal rest stripped from his mind. He pulled over sharply, parking his Dodge pickup on the side of the road, and looked up.

"Together for a better Chihuahua – Guillermo Smith and you," the billboard read. A picture of a benevolent Memo in the center smiling down, surrounded with pictures of road construction, schools, and hospitals made Lalo grind his teeth.

Apparently, Memo had spent his last few years dedicating himself and his money to politics, and even for Mexico, this seemed inconceivable. A high-level, well-known drug trafficker running for governor of the state of Chihuahua would surely have a lot of protection. Killing Memo would be a monumental task, indeed. As Lalo neared Cuauhtémoc, he saw more and more billboards with Memo's face, each one causing his stomach to lurch in protest.

The plaza in the middle of town bulged with the usual crowd of Sunday locals. Young men dressed in their best clothes, boots, and cowboy hats, and the young ladies wore their best dresses. Old men sat on the park benches, remembering their younger days. On the corner were several men who dedicated their time to currency exchange, making money changing dollars for pesos or vice versa.

Lalo parked his truck and walked to an unoccupied shoe-shiner with his face down. People tended to stare at his face, still somewhat disfigured from the shotgun blast. The shoe-shiner chatted amicably while he shined Lalo's boots.

"You know, I was here about four years ago. This place has really changed."

"You are right about that. When Don Guillermo became the mayor of Cuauhtémoc, he did more for the city in three years than others had done in twenty. Road construction, new housing, and potable water. Others only promised those things, but he actually came through. He's a fine man, may God bless him."

Intrigued, Lalo began questioning anyone who would give him the time of day. It seemed Memo didn't have an enemy in town. In fact, not only did the people of Cuauhtémoc love him, but it seemed that word had spread to the surrounding cities and he was a shoo-in for governor. When Lalo said anything about Memo's illicit activities, the person he was talking to would just walk away, their smiles turning to frowns of disapproval, almost as if Lalo had said God's name in vain in church. Lalo had to question how an evil man could have such a hold on everyone.

No matter whom Lalo spoke with, each had something good to say about Memo. However impossible it seemed, Memo had managed to buy everyone's loyalty. Large donations to the local police, Red Cross, and fire department kept the local officials happy, and their departments had the best and newest equipment in all of Mexico. A local boxing gym had been completely renovated and renamed in honor of the trafficker.

Armed guards with high-powered rifles manned small towers and a gate to Memo's mansion. Unfortunately for Lalo, his funds were running low, and since he didn't want to tip Memo off, he couldn't go after one of Memo's loads or cash to replenish them.

There was no way Lalo would be able to get to Memo at his home. Patience was one of Lalo's stronger points. He would tail Memo for a while, recording his habits until he found a point where Memo was least protected.

At a campaign event for Memo, a live musical group played. After a song ended, Memo got on stage and everyone cheered.

"Let's hear it for my cuñados," he bellowed. "Don't they play great?"

The crowd cheered again.

Memo smiled and raised his hand for quiet. "It's been a long and hard campaign, folks, but it is almost over. In two weeks, we'll have the election, and, with all of your help, you'll have a new governor!"

Another cheer rose into the night.

Memo, probably better protected than the President of Mexico, had bodyguards, friends, and family surrounding him everywhere he went. He had a beautiful wife and two boys, a lover and their daughter. Lalo found himself envying the man more and more, but he pushed the envy away. The only emotions he could permit himself to feel were those of rage and anger toward the servants of evil. Drug dealer, adulterer, and murderer were Memo's true faces, not the benevolent community leader he used as a façade. It was time he was dealt justice.

"And now, let's watch the cockfight," Memo invited, motioning the announcer onto the stage.

"Close the doors, ladies and gentlemen," the announcer shouted. "The fight is about to start. Make your bets. The red is Don Guillermo's, and the black is Don Chumando's. Make your bets."

The two rooster handlers prepared the birds for battle. Razors were tied to the legs of the cocks, and the handlers enraged the cocks by shaking them around.

From the very moment of first contact between the two cocks, the red rooster gained the advantage. A cut to the black rooster's eye shocked and confused him, and the red rooster went to work on him, pecking him until he didn't get up. Losing interest in his former adversary, the red rooster walked away while many cheered him.

A grin on his face, Memo shook hands with Don Chumando, the owner of the deceased black rooster, and a large sum of money exchanged hands.

Lalo's hateful gaze penetrated the crowd, and Memo looked up directly at him. Surprised, Lalo turned around and began walking through the crowd, not looking back. The last thing Lalo could afford was for Memo to have the whole region looking for him.

After a few weeks of tracking Memo's every movement, Lalo decided he would hit him on a Saturday afternoon. Every Saturday, Memo picked up his daughter from his mistress's house and took her to his ranch just outside of town. His bodyguards never accompanied him during his time with his daughter, possibly because armed guards were always present at the ranch as well. Not liking the fact that he would have to kill the man in front of the daughter, Lalo tried to stay as emotionless as possible. He'd do the job and be done with it.

Memo and his eleven-year-old girl played at the ranch, out of sight of his wife and other children. They rode horses, played hide and go seek, and even practiced shooting pistols. Using binoculars to watch them, Lalo remembered when he and his daughter played together, and tears formed in his one good eye. Lalo would have liked to have shot Memo with a high-powered rifle while the two were playing hide and seek, but all he owned was his .380 the doctor saved for him in Mapimí. He had just enough ammunition to fill one clip. He would have one chance to kill Memo, and he knew he had to succeed, no matter how bad the odds. God wouldn't let him down.

A bright red Ford Lobo extended cab pulled out of the ranch, Memo in the driver's seat and the little girl in the passenger's side. Lalo was set up on top of a hill overlooking the ranch and a dirt road leading to the main highway. The dirt road entered the highway on the north side at the westbound lane. Lalo waited right at the intersection on a seldom-used dirt road. Memo would have no reason to stop or even slow down at that place on the highway.

As Memo came around the curve in the road, Lalo revved his engine, timing his entrance onto the highway just right. He entered just as Memo was passing him, crashing the front end of his truck into the side of Memo's truck, causing the truck to roll. The truck rolled over twice, stopping once again on its tires. Lalo shook off the crash and tried the door. It wouldn't open, and he could hear Memo's Ford struggling to start again. Lalo busted out the window of his door and climbed out, .380 in hand. Memo got out of the Lobo, hands in the air, his leg bleeding. He looked like he knew Lalo's motive.

"Whoever you are, I'm unarmed," he shouted. "If you are really a man, then let's do this with our fists. If not, kill me and be done with it."

Memo limped away from the Lobo, hands in the air. Lalo realized Memo's only concern at the moment was getting the danger as far away from his daughter as possible. Lalo respected that, but he thought about his own daughter in the grave with her mom and yelled out, "That's far enough, Memo!"

A look of sudden revelation crossed Memo's face.

"Lalo. Back from the dead, eh? That's the second time, though, isn't it?"

Lalo couldn't believe Memo recognized him so soon. "How did you figure it out?"

"It's a small world," Memo said with a pained smile. "I wasn't sure until you confirmed it. You really had everyone going. I knew deep inside you weren't dead this time, though."

"Oh, really?" Lalo raised his eyebrows. "Then why didn't you look for me?"

Memo shook his head. "I don't know. Maybe because I understood your reasoning, however misguided it was."

Lalo raised his gun, sighting along the barrel at Memo's head.

As if to gain time, Memo went on. "You know, I didn't have anything to do with your family's deaths. I'm a fair man, Lalo. I really wanted you dead after you killed many of my close friends, especially Don Rafa."

Memo made the sign of the cross as he said Rafa's name. "May he rest in peace. But I understood you. I might have done the same thing in your shoes. But, like I said, I didn't kill your family."

"Liar," Lalo cried, his arm trembling. He lowered the gun. "Don't ever say anything about my family. You wanted to fight, right? Let's do it. I'm going to give you the chance that was never given to my family."

Lalo dropped the gun to the ground and stepped forward.

When Lalo and Memo clashed, Lalo felt a tremendous crash of thunder within his skull. Memo hit harder than ever, age apparently not affecting that factor. Lalo was incredibly strong, his mixture of steroids and growth hormone was a literal power cocktail. He hit Memo in the chest so hard that he actually heard ribs crack. Memo fell to his knees, and Lalo hit him in his head with his knee, following up with a straight right to his temple, forcing his head down further. Blood gushed from Memo's eye. Lalo rushed in for the kill, but Memo surprised Lalo by rolling out of the way and jumping up. Obviously, he had picked up on the fact that Lalo had lost the vision in his right eye; Memo pummeled his right temple and jaw with left hooks.

Whatever advantage Lalo may have with his size and strength was lost. Literally seeing stars, Lalo fell to the hard ground. Remembering how Memo's rooster had easily finished off the other man's, Lalo grabbed the .380 he'd dropped earlier, which was now under his leg.

Memo still talked, as if trying to distract Lalo. "You don't understand, Lalo. I investigated what happened. I had nothing to do with the explosion. I was barely starting up my business at that time. I never killed innocents."

Lalo raised the gun again, and Memo backed off, breathing heavily.

"The man who gave the order to have you killed was a guy named El Soldado. Shortly after your family's death, I killed El Soldado and his people because he tried to do me in too."

Lalo watched Memo carefully, his gun never wavering as he got to his feet again.

"It doesn't matter what you say, I don't believe you. You're evil. You might have fooled the people here with your good deeds and throwing your money around, but you're just a drug dealer. I'm here to deal justice to you. God gave me this mission."

"Jesus, you're fucking nuts," Memo laughed harshly, taking a quick look at his nearby truck. "Don't you understand? I investigated you, man. You were told by your peers and superiors to let the Medina case go. But you couldn't, even when it put your family in danger. You act like I'm the worst criminal in the world. At least I'm not a hypocrite."

Lalo followed Memo's gaze, but there was no movement in the truck.

"You have been killing people in the name of vengeance for years," Memo stood quietly now, still recovering his breathing. "You want to find the person responsible for the death of your family? All you have to do is look in the mirror."

"Shut up, you fucking dog, you don't know anything! I'm not in this for revenge. This is for God!" Lalo shouted, but Memo's words cut deeper than he wanted the other man to know.

Memo seemed to detect something. "You fool," he said with a laugh. "I was a cop too. Your wife probably begged you to get off this case, look for another job, anything. But justice meant more to you than the lives of your wife and child. Whatever drove you, you could have just moved on, and nothing would have happened to them. You're as much at fault as the guys who put the bomb in your house."

Lalo couldn't take any more. Memo's words were of the devil, meant to confuse and deviate him from his mission. A sudden movement caught his eye. As he trained the gun on Memo, who yelled something toward his truck, pain pierced his chest. Lalo reacted, firing toward where the gunfire originated. Looking up through his bloody eye, Lalo could barely make out Memo running toward the small figure standing outside his truck.

As the small figure fell, Lalo realized the girl held a gun. Memo caught the young girl in his arms, and Lalo felt his life slipping away from him. Trying to raise the pistol once more in a vain attempt to shoot Memo, Lalo's arm refused to move. He didn't want to go on anymore; the realization of what he had done had finished with his will to continue.

As his vision dimmed, a bright light appeared to him, then two figures beckoned within the misty realm. Finally, Lalo felt he couldf rest from the constant torture that had been his life.

Hearing the sounds of anguish coming from Memo, Lalo felt pity for the man sitting in front of the wrecked truck, his daughter's lifeless body in his arms. He'd done what he intended; although not physically, he'd taken Memo's life. No longer were there two figures pointing at him, but three, and suddenly his peacefulness turned into fear and remorse.

About the Author

Guillermo Paxton lived and worked in Mexico during the most violent years of President Calderon's drug war. He has a background in both the military and law enforcement and drew upon his experiences while working undercover to write *Cartel Rising*. His other books include *The Plaza* and *Lily Without*.

www.ingramcontent.com/pod-product-compliance
Lightning Source LLC
Chambersburg PA
CBHW070653180626
46817CB00006B/2353